STEPFATHER BANK

D.C. Poyer

ST. MARTIN'S PRESS/NEW YORK

STEPFATHER BANK

Copyright © 1987 by D.C. Poyer.
Cover art by Paul Lehr.

Library of Congress Catalog Card Number: 87-4376

ISBN: 0-312-91045-2   Can. ISBN: 0-312-91046-0

Printed in the United States of America

St. Martin's hardcover edition published 1987
First St. Martin's Press mass market edition/September 1988

10 9 8 7 6 5 4 3 2 1

STEPFATHER BANK

hello
HELLO, YOU ARE LOGGED ON. GO AHEAD.

got him study assignment, histry of 22nd century
SPECIFY DATA YOU WANT, PLEASE . . .

econ, polit, socio, genetic—everything i guess
**THAT WILL TAKE YOU UPWARDS OF TWO
THOUSAND YEARS TO SCAN. WE SUGGEST YOU
NARROW FRAME OF RETRIEVAL**

how
**GIVE US A REFERENT—A KEY PLACE, EVENT, OR
PERSON**

how about monagan burloo
****PROPER SPELLING "MONAGHAN BURLEW."
SPECIFY START DATE OR LEAVE TO PROGRAM?**

leave to program
**START DATE WILL BE 2110. DO YOU DESIRE
LINEAR OR ANALYTICAL PRESENTATION?**

linear
TEXT OR ANIMATED?

text
FACTUAL OR DRAMATIC NARRATION?

which is more fun
DRAMATIC

ok turn me
**LINEAR DRAMATIC TEXT NARRATION SELECTED
APPROXIMATE RUN TIME 3.0 HOURS
STANDBY
START**

The year was 2110, and Earth groaned under the iron heel of invaders from the stars.

No.

The year was 2110. From beneath the rubble of nuclear catastrophe, a mutated humanity struggled upward into a harsh new dawn of barbarism and savagery.

No.

The year was 2110, and the Bank owned everything.

Yes.

It was called simply the Bank because its full name was sixty-six words long. It had begun in the late 1990s as a merger of Dai-Ichi Kangyo, Citicorp, and Barclay's, followed within a few months by General Motors, Mitsubishi, Messerschmitt-Boelkow-Blohm, and Compagnie Tunisien des Petroles. Over its first ten years it gained controlling interests in IBM, Deutsche Anilin, Brazil, the AFL-CIO, and the Mafia, among many other international or multinational organizations.

That was early on. After the Last War and the intereconomicum of the Big Overcast, the Bank emerged as the strongest contender for what had long been predicted as the final stage of economic evolution: monopoly. Caught between the Bank's ownership of "Doctor" Gnath Greatmother's research and the newly dominant rational-unitarian philosophies of Mihailovcic and Frassatti, the remaining conglomerates, international corporations, cartels, and zaibatsu panted to interlock their

1

directorates with it. They were not refused. When Communism filed for bankruptcy in the thirties, the New Soviet Union and its satellites (in both senses) were swallowed in one mouthful.

By the year 2110 the Bank had owned Earth (et cetera) for four generations. It was fully automated and computerized. It had eliminated armies and armaments, governments and war, money and crime, discrimination and religion. Over the span of a hundred years it had transformed the world genetically, scientifically, culturally, and economically. Its philosophical and financial underpinnings were solid as basalt. Every human transaction took place through it and was taxed at a flat rate. It employed, was owed by, and so ruled everyone. Everyone in the world.

Except Monaghan Burlew.

Burlew was a free-lance poet. He had styled himself one since the day he turned fifteen, completed minimum schooling, and became of Working Age. Since that day he had never earned a currency unit and never spent one. Therefore, by law—and the Bank was rigidly legalistic—he paid no percentages and owed no taxes. He owned nothing, bought nothing, owed nothing; and so the Bank could not "assist the client in question to find the most suitable employment, considering both said client's talents and the needs of the world economic community"—i.e., tell him where and at what to work. He was the only man on the planet who was outside the System. The only one who was free.

This, unfortunately, did not make him a heroic or even an appetizing character.

Burlew was grossly fat. Of Class V (unknown) parentage, he had not been educated beyond Low English and basic computing. He seldom had intercourse or bathed.

2

He spent a third to half his time sleeping. His one pair of green joggies, found in a trash can in Warsaw, stank like a Neapolitan beach at low tide. He limped because his bare toes had been chewed by dogs one bitter July night in Sydney. He owned neither razor nor microdepilator and did not cut his hair.

Nevertheless, Burlew was happy, in his way, because he felt he was free. But he was also restless. He felt dimly that there was something he had to do, although he did not yet know what it was, or how to go about it.

In 2110 he was thirty years old.

The Single Grain
of Sand

The ten-klick runwalk, humming coolly, bore the fat man along under the rainbowed buildings of New Fifth Avenue.

"Yam, New Newyork," he said aloud. He turned round and round on the vibrating pavement, head back, devouring the mile-tall skyscrapers with his squinty eyes. Above his head they seemed to lean inward, almost meeting. From the narrow blue between them the sun probed toward him with shimmering fingers of fire. "How me loves it. What a top city. It fills me clean."

As he pivoted, as the pavement flowed, his benignant eye glided over the shops and druglets, the workies and

4

flito palaces that lined the Avenue. It came to rest at last on the tired face of the man next to him. "Hey, fren," he said, slapping his shoulder. "Woulj like to fill up on a pome?"

"Say what?" said the client, a clean-shaven Class II in pink business joggies. Idpatches glittered on his chest for BiSex, UpMid, Manuf, and Veget.

"Pome. You top on pomes, si? Give him a turn."

"All right. Turn me," said the citizen, smiling a little as he looked Burlew up and down. The vast green bulk; the tiny blue eyes, almost hidden under cheek-length hair; a sunburned potato nose; the flowing, matted beard decorated with the remains of several recent and enormous meals.

Burlew nodded in satisfaction. He spread his arms in the direction that once was heavenward, exposing two ragged holes at his hairy armpits, and began his declamation.

> "Here I be in New York City
> Where the load be mighty pretty.
> Here I be in NorthAm State
> Where it fill me plenty great."

He paused for a moment, lowering his glance. The faces round him on the moving walk were puzzled. Most of them had never heard poetry before. It had neither rational justification nor economic function. It was not proscribed; it simply produced no profit for the Bank, and so was not published or read.

Burlew returned his gaze to the sky, shook his fists at the sun, and continued:

5

*"Once the nation U S A
Like to have the world his way.
Nation now take zero rank;
Stepfather Bank."*

"Greatmother," said the clean-cut man, his tired face going suddenly white at the last line, "I don't agree with that. No, I don't!" He looked around frantically, then stepped off onto the fifteen-klick walk, which carried him rapidly away. He did not look back.

"Say, who be you?" said an overweight young girl, maybe fourteen, not yet old enough to Work. "Who be you, saying 'Stepfather' out in people like that? Maybe some Adjustor be hearing you."

"Burlew me," said the poet. He looked thoughtfully after the now-distant Class II. "Say, whaj think? That be one fine pome, rite?"

She moved closer to him. This was easy now; a cleared space had appeared around the fat man, and people at the edge of the runwalk were glancing at the two and stepping off. Some were already scratching. "Burlew . . . yam, me heard of you. Kids talk about you. Be you really him? Yam, that a top-rate pome. That Stepson, he not top on that.

"Say, why you be dress so poor, make fun of Bank? You get terminated, no lie."

"Not me," said Burlew. From a tear in his coveralls he extracted a blue plastron square. The girl blinked and looked away as if he had exposed himself. "Gon, look at him Balance," Burlew urged, holding it out. People murmured around them. At last, after repeated assurances that he really wanted her to, she took the telecard.

"Credit . . . zero," she read in a whisper. "Debit, zero.

6

Last fiscal year income, zero. Accrued income to date, zero. Projected lifetime income . . . zero." She looked up at him, eyes widening.

"Stepfather can't terminate you unless you be broke," explained the fat man. "That mean, got debit Balance beyond what you can pay off. Burlew got income zero, outgo zero. No tax, no Percentage. Never can be in Red; can do what me like. Adjustors never touch me, no lie."

"Yam, you got him wired," she breathed, comprehension dawning. She took his arm reverently. "Wow. Real Burlew, here. Look, where you be living?"

"Wherever."

"Wow. Something smell bad along here . . . look, me am got student cube." She tucked the card back into his coveralls, looked up. "Want to stay with me tonight?"

Burlew lowered his voice. "That be Giving, you know. Adjustors fine you for that if they find out. Him Bank not top on Giving outside of Holiday Exchange."

"Stroke the Bank," she whispered. "Maybe be like you, never Work."

"Alrite. Where be your cube?"

"Thirty-third, level twenty-three. We be almost there now, so—"

"Wait," said the poet suddenly, looking around him. The buildings were falling away as they emerged into an open, sunlit plaza. "Where be we?"

"Lennon Square coming up."

"Get off."

"What?"

"Gonna talk."

The square, once they stepped off, was narrower than it looked, edged with uptubes to higher and lower levels. And it was crowded. Thousands of people were crossing it. Their haggard faces looked ahead or at the pavement, each closed, intent on its own concerns, its own tiny facet of the enormous jewel of the Perfected World Economy. Unnoticed, Burlew climbed to the top of a flight of steps, inched from there to the apex of a dully gleaming metal cone. From each of its faces the features of a long-dead musician peered out from the soft metal.

The girl hung back, looking upward. Her stringy hair fell over her face, making her look to Burlew, staring down at the hurrying crowd, like a frog awaiting a shower.

He spread his arms. "Clients!" he shouted.

A few faces turned toward him, then away; the people hurried onward.

"Frens! Fellow account numbers! Pop me the ear!"

At last a few sullen, tired-looking citizens detached themselves momentarily from the crowd by slowing down. Men and women, in the varied clothing of several Cons, bearing the idpatches of many persuasions, many ways of life. They glared up. Burlew took a deep breath. He knew from experience that he had only seconds to hook them, to get his statements so deep under their skins that they would stay for the clinchers. He lifted his arms higher, higher, till he had as much of silence as there could be in the crowded street.

"Anybody here work for the Bank?"

There was a ripple of surprised laughter. "Sure, couple of us," someone called.

"Anybody here *not* be working for the Bank?"

"Helno."

"What him be saying?"

"Be there anybody here, not be a Greatmother Client?"

"*Everybody*'s a Client, fren," called up a severe-looking older woman. As she spoke, two identical twins—stocky, handsome men in neatly cut gray joggies—appeared at

8

the rim of the crowd and stood watching the man who balanced alone on the slippery metal.

"You be wrong, frenita," Burlew shouted. "You be looking at one that idn't rite now. Me."

"Now ask me if I'm impressed."

The crowd laughed. Burlew smiled. He loved hecklers. But there seemed to be fewer every year. People seemed more tired, more submissive—he shoved the thought aside. He had an audience to attend to. "What I be looking like up here?" he called, turning so that they could all see him.

"Like a complete fool," said the woman.

"Like a cockaroacha on somebody's nipple," called someone else.

Burlew roared a delighted laugh. Somebody out there had a remnant of wit. "No. Me be looking like a free man," he shouted.

"Free? What be that?" he heard them asking each other.

"That be old word. Means got no Credit."

"Sir, do you need help getting down from there?" called one of the men in gray politely.

"No way, Stepson," said Burlew.

That got them, he saw. The crowd muttered uneasily. The gray men looked at each other. One of them raised his arm to his mouth.

Burlew turned from them. "Got me one question for you people," he cried. "One question. Be you all healthy?"

They nodded, more or less silently, listening in earnest now. The crowd was growing at the edges in that peculiar coagulating way crowds do when something is going on in a public place.

"Yall got plenty prot?"

"Not *plenty*."

"But enough."

"Yam, mam."

"Like to flit-flit that flito?" called Burlew, swinging his arms and almost falling.

"You bet."

"That's three questions, not one," shouted the woman.

"Stroke can count," cried Burlew in mock surprise. "Must be a Class One."

The crowd tittered. The woman flushed and looked at the two men in gray. They stood patiently, arms crossed now, the same expression on both identical faces, watching Burlew.

"Then got one more," he shouted out over their heads. "Be you all happy?"

There was a pause. "Why shouldn't we be?" some anonymous voice called at last.

The men in gray both smiled, dimpling in exactly the same place.

"Got all we need."

"Got plenty Smile, plenty Happy."

"Got top flito."

"Everything under control."

"Who be this nut? He gets paid for talking in squares?"

"No, I don't get paid for this!" Burlew screamed.

The girl, below him, picked that moment to sound off. "This is Monaghan Burlew!" she shouted. "For real!"

"Who?" "So what?" said several voices at once.

One of the gray men now stepped up to the base of the cone. "Breley," he called.

"Burlew me, dammit. Not 'Breeley.'"

"We have a question for you. Are *you* happy?"

Seeing his look of pained hesitation, the crowd, compassionate as New York crowds have always been, began to howl in derision and throw things. Most of them fell short; Burlew danced about, trying to dodge the remainder without losing his balance. "No, not be happy, exactly," he bawled out. "But then—Burlew at least be—"

"What are you trying to say, fren? Exactly?" the old woman called up. She glanced at the men in gray. "Is it something . . . against the Bank?"

"Not 'against' him Bank," he said. "Bank do plenty good, no lie. But me just be wanting you to . . . well . . . think about things."

"Things be thought out plenty fine."

"Got him Cons for that."

"Be real, fren."

The crowd was dispersing. He opened his mouth to shout, raised his hands once more; then let them drop. Below him the two gray-suited men smiled, waved up to him—each with the same hand, in the same way, exactly—and melted back into the hurrying thousands. In moments the plaza was chaos again. Burlew looked sadly after them, then sat and slid down the side of the cone. There was a ripping sound as he passed over one of the faces. The girl came up to him, and they stood looking at the people for a while, the fat man chewing at the corner of his beard.

"Anyway, I be'd listening," she said at last. "Come on."

She not only took him to her cube, she fed him for a week. She was frightened by his sleeping and taken aback by his smell; but mostly he kept silent. For that week he seemed content, but then one day she returned from her classes to find only a crudely printed pome.

Monaghan Burlew had moved on.

■　■　■

The Board was scheduled to meet in Singapore that week.

The room they met in was anonymous. Quietly luxurious, well-appointed, in the finest taste, certainly, and with powers and functions all its own; yet in general it was exactly the same as forty other Boardrooms in the penthouse levels of forty other World Cities.

The Board had never felt obliged to deny themselves luxury or the trappings of power. But like most people their age, they did not like changes in the furniture.

In 2110 the Board had five members. They now sat waiting around a long table of clear cast glass. All were dressed in conservatively cut Bank gray.

Hakamaro Nagai had always said he was Japanese. He was the senior member, a slight man, shrunken (though he had once been tall); with bright, surprisingly green eyes that missed nothing, and jet-black hair that belied his age. He half-leaned forward in his carven chair, hands folded in his lap. Nagai watched the others with half-amused tolerance, as if they were children and he the only adult.

C. Bertram Boatwright was British. Still erect, still tall, with snowy hair and eyebrows above a seamed, ruddy face, he carried his age like a fading banner. He held an antique calabash pipe, and was searching the pockets of his double-breasted suit, frowning down jovially at the table.

Amitai Muafi was swarthy, still dark-haired, though seams of silver showed in his thinning hairline. He was both Israeli and Arab, one of the vigorous mixed race that had grown up in the long-contested Sinai. He rubbed his mouth, glancing around at the others with an air of slight uncertainty. He too was old. Those who sat nearest him

12

were conscious of a strangeness in the air, a humming, barely loud enough to hear. But that was only one of the strange things about the three of them. They were all old, that was evident; but their age seemed hardly congruent with their keen eyes, the expectant, tensed way they leaned forward over the table, by an oddly anachronistic look of health and vigor and intelligence.

Lady Lakshmi Dawnfair was not old. Twenty? Forty? It was impossible to say. The cascade of shoulder-length hair was the color of autumn maples. Her forehead was wide and rounded, her skin pale and faultless. Her triangular face was ethereal and at the same time sensual, as Botticelli might have painted the hetairae of Athens. If her eyes had been closed, she would have been lovely. But they were open, widely spaced and icy violet under red-gold lashes. The three old men, when they crossed glances with her, smiled quickly and looked away. She sat with her long legs crossed, tapping an exquisitely worked necklace of violet jade impatiently with a long fingernail.

"What are we waiting for?" said the old Oriental, breaking the silence at last.

"He's not on yet," muttered Muafi. He stared doubtfully at the thing that sat alone and motionless at the narrow end of the sheet of blue glass.

The fifth member of the Board had no name—or, rather, had sixty-six names. He was a bankrupt science-fiction writer who had waived Termination to have his cerebrum replaced by a psitelechiric interface. In other words, the last member, for which the others now impatiently waited, was the Bank itself, the worldwide parelectronic mind that controlled the largest, most efficient, most perfectly integrated and logically administered economy in human history.

13

Suddenly the woman leaned forward and slapped its face. The crack made the men present start. "Lakshmi—" said Boatwright.

"Turn yourself on, damn you."

"READY," said the face. It had come alive at the slap; yet not, in a curious way, awakened. It was a smooth face, a blank face. Once it might have been handsome, in a rounded, cowlicked, ineffectual sort of way. Now the lines and tics of whatever rage or joy had come to it in life had been dissolved from beneath by an unhuman passionlessness, detachment, distance. Now it was merely . . . there. "ON LINE. ARE ALL VOTING MEMBERS PRESENT?"

"Yes. And have been for a full five minutes," said Hakamaro Nagai softly.

"THIS MEETING WAS SCHEDULED FOR 10:20 AM ZONE TIME. IT IS NOW 10:19:23."

"We're here. Why keep us waiting?"

"All right, all right. Let's not argue about it, *please*," said Muafi, looking around at the others.

"Shut up, Amitai," said Lady Dawnfair. She uncrossed her legs and leaned forward. One hand caressed the necklace between finger and thumb. "Let's proceed with business."

"THERE ARE FOUR ITEMS ON THE AGENDA TODAY. THE FIRST—"

"Had better be Hades," said Nagai. His voice was so quiet as to be barely audible. But the last word, spoken a little louder than the rest, was clear.

"THAT HAPPENS TO BE THE SECOND."

"You will deal with it first," said Nagai. "Make no mistake. We are in a race with Death himself for this planet—and I have always felt uneasy that we have only one means of winning it."

14

"YOU MEAN THE BLOSSOM."

"We have only two years left. You must complete it and it must work."

"AS YOU WISH: WE WILL ADDRESS ITS PROGRESS FIRST TODAY. THE INCREASED COMPONENT QUALITY AND QUANTITY ORDERS RECEIVED FROM BLOSSOM IN THE LAST SUBTASK PERIOD HAVE BEEN FILLED, THOUGH WITH CONSIDERABLE STRAIN ON PRODUCTION FACILITIES AND WORKERS. CRITICAL WAYPOINTS ARE BEING MET. WE THEREFORE BELIEVE WORK IS ON OR SLIGHTLY AHEAD OF SCHEDULE," said the Bank tonelessly.

"You *believe*!"

"THERE ARE NO GUARANTEES WHERE THE BLOSSOM IS CONCERNED."

"But you say—there's no reason to worry, is there?" said Muafi.

"NONE THAT WE KNOW OF."

All four Board members seemed to relax a bit. "Very well," said Dawnfair after a moment. "Go on."

The next item on the agenda was a proposal to begin large-scale mining of the chromium and agamemnite deposits at Syrtis Major, Mars, a task that would take years, billions of currency units, and hundreds of lives. The Board approved it. The third was a proposal from Res-Con to close down Antarctica, which had lost money for the third year in a row. This was defeated three to one, Boatwright jokingly pointing out that the United Kingdom had been losing money for almost three centuries with no apparent ill effects. The last item for discussion was a Gray report on the activities of Monaghan Burlew.

"Terminate him," said Nagai instantly, as he did whenever Burlew's name was mentioned.

"HE IS SOLVENT AND PRESENTS NO GROUNDS

FOR TERMINATION," said the Bank, its face smooth and expressionless as always.

"What's his balance?" asked Muafi, sounding as if he already knew the answer.

"ZERO."

"That's solvent?"

"BURLEW HAS NEVER PARTICIPATED IN OUR CURRENCY AND EXCHANGE SYSTEM. THEREFORE, HE IS NOT IN DEBT. THEREFORE, HE CANNOT LEGALLY BE TERMINATED OR OTHERWISE PROCEEDED AGAINST."

"Round and round," said Boatwright, shaking his head. "Legality—are we not the law? *Salus rex suprema lex esto.* That's where you differ from us. You're inflexible, not adaptable to changing circumstances. Can't you compromise a little, just once?"

"WE DO NOT COMMIT ILLEGAL ACTS," said the Bank. "BY DEFINITION. WE HAVE LIVED WITH THIS MAN FOR THIRTY YEARS. WE FIND NO HARM IN HIM. AS YOU KNOW, THERE ARE FAR MORE IMPORTANT PROBLEMS TO DEAL WITH. IS IT NECESSARY TO ACT AT ALL? CAN WE NOT LEAVE HIM ALONE?"

"No. We must eliminate him." Nagai scratched at the glass with a withered hand. "He is the only one. He defies us constantly, in speech, in gesture, in the very way he lives when at last we are all working together. He is a single grain of sand in the perfect planetary machine, a fly crawling on the banquet we have made of the world. His so-called 'poetry' spreads a hideous virus of disrespect and noneconomic behavior. I am convinced that it must inevitably impact production and therefore the Schedule.

"Do you know"—he aimed a bony finger suddenly at the Bank, which stared back unblinking—"what he calls

16

you? Stepfather Bank! It's a code word, like 'off the pigs,' or 'foreign devil'!"

"WE DO NOT MIND NAMES."

"You don't? We do. Don't underestimate their power over men. Those names are spreading. People say things like 'Stepfather is watching you'—sometimes right in the Adjustors' hearing! There are anonymous comments about you addressed to the user banks. Obscene comments. Have you scanned them? The top tune among preteens in Morocco is something called 'I Owe My Soul to the Stepfather's Store.'"

"There are other ways," suggested Muafi uncertainly. "Ban the word. Trademark it and sue those who infringe."

"That's treating the symptoms," said Lady Dawnfair. Her hand rose from beneath the table with a small gold tube, engraved to resemble a Sumerian cylinder seal—to be precise, that of Ibil-Ishtar. She placed it to the interior of her wrist. Her hand trembled for a moment. When she opened her eyes again, the pupils were wide and a few droplets of fine moisture had appeared on her forehead. "I think the Senior Member has a point. Production is steady. We approach Hades on schedule. We are secure, *save for this man.* He's a vector of infection, and we've let him circulate for far too long. There must be *something* you can convict him of."

"ALL CRIME IS BY DEFINITION ECONOMIC. ANY MALFEASANCE NOT ECONOMIC IS VICTIMLESS AND THEREFORE NONCRIMINAL. THIS IS A PRINCIPLE DATING BACK AS FAR AS THE NINETEENTH CENTURY. BURLEW DOES NOT ENGAGE IN ECONOMIC ACTIVITY. THEREFORE, HE HAS NEVER AND CANNOT NOW COMMIT CRIME."

"Then how does he live?"

"THAT IS NOT PROPERLY OUR CONCERN."

"This obsession with legality sickens me, frankly," said Nagai. "Can't you convince yourself to use extra-legal procedure? Say . . . the Manifest?"

Boatwright, Dawnfair, and Muafi glanced up at the name. It seemed to echo in the room for several seconds as they sat without speaking.

"YOU ARE AWARE," said the Bank at last, "OF THE CONSTRAINTS GREATMOTHER FOUND IT NECESSARY TO IMPOSE ON THE USE OF PSITELECHIRIC METAREALITIES." There was no trace of reproach, no trace of any emotion in its voice. The mouth, the eyes, the soft pale hands remained unmoved, void of expression. "THOSE CONDITIONS ARE NOT, IN OUR JUDGMENT, ANYWHERE NEAR OBTAINING IN THE CASE OF MONAGHAN BURLEW. AND IN FACT, OUR MACKAY FUNCTIONS INDICATE THAT A DECISION TO PURSUE HIM MIGHT LEAD TO MORE TROUBLE THAN WE ANTICIPATE."

There was another pause. Dawnfair yawned. "Let's forget it," said Muafi suddenly.

"Terminate him, *I* say," came Nagai's whispery voice again.

"Wait," said Lady Dawnfair, lowering her hand from her lips. They all turned in their seats to look at her, even the Bank. The cold eyes were fixed on their reflections in the deep blue glass.

"I don't like it when you smile like that, Lakshmi," said Boatwright, half-jokingly.

"You may this time, Bertram. I may have thought of a . . . viable means of dealing with this situation."

"IT MUST BE LEGAL, LADY DAWNFAIR."

"I know, I know. It will be, even by your impeccably asinine standards."

18

Still smiling, fingering the necklace, she explained. The other three humans nodded. When she was done, the old Japanese chuckled like a pile of brush catching fire. "I like it," he said. "We trick him into destroying himself. Excellent!"

"DO YOU THINK HE WILL DO IT?"

"I assure you," said the woman, still smiling, "he will. I have some knowledge of the nature of men . . . and women. Something, I might add, that will forever be denied to you."

"NOR, WITH ALL RESPECT, DO WE MISS IT, LADY DAWNFAIR."

"Are we agreed, then?"

"Yes," said Nagai instantly.

"I'll go along if . . . if you're sure it's necessary," murmured Muafi.

"Bertram?"

"Of course, darling. In fact, I may be able to contribute just the person we need."

"Excellent," said Dawnfair. She produced a pair of long gloves and glanced around the table. "That's settled, then. You—is there anything else to discuss?"

"NO. WE HAVE SETTLED ALL PENDING BUSINESS."

The meeting was over. The old men, the woman, touched hands and left, each to his own corner of the world. They did not say farewell to the Bank, which had stiffened and sat now staring rigidly into a corner of the ceiling.

They agreed to meet again in a month, to celebrate the fall of Monaghan Burlew.

Three hours later that same day, some seven thousand miles to the west, Jesus y Maria Ramirez realized he was running early.

Jesus (y Maria) was one of the billions of average ordinary working people who lived on Earth, etc., in 2110. He did not think often of the Bank, despite its omnipresent impact on his life. In many ways it was too large for him to see, as no ant has ever comprehended the Sphinx. He thought about his jobs; he thought about his wife; he thought about the few free hours he could find each week for his hobby, which was zippers.

This morning he was occupied primarily with his schedule, and with a slight hangover from too much oporto the night before. He took an escalator up a flight from his cube and stepped out onto the platform. As his runwalk segment accelerated, humming, he blinked in the flood of cold sunlight and leaned into the fresh Atlantic wind. A gull, trying to pass him, dropped rapidly astern.

At fifty kilometers per hour, J. M. Ramirez, tubetech second class, moved down the mile-wide strip of made land and machinery that had once been the Gibraltar Strait Bridge-Tunnel; and before that, long before, the open sea. It was March 20, 2010; and it was 0720 in the morning; and he was ahead of sked. "Don want get head that sked, mam," he muttered half to himself, half to the cold wind. "Him TransCon not be paying a single CU before eight."

As he neared the middle of the strait, he cast a practiced eye over the sea that whipped by on either side. Whitecaps. Decent wind. Perhaps, he thought, WeaCon would give him a good sailing day for a change.

At 0749 he strolled into the lower power room of the East End NorXlantic Frateline, Incoming. Still a few minutes early, he paused on the balcony, looking over the railing at the black maw of the Tube.

The Frateline was the reason why, in 2110, the merchant marine was only a memory; why there were no more aircraft (the few passengers moved by suborbital); why rails were only fading lines of ink on the curling paper of old maps.

As he looked down he heard the distant hundred-hertz hum of an incoming freight.

The first transocean tube, the NorXlantic had been laid about fifty years before, in 2062. Ten meters in diameter, over five thousand kilometers long, it stretched straight as a taut string from St. John's, NorthAm, to the East End Portal, below him. At mid-ocean, four hundred klicks northwest of the Azores, it was five hundred miles below the ocean bed. Laser-bored, titanium-shieldringed, electronically evacuated, through it sped trains of earth-metal canisters propelled by gravity and electromagnetic force.

The warning light above the portal came on. He covered his ears. Around him the hum became a scream as the coils fought the enormous kinetic energy of the incoming load, converting it to power and storing it in the immense capacitors that lay stories down, hundreds of feet below the bottom that the anchors of Nelson's fleet once gripped.

He blinked. Too fast for eye to follow, jolting the concrete beneath his feet and blasting air against his face, the load bolted from the dark lumen of the tunnel: forty or fifty rusty iron cylinders thirty feet in diameter and two hundred long, each weighing more than one of those ancient battleships.

When it had disappeared, switched automatically on its way into Asia at two hundred and fifty miles an hour, he turned from the empty rings and went down a flight. The concrete walls were streaked with old graffiti and he read them absently:

. . . And along with the familiar, a new one. He stopped and reached up to touch it. The burnt words on the wall were still warm.

IF WORK BE MANDY
AND SLEEP BE SIN
THEN WHEN WE WAKE UP?
WHEN LOVE BEGIN?

He frowned for a moment, pondering, and then went on. The rhyme jingled in his hung-over brain. It meant something; he almost understood it . . . something he wanted, but he could not quite remember what it was.

Odd, he thought, and dismissed it from his conscious mind with a shrug. Two flights down he waved the door of the conroom open. "Hola, Jesu. You ready to take him, mam?" said his supervisor, sipping at a mug of sea-prot and glaring out from the cocoon of light that surrounded her.

"Si. What's up?"

"Just took fifty cars New Chicago–Beirut. Next in: twenty-two from Kinshasa to Edmonton; then a big one, 150 thin-wall to Malakal. They be heavy, so monitor coil loading on AL."

AL, Ramirez knew, was the mid-Atlantic segment, the deepest. Subterranean heat made the propulsion/braking coils there less efficient. "Roj," he said. Slipping into the lightwebbed seat, he nodded to ask the trafficomp for a brief. As it began to chatter he saw the woman he had relieved reach up to the wall dispenser. He made a face as she closed her eyes and shuddered briefly; he could use a shot of paranorepinephrine and orgasmopoietic himself.

But for now, he had to Work.

Six hours and 962,000 metric tons of freight later, Jesus was relieved. "What be that smell?" said his relief, sniffing the air.

"Ganja."

"What's that?"

"Never mind," said Jesus. "It be a kind of old-style Smile."

When the turnover was complete, he went up thirty flights to the roof. He lit another bone in the clean fresh air and looked out over the meeting of strait and ocean.

A hundred years before—he liked to watch historical flitos—this had been open water. But fill and turbines, the massed economic power of a united humanity, had long since deleted the Pillars of Herakles from the waterways of the world. A solid bridge of earth and metal stretched from Europe to Africa. To his right, low on the northern horizon, he could make out the heat-exchange towers and dikes of the Farms. Once shallow water, dangerous to seamen, now the fusion-heated ponds produced seaprotein. Most Western Europeans lived on it, in various forms. Jesus tired of it sometimes. But once in his zipper he had caught a wild fish, and it had tasted very strange. The seaprot, he had decided then, was better.

The Bank managed Earth for the good of all.

"How be weather looking?" he asked his wristcomp.

"WINDS ARE NORTHERLY, TWENTY-TWO K.P.H. SEATEMP 24 DEGREES, AIRTEMP 30.5. SEA STATE TWO. GOOD ZIPPING WEATHER, JESUS."

"Sound like it. Will it be staying like this, mam?"

"TILL MIDNIGHT. WAIT ONE . . . RIGHT, RAIN

WILL BE DUE IN FROM SEAWARD FOR THE FARMS THEN."

"Got him," said Jesus, deciding suddenly. He had three hours till his night job started. Normally he spent them flitting, or just sitting in his cube, sleepatch prickly on his rump. Today he would sail. "Get me Avien," he said.

"CALLING," said the WC, and then his wife came on. "Jesus? That you?"

"Hey, stroke. Top on sailing?"

"Wait . . . Yes, can do. For a couple of hours, anyway."

"Roj. Meet you at him pier."

He decided to go there right now and get rigged. Stepping into the downtube, he dropped fifteen stories to sea level and walked out a floating platform to the pier. Strictly speaking it was reserved for Class I's; but, as he worked here, he could shift his own boat from berth to berth as necessity demanded.

Halfway along it he stopped. A fat, brown-bearded man in dirty green joggies was looking pensively down at his zipper. Jesus hesitated. Trouble? But he looked like anything but an Adjustor. In fact . . . the model of the world he carried within his brain adjusted itself subtly. It had never contained anyone who looked like *this* at all.

The man glanced up, saw him watching, and gave him a strangely charming smile.

"This be your boat, fren?"

"Uh . . . yam."

"Top looker. These others, low class."

"Thanks," said Jesus, growing even more puzzled; his instinctive check for idpatches had found none.

"Sail good?"

"Plenty fast," said Ramirez. Zippers had been clocked

at over a hundred k.p.h. "But she be mucho hell to handle, no lie. Capsize easy."

"Capsize?"

"Old sailing word. Means to turn over."

The fat man stroked his beard gravely. His clothes, Jesus noted, were worn and ragged, even dirtier than he had first thought. The wind brought the smells of body odor and . . . peanuts? The stranger looked bewildered, like a big, hairy, lost child. The tubetech's suspicions disappeared, replaced by a spontaneous sympathy. "Hey," he said. "Wife be coming down for a sail. Zipper can take three. Want to come?"

"Well—sure, yam. Where you be going?"

"Just out and back."

"Thanks, fren."

"Nada," said Jesus. He bent to jump down to the boat. Then he looked up. "Say. You not be a Class I, be you?"

"No," said the fat man gravely.

"Not tube worker."

"Nyet-o."

"How you be get out here? Only be tube personnels on island."

"Well, don't tell him Stepsons," said the bearded man. "But Burlew—that be me—come over from NorthAm in cargo. Stowed away."

"Greatmother," said Jesus, appalled. "How you pull those G's? No, mam. No human can ride tube and live."

"Till Burlew."

He squatted on the pier and waxed conversational as the tubetech began rigging the boat. "Need two things: big trash bag, and right cargo. Found canister peanut oil this time. Screw open inspection hatch, drop in, reverse hatch and screw tight from inside. Plenty air in expansion ullage. Accel and decel, fluid be taking pressure

25

same as you. No party, but Burlew can handle for two-three minutes before free-fall start."

"What trash bag be for?"

"Breathe from him when pressure comes," said Burlew. "So lungs don't pop."

"*Madre de dios*," said Ramirez. "But why take tube at all? Why not just Charge ticket on suborbital?"

For perhaps the ten-thousandth time in his life, Burlew began to explain.

An hour later the poet, Ramirez, and his wife, Avien Dreen, were five miles to seaward on a port tack. Dreen, Burlew learned, was an engineer with GeneCon, in the experimental division. Her current project was the development of a stoolless cat. A feline had actually been designed which excreted all wastes through exhalation, rather than in a litter box, but its breath had been so bad that no one could stand to have it around. She was persisting, though, and had ideas of someday extending a workable system to humankind. Burlew asked her dozens of questions about human quality control and the methods and goals of GeneCon (not without lust in his heart, for she was beautiful) as Jesus maneuvered the boat around a floating electrolysis plant. The tang of free chlorine reached them on the wind, smarting their eyes.

Ramirez tacked, tilting the zipper precariously. Spray doused them as it sliced over a wave. Its twin torpedo hulls were entirely submerged; the three passengers lay on a mesh platform set above them on narrow struts that also acted as rudders. It was as fast and as unstable as Jesus had promised. Burlew looked down from the snapping telltale on the starboard mast to hear Avien finishing a remark to Ramirez: "So what we have to decide is, what to name him/her."

26

"Who?" said the tubetech, frowning into the wind.

"The neonate."

"What baby?"

"The one that's coming next week," said Dreen. "You haven't been listening."

"I be'd thinking about the wind. You say we sked for baby issue? Where we find the time? Work twenty hours a day now." He was growing more and more confused, trying to handle two tillers, six sheets, a planer coming fast across his bow, and what his wife was telling him. "This about baby assignment, this be pretty sudden. GeneCon say him, no lie?"

"No lie."

"Him not be ours, though."

"This way is socially more logical, Jesus. 'Trade neonates for truer democracy.' I can hardly argue against my own Con."

"Guess not," said Jesus; but Burlew, watching them, saw the puzzled, hurt look in his eyes.

The three said nothing more for a time. Burlew, lulled by the slice and burble of the hulls through green seas, the whistle of wind past semirigid plastron, sat with his bare feet dragging in water, and thought. No. Not thought, precisely. He felt.

It was the same odd pressure of ideation, some as yet inchoate insight, that had touched him in Lennon Square; and before that, in what had once been Oahu; and before that in the Bolivian Lowlands, where he had lived on tapioca and wild cocaine for six months before being thrown out by the anthropologists who ran the headhunters' collective; and before that in all the various rat holes and mouse corners of the world that he had known in the fifteen years of his Creditless odyssey.

Now he looked at the two silent people in the boat, and pondered anew.

Take them, for example. What did the worldwide dominion of the Bank mean to them? They had all the twenty-second century had to offer. Demanding careers, at least roughly matched to their talents; a twenty-by-twenty cube; each other, again screened and matched for compatibility and contribution to a stable society; enough recreation and Smile and sleep supersessives to keep them working efficiently. And now, a baby. Though none of it was voluntary, they did not seem to regard themselves as exploited. Even the neonate issue would bring compensation: a larger cube, raises for both of them.

All logical, he thought; all good, beyond doubt; and all provided by or through the worldwide economic union and omniscient administration of the Bank.

Why then did he, alone, feel he had to ridicule the source of so much good? Why did he fear the times to come; and why had the same dream wakened him shaking again and again through the years in whatever wretched basement or alley he had chosen as home for the space of a night?

No, it was not logical. He made no sense. The crowds that scoffed when he spoke were right. Yet still he felt that steady pressure. Its source not yet revealed. Not yet plain. But it was there.

"Fren Burlew. Where you be going from here?"

"Sabay. East maybe."

"You don't know where you're going?" said the woman.

"No."

"No mate? No home?"

"Never assigned one, and don't be owning nothing,"

said Burlew. "So noplace home. Or everyplace. Which-ever way you be wanting to say him."

"If you can ride him fratelines, you be going anyplace you want," said Ramirez. "Got him three lines meet at Gib. Next stop east—can help you aboard for Malta if you want."

"Thanks," said Burlew.

Once more, for the moment—and what more was there?—he knew where he was going.

Three days later he found himself in the narrow streets of Old Valletta. He wandered without aim, eyeing the graceful jet-eyed women and blinking in the sunlight. His lips moved as he strolled, bare feet slapping warm pavement. There was meaning to his life somewhere. There was something he needed, something he had to do . . . but for the moment it was out of mindshot, re-mote, unthought-of. He was happy, though his stomach growled and his fleas were stimulated by the heat.

He was composing a pome.

> In Malta strokes be black the eyes,
> They beauty come as top surprise.
> The edge of sea be blue

He worried at the last line. Shoe, frue, sue, two . . . no good. Have to change the line before. "How about," he muttered, "The edge of sea be green. But dammit, it not *be* green—"

He was so engrossed that he walked by the alleyway. But his eye had registered the scene within even if his mind had not, and a few steps later he forgot the pome suddenly, spun around, and urged his bulk into a sham-bling run.

A thin figure gesticulated from atop an archaic metal trash can. A knot of silent listeners, wrapped in black wool against the fierce heat, stood elbow to elbow around it. Burlew's eyes widened. He stepped cautiously forward to join them and caught the words.

"Slaves of monopoly capital, universal state capital! Yes, you have work in the parts factories, but who really buys? Who really sells? Do you know?

"The Bank! And skims its ten percent *ad valorum* from everything you produce or need. Clothing, wine, medicine, bread. It sets price and determines supply—not only of goods but of labor; and that means us. It owns you, brothers and sisters. Owns all of us!"

The dark figure's fists flew in angry counterpoint to its words. Moving closer, Burlew saw that it was a black woman. Ratitic, awkward, but with eyes of fire set deep in an intense, ascetic face. Who she be? he asked himself. Open defiance like this, speaking in public against the Greatmother Corporation . . . it was suicidal. He himself had never dared it, reciting his most seditious compositions only to individuals in passing, furtively, or leaving them scrawled on walls in dead of night.

"Who her, fren?" he grunted, nudging the nearest Maltese in the ribs.

The man flinched around. He stared for a long second white-eyed at the shabby fat man, and then bolted, screaming. The rest of the crowd turned, started guiltily, and scattered like chickens to a fox. In seconds, Burlew and the woman were alone in the alley. She lowered her hands slowly and looked around as if awakening.

"Top-rate talking," said Burlew uncertainly. "Hey, stroke. Who be you?"

She stepped down from the makeshift podium, her shoulders slumped. For answer she held out her hands.

Bony wrists emerged from the too-long sleeves of worn student-pension joggies. "So take me in," she said tonelessly. "No more talk, Stepson. I'm ready to drop this load."

"Stepson! Hey, you think me be cop? Look at me! You be seeing any gray on me?"

"Who are you, then?" she said, peering past him suspiciously toward the entrance of the cul-de-sac. *Like a cat*, Burlew thought in one of his few flashes of genuine poetic imagery. Like the ill-nourished cats of the night that had till now, aside from him, been the only free beings left in the *weltstaat* of 2110. And with that thought came a touch of jealousy. Something in him had prided itself fiercely on his own uniqueness, shabby though it was.

He explained. She flattened her back against sandstone, eyes gradually widening.

"No Credit!"

He showed her his telecard. Reluctantly, she took her own out of her sleeve and tipped its face to him. The telesensitive plastron had changed from its normal healthy blue to a flushed red, and the characters on it glowed like the black fire of her pupils:

```
CREDIT                                        00.0 CU
DEBIT                                      4239.7 CU
LAST FY INCOME                             1320.0 CU
PROJ FY INCOME                                00.0 CU
PROJ LIFETIME INCOME                          00.0 CU
FINAL NOTICE *************************OVERDUE
REPORT TO NEAREST OFFICE OF ECONOMIC
ADJUSTMENT FOR IMMEDIATE SERVICE
```

"Burlew wondered," he said, glancing uneasily up the alley himself. "You Overdrawn already. That be only reason you not afraid to talk, not fear breaking law. Whaj do?"

"I'm sorry—I don't understand Low English very well."

"Whaj do? Why you be so deep in Red, frenita?"

"Oh. I'm—I was a student. Postdoctoral, mathematical economics. I wrote a paper. A macroeconomic indicator analysis of certain aspects of the credit and exchange structure."

"You didn't top on him Stepfather."

"I . . . top on? And who is—?"

They stared at each other. Burlew had the sudden feeling they didn't understand each other at all. "You didn't like him Bank?" he repeated.

"Oh. No, it wasn't really antiestablishment. My thesis was on certain regressive aspects of the flat ten percent rate on goods transactions. How this was a special hardship for the Class III and IV consumer. And why ten percent? That seemed too high from my analysis. I calculated two-point-five would cover the social overhead and administrative . . . well, never mind that now," she said, sensing Burlew's complete lack of comprehension. "Anyway, I received the order to report to the Adjustment Office the day after I turned it in."

"But how you be Overdrawn?"

"Oh, that. I had a scholarship. It was . . . canceled. I'd already put it all on Credit for the postdoc. But there seemed to be no position available for me."

"Where you be from, stroke?"

"New SanFran. A . . . friend put me on a suborbital. Thought I could get away somehow, but I guess I wasn't thinking very clearly. Now I'm here. Nothing left now. But I'll starve before I serve them again."

"No lie," said Burlew. Like amino acids circling a replicating molecule, something was warily assembling itself in his mind. He took her hand, felt it trembling with the fever of appetite. Thin black fingers against dirty white ones. His lifelong solitude balanced briefly against that touch. Then he thought: maybe just for a day or two.

"Look. You seed my Card. I be'd out here for fifteen years now—no Credit, no Debit, Balance Zero. You sabay? Been Free. Want to give him a turn with me?"

The thin fingers tightened in his hand, and her eyes searched his face with an expression he could not read.

"What have I got to lose?"

The waterfront shimmered, the glowing pastels of its buildings reflecting and cooling the crushing flare of Mediterranean noon. Curving stone lapped by sea ended at a palace in cool white. She followed him down the ancient quay, but hung back as they approached the door. "You—Burlew—this looks like the most UpUp class restaurant on the island!"

"Yam. This 'rant run top-rate prot."

"But the price—when we can't pay it, the Grays will be here in seconds!"

"No, they won't." Burlew patted his stomach fondly. "See him? And hardly ever use zeos. Burlew know a few tricks. Sabays the scam, gets round the Charge. Come on. Or you decide you not be wanting to eat?"

She looked around the harbor, and then at Burlew. She lowered her eyes.

They went inside.

An hour later Burlew shoved himself back from the table and belched with great concentration. The woman, who had stopped eating many courses back, was staring at him over the debris-strewn cloth. Burlew grinned disgustingly and picked at his teeth with a dirty thumb,

33

looking right back at her. She was thin, he was thinking, bony, and rather tall; but she seemed intelligent, at least.

"Absolutely Rabelaisian," she said.

"What?"

"Nothing."

He belched again. "Top on that prot, stroke? Telled you Burlew fix."

"But how do we pay for it all?"

Burlew slid his eye toward the Desk, fantastically distorting his face as he mined for a piece of teriyaki beef behind one decaying molar.

The 'rant, fully autoed, had taken their orders, cooked, served, and carved with flashing servo-driven waldoes. It would now clear away, and all without word or question. The reckoning would come as they left. The Desk would not let them past without Charging them. Charging was as simple here as at every other shop on earth. The patron placed his hand over a reader port. A microsecond-long stab of maser gasified a bit of dead surface skin. The genetic data was recorded in short-term memory and the customer allowed to pass. Four times a day Charge data from all commercial, production, and service units was multiplexed to the Bank, converted to digital genetic coding—the basis for all the transactions once handled by money—and Balanced. The client's telecard silently and faithfully reflected the change.

Fast. Simple. And foolproof.

The poet shoved one of the used plates aside and picked something up, palming it skillfully. "Follow Burlew," he said. They sauntered toward the Desk, waited for a moment as a casually dressed, graying man, id-patched for HetSex, UpUp, Exec, and Lifex, checked through. When his turn came, Burlew's porcine hand covered the reader port. The maser pipped, the door unlocked, and the Desk said politely, "THANK YOU, SIR, MADAM. WAS EVERYTHING TO YOUR SATISFACTION?"

"Him oysters not be as good as last time me be here," said Burlew. "But alrite feed."

They stepped out into a wave of brilliant sunlight, a boil of air. Burlew opened his hand to show her the slice of meat before tossing it into the water. "In hour or so," he explained, strolling down the quay, "Him Bank be plenty puzzled. Ham be enough like human genetically to pass Charge. But later on, end up with pattern him can't match to an account. What to do? Only one thing: write off to error and send RepRob to tune up Desk."

"Won't they catch on to that after a while?"

"Only pull ham scam two or three times a year, in different place. Yam, him Burlew got plenty more." He smiled down at her. "Got plenty more scam. Top on scam? Stay fat, no units. Harder for you—you got red card. But—" He hesitated. "You got name, stroke?"

"Name be Jaylen," she said, obviously straining to follow and imitate his dialect. She smiled for the first time. He found it bewitching, but at the same time sad, like one of his more ambitious works, "Fate Stroke Him Hairy Rat."

"You were saying. . . ?"

"Oh. Be saying"—the fat man looked at her intently—"Maybe we doose up for awhile. Whaj think?"

They spent their first night together on the roof of a workie in the Old City. The full moon rolled like a silver ball down silver rails of cloud, and the silver stars shone down on them without Charge or quota.

Free.

SUPPLEMENTARY DATA FOR ORIENTATION: REFERENCE DATE 2110

The world of 2110, through the interstices of which Burlew and Jaylen Mcgreen were to filter their way by silence and scam, was a patchwork of primitivity and advanced technology. The key words, as they always were for the Bank, were efficiency and marginal economic return.

The recovery from the Big Overcast and the economic imperium of the Bank had been made possible by four inventions, each revolutionary in itself, but in synergy the kind of advance that made Otto and the Wrights look like children tinkering with toys at Christmas.

The first had been parelectronic. The second, genetic. The third, nutritional. The fourth, biochemical. In contrast to the advances of the Bloody Twentieth, they were all the work of one person, the kind of synthesizing universal genius who lives perhaps once in a thousand years—"Doctor" Gnath Greatmother.

The parelectronic (para-electronic) revolution had grown out of solid-state electronics, but resembled it by 2110 about as much as a late twentieth-century microcomputer resembled a Leyden jar. Given enormous impetus by the technological competition that had preceded the Last War, parelectronics freed the processing of information from its matrix of digital electronics—crude, rigid, and snail-slow, even compared to biological systems—and explosively proliferated it into a dozen new technologies using light, x ray, and gamma bandwidths. The last human being to contribute to parelectronics (after her it had exceeded human mastery and been taken over by a subdivision of the Bank), Greatmother's first solid work had been to formulate and breadboard the heuristic algorithms that led from artificial intelligence to synthetic consciousness.

The parelectronic revolution also made it possible at last to truly model reality, rather than represent it by large-scale abstractions. And with a true model in real time of a system—say a worldwide economy—it becomes possible at last really to plan it.

The second revolution was genetic. Also foreshadowed by advances in the twentieth century, it had suffered in the scientific hiatus following the twin catastrophes of war and winter until taken in hand by Greatmother. Her contribution had been the final codification of the human genome and its interpretation in mathematical terms rather than the crude analogies of engineering—what she called Skinner-Leontieff stimulus-response input-output tables. Married to the new processing power, S-L tables made it possible to derive high-information functions that predicted not only the biological possibilities of a postulated genome but, with a reasonable amount of determinacy, its functioning within a given social and economic framework.

In effect, not only could the complex and unified social machine that philosophers since Plato had dreamed of be designed at last, but its human components could be molded to fit and function free of the imponderables that had balked utopians and dictators alike from the beginning of historical time.

The third revolution, and perhaps the most important from a long-term point of view, was dietary. By 2110, every person on earth ate a thimbleful of the Moon every day.

This was not a perversion; it was a Malthusian triumph. The theory was simple. Zeolites had been used in industry since the 1960s. Complex naturally occurring crystals of various metallic elements, bubbled full of interconnecting microchannels during the volcanic processes that formed them, they acted as incredibly powerful catalysts. Their most remarkable property was that they did so at low temperatures, lessening the transition and boundary energies for molecular interaction. At first, as the simple corporations that preceded the Bank investigated their properties, they were used in industrial processes, in petroleum refining and drug manufacturing and soil amendments.

In 2038 all that changed.

It was in that year that Greatmother, on the Moon as part of the Bank's first expedition of rediscovery, made a major find in the Mare Imbrium. She mapped hundreds of square miles of natural zeolites, buried under sixteen to sixty feet of lunar dust and the remains of kamikazied meteorites. And every kilometer their properties changed. Vacuum, heat, the varied gases present when they flowed out upon the freezing or roasting surface— there were thousands of combinations, olivines, tectosilicates, biotites. She put in a year of prospecting, footing it alone over the gray-white silences, and came forth with the greatest advance in nutrition since wheat.

Simply put, a diet augmented with certain lunar zeolites enabled human beings to metabolize more complex polysaccharides than evolution had equipped them for. Zeos broke down into simple sugars organic material that was formerly eliminated as waste. Vegetable matter such as fiber, grass, stems—all became edible. Even long-chain molecules like cellulose, formerly tasty only to termites, became human fare. There was an increased risk of bowel malignancy, but Greatmother solved that in a single intense week of work by designing an injectable, self-reproducing white blood cell that produced appropriate lymphokines on contact with a carcinogen.

It was equivalent to a forty percent increase, across the board, in the food supply of the world, almost making up for the loss of crop-producing area in the War. And all it took was a thousand tons a day from the torsion catapults at Mare Imbrium.

Greatmother turned all data over to NutriCon, and refused the emoluments and honors tendered by a grateful planet. She asked only for a modest level of support for her next researches, into what she had long seen as an irksome defect in mammalian adaptation to diurnal rhythms: sleep.

And that was the fourth revolution.

From Valletta they went to El Iskendriyeh, hitchhiking on a short-run cargo planer whose captain, a crotchety Melanesian, Burlew amused with a heroic cycle of porno pomes. The poet, lolling, composed them *ad libitum*, varying the entertainment from time to time with songs, juggling, and sleight-of-hand. He and Jaylen stuffed themselves mercilessly in the crews' quarters during breaks. When they ran the ramp in Egypt, it was too late to look for shelter. Instead Burlew cornered a city cop—not a Gray—and insulted him in broken Low Arabic until he lost his temper. That night they were housed, fed, and generally made much of by the staff of a two-cell jail that had been untenanted for years. At dawn they were released (after breakfast) by an apologetic desk sergeant; the CrimeCon terminal had given the predictable response that since there had been no economic activity, therefore there was no crime. *De minimis non curat lex.* The Bank offered them 200 CU damages. Burlew turned it down. "Why?" whispered Jaylen, staring at him as the sergeant shrugged and turned away. "You don't even *take* money?"

Burlew looked at his hands. They were pudgy. They were dirty. Two fingernails were missing. He spread them. "No."

"Why not?"

"Think up, stroke! Burlew use it—even once—and then him Bank got me. Tell me where to live, what to do, Terminate me if too far in Debt. Steering clear of that. If found Credit lying in street, would edge around it, no lie."

"But that's crazy. No one can live that way."

Burlew spread his hands farther, and then patted his stomach, smiling. Her eyes narrowed as if she doubted what she saw, or hardly knew how to evaluate its truth.

The poet was gnawing his beard. "Now for you it be different. Let's see, maybe could accept it, apply it to your Debt, keep on repping that scam till you be paid off—"

"No," said Jaylen. "They can find out where we are from that, can't they?"

"Rite. Any transact, they id us for receipt. You be rite. Gave false names, but better be moving on allee samee."

From Alexandria they followed the Nile south, headed vaguely for the bustling new parelectronic production facilities of the PanSemitic Sudan. They walked, hitched, scammed their way along.

Burlew, hiking beside Mcgreen, found himself from time to time glancing at her aquiline profile, the high cheekbones, the skin like plane-smoothed mahogany. The twenty-second century's mastery of genetic engineering had long ago obsoleted the idea of "race." But he was not thinking of that. He was trying, somehow, to feel what she was, what she meant. At times he caught a cool, examining gaze that made him uneasy. Her long stride kept him hustling along the dusty roads till he had to remind her angrily that they were, after all, going nowhere in particular and there was no point in arriving exhausted.

And at that she would laugh—tossing back her fine, too-narrow face, sending shoulder-length black hair flying through dusty space—and slow to match his rolling shamble.

As the days passed he grew used to her company, and began to teach her the Road. She quickly grew adept at the centuries-old Stone Soup routine, and learned to find shelter in the Cynic style. More, she seemed to enjoy it. He found an unaccustomed pleasure at being questioned, challenged, and at times looked up to, although he was unsure how much of that might be subtle mockery behind her dark eyes, so intent on him at times that he felt like an adolescent before GeneCon's Board of Evaluation. She was intelligent despite her advanced education. She picked up languages more quickly than he, and had a knack for making herself trusted that at times even he envied.

As the weeks went by they learned to operate as a team, pulling more complex scams than could one person alone; and in these escapades the thin, intense woman became more and more often the lead, the operator, and Burlew simply bagman. She learned fast; she was clever and audacious, with the heart of a born scavenger, a hardened tramp.

Little by little he grew proud of her.

In the evenings their roles of teacher and taught turned about. Camping out in the brush or on roofs, in

41

jimmied shipping containers or on dry wadis filled with the smell of distant factories, they talked. Burlew, brow furrowed and fingers in his beard, tried to understand what she told him about the world economy of 2110. It was something he had always considered a mystery. Or, more exactly, as an immense confidence game put over on everyone but him. He lived on it, used it; but he had never understood how it worked, how it had begun, how it had come—over two centuries of trial and war, plenitude and want—to be The Way Things Were.

Under the rustless wing of a shot-down MiG-31—the rest of the ancient wreck was scattered across an immense dry plain of sand—they sipped their water sparingly and talked.

In the dim pews of a TotiUnitarian church they shared jolts of Mystic and nodded together in ersatz reunion to the subsonic five-hertz *om* from hidden speakers. In the red-flickering recesses of what once would have been an altar, four visages peered out at them: Frassatti, Mihailovcic, Greatmother, and an Oriental-looking man Burlew did not recognize. He made his confession to the Bank-run microphone. It was safe; his voice was not recorded, the RevComp said so; and he and everyone else on Earth knew that the Bank never lied. That was one of the things that made its black tyranny so hard to shake off. When the drug receded, the lessons resumed in the choral loft, among the now softly humming black-robed robots.

"You've got to know more about mathematics, Monaghan, and a lot more about economics. The two most important studies in the world. One describes the universe; the other, how men get along in it."

"Be listening," said Burlew equably. "You be saying last time something about Bank being inevit—ah—inevitable."

"I was talking about its economic justification," Jaylen said. "The central question that split the world two hundred years ago and made that century the Bloody Twentieth was: Who owns capital? Now, we already discussed capital. What is it?"

"Be frozen labor."

"Rite. Work hours that instead of being used directly to produce goods go to produce tools or machines that can make more goods in the future.

"Who owns those tools, machines, buildings? Once it was priests and kings. With the industrial revolution it became those who controlled money: the capitalists.

"Since the labor originally belonged to the laborer, Marx saw any diversion of it from him as theft. But capitalism saw its appropriation of surplus value as a reward for management and risk-taking.

"Socialism was government expropriating control of capital in the people's name. But socialism, in its Communist incarnation, exploited the worker as consistently and ruthlessly as capitalism ever had, and was also less efficient in that it tried to direct an economy centrally without having the data to do so.

"The Bank cut the Gordian knot of ownership by arrogating control to itself, while national governments, weakened by war and popular blame for it, withered away. This was logical, since following the Big Overcast, only the Bank had the data-processing capacity to formulate the plans necessary for recovery. With perfect information and instantaneous processing, the world economy could thus approach optimal efficiency."

"But only if everyone do what him be told," said Burlew.

"There you have it. Steadily the Greatmother Corporation has extended its control over humanity. Sex, medicine, art, religion: no human activity now exists free of

43

the Stepfather. From an instrument of salvation after the War, the Bank has become an oppressor. I suppose that any monopoly of power will eventually become evil. But this one will be harder to overthrow than any before it."

"You be thinking so?"

"It has to do with the people, Monaghan. They're different now. It isn't just GeneCon. After the Overcast, I think humanity became less independent. Those who huddled together survived; those who went it alone perished.

"It's harder to light a fire in people nowadays, Monaghan. They know a little history; they accept the Bank as the cure for the national-state system that caused the Last War. The Bank doesn't lie, but it does restrict and dominate the flow of information. A police state? Not exactly—but with a worldwide network of economic sensors, the Bank can keep order with only a few hundred Adjustors."

"So you think it be impossible to change things?"

"Maybe so," she said, staring at him in the darkness while behind her a robot turned its head slowly, humming a tune that once had been *Messiah*. "And maybe—if it was done subtly, cleverly, by people who understood what they were doing—maybe not."

And as they penetrated deeper into Africa, they found that at times they didn't even need to run a scam. In some of the smaller towns they could ask for food, explain they were Creditless, and sometimes shopkeepers and common clients would slip them soyloaves or zeo capsules in spite of the illegality of Giving.

"Him Bank be losing load," he mused to her as they munched oranges from the orchards of the Saad el Aali late one blazing day, overlooking Lake Sadat. The road

44

had been dusty and the sun intense, and Jaylen had loosened her joggies and leaned panting against the bole of one of the date palms that lined the road.

"Why do you say that?" she murmured.

The poet, watching her, felt unaccustomed emotion. Her glossy hair was wet with sweat, and the skin of her throat was pale under her face. *She be filling out*, he thought. The food and exercise of the Road were rounding her in places he had never expected.

A smile twitched the corners of his mouth under the beard. The life of a free-lance poet in the twenty-second century was not François Villon's. He had never found a woman willing to travel with him before; and though some had been desperate enough to take him in for a night or two, none of these had been a tenth as beautiful, he suddenly realized, as Jaylen Mcgreen was to him now.

Musing, he looked away from her closed eyelids, pulled four fresh-picked oranges from his baggy pockets, and began to juggle them. The bright spheres floated against the hot sky like independent planets, up, around, in the smooth wheel of destiny. . . .

Jaylen muttered something. "What?" he said, still watching the miniature system revolve before his eyes.

"I said, Why do you say that? About the Bank?"

"Oh. Them—*those*—people in last village, they not act like Stepsons. I think here in PanAfric they not so top on Bank anymore."

"It would be nice if it were like that all over," she murmured. She had still not opened her eyes. He glanced at her; she was frowning. "But it's probably traditional. They used to have Dervishes here, not that long ago. A custom of kindness to wanderers. . . ."

"Uh—yam. Well, we get along top in Sudan. Remember Malta? Told you then, you stick with Burlew, we be living plenty good. Who needs Credit?"

"You know, Monaghan, I've been meaning to ask you that." Her voice was muffled now by the arm she had put over her eyes. The sun burned down between the fringed shadows of palm fronds. "What made you so different? Why did you decide, back when you were fifteen, that you weren't going to cooperate like everyone else?"

Burlew stopped juggling. He caught the falling fruits one by one, weighed them in his hands while his look sought the blue of the distant lake. When he spoke his voice was soft, introspective, a tone she had never heard from him before. "It be'd a . . . dream, Jaylen. When I be'd small, alone in the kibut. A dream of bad time. Dark Time, I been calling it."

"Dark Time—you mean the Big Overcast?"

"No. Not in past. In future. And then, seeming in the middle of the dark—brilliant light. So . . . hot." Despite the heat around them he shivered. "It be'd a strong dream."

"And it told you to stay out, stay free, and you'd survive?"

Burlew grimaced. Sweat dripped from the end of his nose. "Dreams don't talk clear, Jaylen. Not sure what it meant. Seemed to be saying, the end of something. A time of dying. Seemed like I was outside, but part of it. And that me—I—be trying with all my might to stop it happening."

"I see," she said. "Tell you what. Come over here by me."

They sat side by side, backs against the rough bole of the palm, for what seemed to Burlew a long time. Then, one arm still over her eyes, he felt a hand grope for his.

"Monaghan."

46

"Yam."

"I'm going to ask you for something. To do something for me."

"Sure."

"Don't say that till you know what it is."

His hand seemed to tighten on hers of its own accord. He looked at her closed eyes. "What be it? Can't think of much I wouldn't do for you."

"That's it, Monaghan."

"What?"

"Don't do anything for me."

"Hey. Riddles, rite?"

"No. Listen, I mean what I'm saying. Don't ever do anything for me you wouldn't have done if you'd never met me. Do you understand? Promise me that."

"Sure," said Burlew, by now thoroughly confused. "But . . . well, sure. Say, you be all right? Talking kind of strange."

"I *feel* . . . strange," she said, putting her other hand to her head. The frown deepened between her closed eyes.

A moment later she toppled slowly over into the sparse broom grass.

"Stop! Stop!" screamed Burlew, running out onto the highway. An old-fashioned wheelcar braked and skidded to avoid hitting him. He pounded on the locked door, coughing in the dust, while the driver's frightened face stared out at him. "She be sick! Yam, you got to take us to medcen, no lie!"

The man knew no English, Low or High, and Burlew's Arabic was more suited to insult than entreaty, but at last he got the door unlocked and Jaylen bundled into the back seat. She lay limply in his arms, sweat drying on her face in white patches of salt.

The driver dropped them in front of a medcen in Wadi

47

Halfa. Burlew had her in his arms again and was running for the entrance; was only a few steps distant when he stopped.

If he took her into a medcen they would do a genetic pattern as a routine test. They would find out who she was. They would discover her negative Balance. And then they would call the local Adjustors.

And she would be Terminated. Alive, she was worthless to the world economy. Dead, she had considerable value—as organs, enzymes, tissues for the lucky few who merited Lifex.

Stepfather was honest. In return for her body, it would cancel her Debt.

He stood on the hot pavement for several seconds, feeling her warm weight on his arms, feeling the blood ebb from his face. And then he turned away. He found an alley back of a closed 'rant, out of sight of the street, and tried to make her comfortable with rags and paper from a pile of trash drifted up in a corner.

"Jaylen. Don't drop load now. Yam," he whispered, and left her there. He pounded on doors, made signs for water. Returning, he found several bony dogs gathered speculatively around her. Sydney! He saw red—since they had mutilated his feet, he hated dogs—and kicked and cursed them away from her motionless form. He knelt over her and dabbed warm water on her burning face, searching for words. "C'mon, stroke," he muttered. "C'mon. Pop a lip for Burlew, nyet?"

She shuddered at last and opened her eyes. They were dark, the pupils wide, whites bloodshot; the flesh under them was growing puffy. "Bur . . . lew."

"I be here. How you be feeling?"

"Bad. . . ."

"Think you got too much sun."

"No. It's something else." She was drifting, he saw, hardly conscious of what she was saying. "Immune systems . . . no good. GeneCon must have . . . slipped up with me. . . ."

"What? You need a medicine? You tell me, I get it, no lie."

She rolled her head from side to side.

"Tell me! Burlew get it!" He was wild with fear; she was gray as the old rags under her head. He felt for her pulse. It was weak, rapid, and it seemed to him that her flesh was hotter than the paving stones. He leaned his bearded anxious face close to her. "Stroke, you be looking bad. *What medicine?*"

At last she told him, and then lapsed, her words trailing off into delirium. He jumped to his feet and ran down the alleyway. As he had hoped, a druglet was across the street from the medcen. "Talk English?" he gasped out to the clerk, a tall fellow with officious eyes.

"Leetle Enlish, yam," said the clerk, smiling. "You want?"

"Need medicine, DNAsub two-seven-three-dash-two, two-eight-dash-eight-oh-four, R. You got him?"

The man punched a button or two lazily, turned to scan his shelves. "Got him, yam. That be for restarting zappo immune system. Not need him much, but—"

"That be him."

"Here he be." The attendant took down an injection tube, and then hesitated. He eyed Burlew over the counter, seeming to notice for the first time his customer's ragged clothes, his matted, overgrown hair. The poet could see his nose actually wrinkling. "That be feefty CU."

"Emergency," said Burlew, reaching over the counter. "Need him real bad, now."

"Just take a minute to Charge," said the clerk, evading his hand and pointing to the reader port set flush in the druglet's counter.

Burlew looked desperately around the shop. There were racks full of drugs, but there was no substitute for his flesh. He thought of Jaylen lying helpless in the alley, her eyes open perhaps as the dogs closed in.

The dogs. He shuddered. "Look. Need him right now. Can't pay. You give him to me, yam? You be top man with me solid, no lie."

"What? Can't pay? You want me to *geeve* him to you? Say, you be Overdrawn?"

"No. See? Blue." He held the card out, breaking the universal taboo. The clerk's eyebrows rose, but he shook his head and put the tube back on its shelf. Burlew's eyes followed it.

"I be sorry, mam. But you pay, or no mediceen. If it be gone and no pay, I lose license, no lie. Got to have Credit."

"Credit," repeated Burlew. He looked down at the port. It was an open mouth, waiting to devour him.

As he hesitated, the outline of a scam formed in his mind, a modification of one he used sometimes to get food in factory complexes. He could enter the medcen nearby through a rear entrance, find the laundry room. No one ever guarded dirty laundry, but joggies of the proper color would give him access to most areas of the hospital. Somewhere there he could find drugs . . . but even as it formed he knew it was hopeless. It would take time to pull the con, time to find the right medicine. And time was the one thing he didn't have.

He thought of his freedom, and of Jaylen's face. And he realized, for the first time in his life, that he loved someone.

Very slowly, he reached out and put his hand over the desk. Sensing body heat, the maser popped. The clerk grinned and handed him the tube. Without a word he took it and walked out of the shop, looking down at his telecard in his other hand. Still blue. But by morning it would be red.

And he would belong to the Stepfather.

In the street he broke into a run. The dogs scattered as he tore into them, and his bare foot caught one and he felt its ribs break and the pack went yelping down the alley.

She was cold now, her face flushed, shivering violently. A dozen different infections, unopposed by her body, were racing to corrupt her flesh. He placed the injection tube to her neck and triggered it into the carotid. Then watched, holding his breath, as seconds and then minutes passed. At last the shivering lessened; she seemed to relax, though she was still unconscious; and he knew that the DNA transfer had pulled her back.

A few hours later, after dark had fallen, she awoke. "Hello, you," she whispered.

"Jaylen. How you be feeling?"

"Stronger." She touched her neck with a trembling hand. "Stings . . . you injected me there?" He nodded. She rubbed it, looking troubled. "How did you get it?"

"Bought it."

"Did you . . . you didn't Charge it?"

"Had to."

"Monaghan. You know what that means? They can make you Work now. Terminate you if you don't?"

"Yam. Burlew know," he said. They looked at each other.

Mcgreen began to cry.

The hand he took was warm now, the grip strong. He frowned down at her. "Now why you be crying, stroke?"

"Because I'm so ashamed. Because that's what they sent me for."

"What?" said Burlew.

"The whole thing was a trick. A scam."

"Scam," he repeated. "Look, think you better rest. You still be—"

"Mixed up the head. I know. I'm not. They sent me. To find out how you lived, and how you could be trapped. Understand? To make you use the System, to compromise that unique immunity you have—I mean, had.

"Monaghan, I was helpless. I didn't know what you were like. I agreed."

He tried to follow her words, but it was like groping through a fog toward something too vast and terrible to comprehend. "You mean—you not be Overdrawn? That you . . . *work* for Stepfather?"

"That's right. Oh, part of it's true. I *was* a student, I *did* write a subversive thesis. They called me in, threatened me. They use people like me, the weak ones. The strong they Terminate. I wasn't strong. I had never known anyone to defy the Bank. I agreed to work for them, for a man called Boatwright."

"You mean you don't care about me," said Burlew, in what was perhaps his first complete sentence in High English.

Her eyes flew open and she pulled her hand away. "You ape! Would I be telling you this if I didn't? Hell, no, I'd just disappear. Your code in that reader was all they wanted. And you gave them that—because you loved me.

"I didn't mean for it to happen this way. After the first

52

week with you, I didn't mean for it to happen at all. But I couldn't think how to tell you. I never thought I'd have an attack here, now. But since it happened this way—you know, I'm kind of glad.

"See, they went wrong, Monaghan." Her words tumbled out now. "They were too smart. They wanted you to fall in love with me. That was easy." She laughed, her eyes flashing. "But it works both ways! You're no prize, Monaghan Burlew, but you're real. You know what your life is for. You talk like a slob, and look worse. And frankly, your poetry stinks. But hell, most of that they forced on you. You're the only one who hasn't knuckled under. The only one! And Burlew, that's why I—well—why I feel the way I do."

The fat man stood up slowly and looked up and down the alley. Anger began to darken his face. He picked a flea out of his beard, crushed it savagely between his nails, and stared down at her. "You saying—?"

"That I love you. That I'll stay with you!"

"They be hunting us now."

"*They* be on their way out."

Burlew took out his card. He looked down at it, and his teeth made a grinding noise in starlight. "What nell you talking, stroke? Now I be in debt. What you be meaning, you're 'kind of glad'?"

She sat up against the grimy wall. "Because I wanted to join you. Work with you. But what we're going to do, have to do, can't be done in the open. We'll both be outlaws, be underground.

"I know you, Monaghan. You're stubborn. You've had to be. You wouldn't give up your precious immunity for anything else in the world. So I'm glad we'll be outlaws together."

"Outlaws? What you be talking about, stroke? We be finished."

"Wake up, man! You've been out here fighting the Stepfather, in your own way, for fifteen years. You've done a lot. Ridicule is effective, it travels fast if it's put in a nutshell; believe me, the Board fears your pomes. But there's something you've missed."

"What be that?"

"That the Bank isn't necessary."

"What? Greatmother! Course it be. You say first, inevitable. Now why you say not?"

"Because Credit isn't necessary."

"Not be necessary!" He turned the astonishing words over in his mind, so startled he forgot his anger. He himself had never used it, but he had certainly, though indirectly, lived on the Bank-organized system of world production and distribution. In one of his pomes he had compared himself to a fly. Living off a cow, ridiculing it, but . . . where would the fly be without the cow? And where would Earth be without a Stepfather? He shook his head. "No. How things be made without money? Why people work? And how they buy and sell without Credit?"

And in the first light of the rising moon, in a stinking alleyway deep in the Sudan, she reached up, brought his angry and doubtful face close to hers, and whispered the word that would shake a planet.

"*Barter.*"

In New Moscow, high in a reproduction of the obstreperously "modern" skyscraper Stalin built smack in the middle of the thirteenth-century Kreml, there was in late 2110 a specially furnished room. It was special in that it was never used by the thousands of functionaries who administered that division of the world state that had once been the New Soviet Union. In fact, it was never used at all except by a single committee, and that only perhaps every five or eight years.

"Good news?" said Amitai Muafi hopefully, glancing around at the other members of the Board.

"STABILITY CONTINUES," said the Bank. It sat, like a slowly breathing sack, at the end of the table. In this Boardroom the table was of Circassian walnut. It had once belonged to Peter the Great. Centuries of Russians had pounded on it for vodka, and the imprints of their mugs still marred the ancient wood, one side of which had been flash-charred by a 20-KT Chinese nuclear warhead. "ALL SYSTEMS ARE GO. TOP DRAWER. BUSINESS AS USUAL."

"Don't be flippant," said Hakamaro Nagai.

"WE ARE TRYING TO DEVELOP MORE PERSONAL INTERACTION WITH OUR HUMAN ASSOCIATES."

"Don't bother," said Boatwright. "Please. It's all I can do to stand Lady D. a few times a year."

At the mention of her name, Dawnfair stirred, flashing the old man a look of contempt. She turned to the thing at the end of the table. "You. Stop playing furniture and talk. What's the news?"

"PRODUCTIVITY CONTINUES ITS PLANNED 2.1 PERCENT INCREASE. WE ARE STILL HOLDING SLIGHTLY AHEAD OF SCHEDULE ON THE BLOSSOM. SEPTEMBER RATES OF POWER AND FOOD PRODUCTION—"

"About Burlew, idiot," said Dawnfair. "And the girl. You can take care of the rest of it."

"VERY WELL. AS YOU KNOW, MR. BOATWRIGHT'S OPERATIVE SUCCEEDED: BURLEW IS IN

DEBT. HOWEVER, SINCE THAT REPORT FROM PAN-AFRIC, WE HAVE FAILED TO MAINTAIN CONTACT."

"Failed to—?" repeated Nagai, his wizened face shocked. "What does that mean?"

"WE DO NOT KNOW THEIR WHEREABOUTS."

"But how is that possible?" the green-eyed old Oriental whispered. "What about electronic means?"

"UNSATISFACTORY. AS YOU KNOW, MOST OF OUR SURVEILLANCE DEPENDS ON TRACING OF CREDIT USAGE. THESE TWO DO NOT USE CREDIT OR TRANSACT PURCHASES."

"What about Adjustors?" said Boatwright.

"THERE ARE INSUFFICIENT PERSONNEL IN THE DEPARTMENT OF ECONOMIC ADJUSTMENT TO CARRY OUT A SEARCH EFFECTIVELY. THEY WERE NEVER INTENDED AS POLICE. ALSO, BECAUSE OF THEIR GENETIC IDENTITY, THEY TEND TO STAND OUT SOMEWHAT IN SURVEILLANCE ROLES."

The Board members sat in silence for a moment. "Well, at least he's out of sight now," said Muafi. "I know that won't satisfy you, Lakshmi, but at least he isn't making any more speeches."

"Shut up, Amitai," said Nagai. "I don't like it. At all. I never felt comfortable with him at large."

"Come on. He's a thirty-year-old bum. He has no Credit, no following. He can't even talk correctly. It takes money to make an impact in a world this large; at worst he's traveling around, giving away his 'pomes' and talking to one or two people at a time."

"Like Jesus—or Lenin?" said Nagai viciously. "Lakshmi. It's all your fault. All this subterfuge, cleverness, it's folly. Worse, it's stupid."

"SHALL WE PROCEED TO BUSINESS?"

"Wait," said Boatwright. "Perhaps Hakamaro is right.

Let's take steps. If we need more Adjustors, let's start the cloning and training now. Maybe even some who can blend in better. The old spysats are still up, aren't they? Let's see if we can get pictures from them. And let's start checking up on people more. Forestall trouble before it starts."

"WE DOUBT THAT THIS IS AN EFFECTIVE TACTIC. REPRESSION OFTEN LEADS TO EVEN MORE—"

"You do? I call for a vote on it, then."

The vote was unanimous. "VERY WELL," said the Bank expressionlessly. "WE WILL INCREASE SECURITY."

"And reduce dissent," said Lady Dawnfair.

"DISSENT IS NEGLIGIBLE—"

"Reduce it anyway."

"UNDERSTOOD," said the Bank. "WE DON'T KNOW WHAT WE WOULD DO WITHOUT YOUR WISDOM AND GUIDANCE."

"That's right, you don't," said Dawnfair. She leaned over the table till her eyes locked with the dead orbs of the Bank. "You don't really understand what's at stake, *at all*. You natter about legalisms when the slightest error, the slightest shortfall or mistake, will mean the greatest disaster in history. *Fool! Idiot machine!* Who is one man, that he should stand in the way of life itself for billions?"

"WHEN HE AND THE WOMAN ARE APPREHENDED," said the Bank slowly, "THEN WHAT IS YOUR RECOMMENDATION?"

"Terminate him," said Nagai instantly.

"I suppose. . . ." said Muafi, glancing around.

"Along with the woman," said Boatwright.

"Immediately," said Dawnfair, nodding.

"WE SEE THAT WE ARE OUTVOTED," said the Bank. "VERY WELL. OUR RECORDS SHOW THAT

BOTH MONAGHAN WILLOUGHBY BURLEW, KK-187-41-5389-23, AND JAYLEN SERAPHINA MCGREEN, KM-410-38-5101-86, ARE OVERDRAWN. NOT HAVING RESPONDED TO COUNSELING NO-TICE, THEY ARE HEREBY ASSIGNED SERVICE FOR ACCOUNT TERMINATION, TO BE CARRIED OUT WHENEVER, AND WHEREVER, THEY SHALL BE FOUND."

Under Ground

Once the abyssal depths of the Philippine Trench had been untenanted, save by corpses. Outriggers and galleons had sailed over it; fleets battled; mighty war-ships sank roaring into its endless night.

Now it was an industrial center, a long valley lit by cold-light floods and sonar, as slowly rolling machines chewed at the vast deposits of precipitated metals.

In the waning weeks of 2110, Seafloor Twelve was a kilometer long, five kilometers wide, and eight full levels deep. A city of two hundred thousand souls, it lay a hundred meters beneath the ocean floor, five miles beyond the last rays of the sun.

Their steps echoed between walls of raw basalt whose edges gleamed in rainbows like Depression glass. When they came to the tunnel's end, the woman turned to the man and smiled.

"Here we are," said Jaylen. "What do you think? This will be good for the night at least—maybe a few days, yam?"

"Yam, this be okay. Top thinking. Adjustors never look for us here, no lie." Burlew looked around at the transparent plastron tanks that lined the walls. The vast room was silent save for a chittering and scraping, a clicking and whistling at the far supersonic edge of hearing. He reached over a barrier and pulled a block of whitish-green substance from one of the feeders. Bit into it. "Fishy," he said. "Krill-and-seaweed. But not too bad. Got a zeo?"

"Snatched a pocketful. Here."

The zoo's inhabitants stared back at them, a thousand bulging, tiny, opaque, lidless, blind eyes, as the fat man chewed moon thoughtfully. The sharks, the rays, the varied fauna of the deep sea. Evicted from the ocean above to maximize a later predator's protein intake, immured in the city's zoo, they watched as Burlew scratched a pome onto basalt, using a wet clamshell as chalk:

> *Trade things and save ten percent.*
> *Tell the Bank to go get bent.*
> *Think your wages are too low?*
> *Barter is the way to go.*
>
> *I love you and you love me.*
> *Give each other things, for free.*
> *Men will say this how we sank*
> *Stepfather Bank.*

In Xishui, a parelectronic manufacturing center outside Wuchang, in what once had been Hubei, a dam burst.

Burlew and Jaylen lived there for a week, standing in line for the scanty relief supplies and talking to the people. By the time they left, fifty of his pomes had been translated into Hakka Chinese.

In Amundsen City, Greenland, Jaylen persuaded a despondent MidMid to lend her his workpass. She put in two days as a genetic counselor and took her pay, 210.4 CU, in small items that could easily be traded: cosmetics, marital aids, active jewelry, recreational drugs, flito tapes. Burlew spent the first few days of the New Year reprogramming the Classical Literature program at Christianshòb University.

CALL
RPB
RU
EL 422
LSN 46 ✳✳
WHAT LITTLE HAS COME DOWN TO US
CONCERNING SIR THOMAS WYATT SUGGESTS
THAT HE WAS ALLIED WITH THE GOODFELLOW
FAMILY, AND THUS RATHER FIERCELY DISPOSED
TO FAVOR HENRY VII AND THE LANCASTRIANS.
BEFORE HIS POISONING, HOWEVER, HE
PRODUCED THE FOLLOWING VERSE (CIRCA 1540),
RATHER IN THE STYLE OF CHAUCER, WHO HAD
DIED OVER A HUNDRED YEARS BEFORE (FOR
CHAUCER, G., SEE FRAME EL 361):

Credit be the root of sin
And that root with Bank begins.
Barter only is the key;
Trading between you and me.

Leave the Grays out. Why should they
Get ten percent as their pay?
If neighbor needs it, Give your stuff.
Tell the Bank we've had enough!
❋❋

A Class IV production worker in what once had been the
Paracel Islands saw something flutter down from a clear
sky. She picked it up and examined it closely. At first she
was puzzled—high reading skills were not demanded in
her foundry—but then she realized that it was a pome.

> Anh nghĩ anh nọ "Nhã Bắng" cuộc sống,
> Bởi vì ngùòi Cha Nuôi không tha thủ.
> Ńếu anh nghi diêùtôt vâñ lã văng,
> Nhìn lại cuộc đời khi anh đã giã.

> Sẽ có ngaỳ:
> Đaǹ ông tụ do, thoát voǹg "U Aḿ",
> Dủòi aǹh mặt tròi, sức khoẻ đôì dạo.
> Gọi chuńg ta, nhử ñg đủa trẻ "Mô Côi",
> Sát cánh nhau tiêñ vào đồi tuồi sáng.

The Director of the New Auckland Fudge Production
Facility rubbed his fingers over the bridge of his fleshy
nose. The news was staggering. His budget had been cut
five percent in the amended Plan. Five percent, yet his
targeted output was the same!

He had heard rumblings of this at the Club. The other
directors told of plan amendments, belt-tightenings, orders to cut down on breaks and opportunities for the
workers to talk. There was something going down. He

had no idea what it was, but it was obvious that someone upstairs was nervous as hell.

He groaned again, pulled open his desk, and brought out a flat square package. The metalloid was cool. He pulled the kookstrip and waited a moment, then juggled the hot fudge and blew on his fingers as he bent to the wrapper. Though he was fifty years old he still—like everyone else in the southern hemisphere, where NAF was shipped—read the jingles printed on the inside. Folksy, funny, they were actually generated by a computer—a branch, of course, of the Bank. Halfway through it his fingers began tightening, heedless of the heat. A moment later a shapeless lump of chocoloid thudded onto the carpet.

> *Gotta make a credit*
> *Gotta make a coo.*
> *Gotta work night and day*
> *For You Know Who.*
>
> *Gonna be so old soon*
> *Gonna be so sad*
> *Don't you think the way things are*
> *Oughta make you mad?*

The leader of the little group of nomads picked his way carefully across the hot surface of the *kavir*. It was a treacherous route. The puckered cakes of effloresced salt were almost an inch thick. They crunched under the soles of his boots. So far, the ground was solid. But under the salt, he knew, there was not always solidity. *Shatt*, channels, wound unpredictably through the *kavir*. The deliquescent salts of this peculiar desert sucked the few molecules of moisture from the dry air and filled the *sh*att with a viscous quickmud more than deep enough to drown a mule—or a man.

In one step, the Desht-E Lut could turn from highway to death trap.

He would not have attempted it, but the loudspeaker from the gray verticopter that morning had been peremptory. They would report to the nearest village for questioning and a lecture.

His tribe went, but they took their time about it. The Afshar had wandered the forbidding plains of eastern Persia in defiance of going on six thousand years of government orders.

As they came up on the water hole the leader slowed, pulling his djellaba closer about his sun-scorched face. Something white flickered on sticks, stuck upright around the scummy brown. As the mules bent their heads to it, the children scampered back with the papers. The leader raised one to his polarized phototints, tucking the ground-density scanner into his knife belt. Despite his traditional appearance, he was not illiterate. In fact, he was a highly trained desert-reclamation engineer, in charge of a slowly mobile solar-energy plant that extracted magnesium and calcium from a slimy mineral pool deep in the interior.

He perused the paper. To his surprise it was in Afshar. Then he grinned.

. . . And the pomes, the couplets, the lilting and incredibly bad doggerel, were read furtively, passed from hand to grimy hand. They were easy to memorize, to quote, and then—to imitate. They began appearing as smudged, reprographed handbills; were laser-burned on freshly painted walls and buildings; were scribbled on

64

the stalls in factory toilets, accompanied, inevitably, by anonymous contributions concerning the amatory proclivities and shortcomings of the local Stepsons, cops, the upper Classes, and the Bank. The Grays followed close behind with paintsprays, handcuffs, and reeducation. But they found that their activities met less cooperation, more resentment, the harder they tried to suppress the hydra of discontent.

Six months passed.

"THIS MEETING WILL NOW COME TO ORDER. MR. MUAFI, PLEASE TAKE YOUR SEAT. GENTLEMEN. GENTLEMEN!"

Unwillingly the three old men, the single woman, quieted. They glanced uneasily around the room, as if fearing hidden assailants. It looked like every other Boardroom. Quietly appointed; luxurious, certainly, with deep Bukhara carpets, and carven Tibetan temple dogs guarding either end of the low porphyry-topped table; but in no way reflecting or revealing the true power and wealth of the worldwide empire that was here, today, concentrated in the persons of the Governing Board. Through a slanting window on the far wall, they looked down on the winding white and blue of ice, of a glacier, trapped and tortured by the stony peaks of the Vatnajokull.

Fifty million cubic feet in capacity, seven and a half times the size of the *Hindenberg*, the fusion-powered airship bored steadily westward, eight thousand feet above the highest peaks of Iceland.

"THE FIRST ITEM ON OUR AGENDA TODAY IS WORLD ENERGY BALANCE. WE ARE BEGINNING TO SEE THE INCREASED ULTRAVIOLET OUTPUT PRE-

DICTED BY "DOCTOR" GREATMOTHER AS HADES NEARS. THE HURRICANE SEASON THIS YEAR—"

"My dear sir, that is not the first item of business," interrupted Boatwright. He looked tired, somewhat thinner, and his normally jovial face was drawn in a way that suggested not one but several nights of strain in the week just past.

"WHAT DO YOU MEAN, MR. BOATWRIGHT?"

"I mean that we have a far more serious problem on our hands, one that we must deal with immediately. I think this is the sense of the Board."

"Hear hear."

Around the table, heads nodded in agreement.

"AND THAT PROBLEM IS?"

"Spreading unrest. Insubordination to clerks, managers, supervisory personnel, and especially to Adjustors. Absenteeism. Giving."

"Stemming, as we all know, from one person—Burlew," hissed Hakamaro Nagai. He turned an accusing gaze on Dawnfair, who sat remote from the rest, drawing circles on the smooth stone of the desk with one impeccably manicured nail. "Now accompanied, and no doubt aided by, that . . . *woman.*"

Dawnfair raised her violet eyes slowly. She studied him, but said nothing.

"Neither of us can be held responsible for that," said Boatwright. "Lakshmi's idea was good. And as far as our choice of Mcgreen, she seemed absolutely malleable—I had no idea—a woman, you know—"

"PARDON US," said the Bank, slowly, impressively. "LET US WORK TOGETHER, NOT AS ADVERSARIES. OBVIOUSLY IT IS COUNTERPRODUCTIVE TO PANIC. IT IS BEYOND THE CAPABILITY OF ANY ONE MAN TO DO SERIOUS DAMAGE TO THE PERFECTED FINANCIAL STRUCTURE OF THE WORLD."

"Maybe not," muttered Muafi.

"His ridicule was always disturbing," said Boatwright. He drummed his fingers angrily. "Not personally—a little humor doesn't offend us, old as we are, we're beyond *that*—but in terms of legitimacy. Few things are as potent as a well-aimed joke. When a regime becomes the object of derision, it's on the way out, no matter how strong it looks.

"But of late—perhaps that's something you can't appreciate—his output has changed. It has become charged with a certain ideological content foreign to his earlier 'pomes,' as he calls them.

"I have here several of his works, if that is the word, found in widely separated places. Some have been reprographed, some spliced into housecomp programming, some reproed by voxriter, and a few even done in pencil, with illustrations—unflattering ones. They seem to be passed from hand to hand in the manner of twentieth-century anti-Soviet *samizdat*." He tossed them onto the table. The Bank pulled one over and read it.

"HIS STYLE SEEMS TO HAVE IMPROVED."

"That would not be difficult to achieve. But note the increased emphasis on four themes. First, barter, or trade; second, Giving; third, eschewing flito and recreational drugs; fourth, suggestion that our rule can be ended."

"AS FAR AS WE CAN SEE, BOATWRIGHT, IT'S HARMLESS. BARTER? YOU CAN'T RUN A PLANET-WIDE ECONOMY WITHOUT MONEY OR CREDIT. BE-SIDES, BARTER AND GIVING ARE ILLEGAL."

"You must realize that, unlike you, people do many illegal things." Nagai tucked a fold in his kimono and allowed the trace of a refined sneer to occur at the corner of his mouth. "They haven't your fine moral instinct.

67

Worse, disobedience is a progressive process. If enough of the population becomes convinced that a thing is right, suddenly one day none will permit its illegality to stand in their way. And another point to consider: they are still convinced that it is they and not we who make the laws—a conviction that we must take care not to challenge openly."

"BUT IT IS UNWORKABLE. IT IS GROSSLY INEFFICIENT. ENGELS SAID BARTER IS VIABLE ONLY IN THE MOST PRIMITIVE SOCIETIES. FRASSATTI PROVED THAT IT IS INCOMPATIBLE WITH DIVISION OF LABOR BEYOND THE THIRD DEGREE OF SPECIALIZATION. OUR OWN ANALYSES"—here the smooth-faced man paused for the merest fraction of a second—"INDICATE THAT A COMPLETE REVERSION TO BARTER WOULD CUT GROSS WORLD PRODUCT BY OVER EIGHTY PERCENT."

"What is current GWP, by the way?" asked Muafi.

"NINE POINT THREE SEVEN TIMES TEN TO THE ELEVENTH CU."

"Is that up? Down?"

"DOWN FROM LAST MONTH'S FIGURES. A TEMPORARY DROP DUE TO DIVERSION OF PRODUCTIVE RESOURCES TO INCREASED SECURITY AND TO FLUCTUATIONS IN CREDIT TRANSFERS."

"How much of a drop? Percentage-wise?"

"THREE POINT EIGHT PERCENT."

Muafi let out a long whistle. The others betrayed varying reactions of surprise. Only the human/parelectronic interface kept its expression calm.

"Can you suggest a cause?"

The Bank was silent. The other members of the Board stared at one another. "Could it be," said Lady Dawnfair, "that certain elements are not using our established infrastructure of Credit, and trade for their purchases?"

"BARTER IS UNWORKABLE," said the Bank. A hint of angry stubbornness, some mysterious hypothalamic feedover from the remnant of human brain through which it spoke, seemed to be creeping into its voice.

"It is, certainly, we agree," said Hakamaro Nagai suddenly. He smoothed one eyebrow with an elegantly long fingernail. "But let us examine it a little more closely. Shall we?"

"WE ARE AWAITING YOUR INPUT."

"Trading goods for goods is often the first symptom of a breakdown in the currency system," the old man said thoughtfully. "I have . . . read of this many times in my studies of Asia's long past. Bertram, bear me out on a few technical points."

"Gladly, Hakamaro."

Nagai placed his fingertips together and looked out the window. He spoke slowly, ruminatively, as if to the distant and slowly moving peaks. "When confidence in a 'soft' currency begins to decline—and what is softer than invisible, electronic money?—men tend to revert to improvised substitutes. In the past this was often gold, but other items of high demand or intrinsic value have also been used as media of exchange during war, depression, and panic. Jewels. Tobacco. Food, chocolate, sexual favors, wine, opium. The older national currencies, such as the 'dollar' or the 'pound.'

"But neither simple barter nor currency substitutes can replace money. It has to exist, because without it, as our colleague has pointed out, specialization of labor becomes impossible, production drops precipitously, and the consequence is shortage or even famine.

69

"Therefore, after a period of chaos those rich men and cities who first reattain stability begin printing or coining their own currencies. These are generally accepted at face value within a given radius, and at a discount by traders farther away. Bertram . . . correct so far?"

"Yes; very lucid."

"Though I am not an economist," said the old Oriental slowly, "I sense this beginning. You, the Bank, are correct in that barter alone is economically impractical. But it can operate as a psychological catalyst. It reduces trust in the established system; that reduces production; that further reduces trust; and people turn in ever-increasing numbers to these substitute currencies. If memory serves me still, there was once a term for this process—"

"A run," said Boatwright. "It was called a run on the bank."

"A Run on the Bank. Exactly.

"Frankly, lady, gentlemen, inanimate—" His last words hung in the still air of the Boardroom, motionless, serene, though moving now at a hundred and twenty miles an hour across the coast and out over the Faxafloi. "If things are allowed to go on as they are, we face certain and irretrievable ruin. And if we fail, so does the Blossom—and Hades takes us all."

But six more months went by; and still, amid the teeming billions of Earth, the two tiny atoms managed to evade the vast cold scrutiny of the World State.

Slowly, the process accelerated.

In an underground city in what once had been Siberia, a bent woman muttered to an endlessly flowing stream of plastron in Low Russian. The machine—a tiny, half-intelligent tentacle of the central octopus—listened, chose, acted automatically in response. From its hundred thousand items of stock it selected small boxes, plastron cans, sealed gamma-irradiated packets. Four kvass-flavored soyloaves, a jolter of Tranquil spray, a charge pack for a portable radoven, a pair of realwool socks (an unattractive style, but then the Bank had never displayed an eye for fashion). As each slid from its bin the Alfeld coils sensed the lightened pressure; a transducer flickered briefly; and thousands of miles away another number clicked over in the incredibly detailed parelectronic model of the economy that was only a part of the omniscient Stepfather.

"Wait," she ended. "Cancel Tranquil. Get—get instead liter bottle pepper vodka. Him used to be liking when we be'ed young," she concluded, rubbing her work-reddened hands across her aching eyes.

The manager of the store, walking by on his way to the bathroom, overheard her last remark to the retailer and stopped. "*Izveenitye*, frenituchka," he said. "We don't be selling liquor at this outlet, mam."

She nodded. The first items of her order began to emerge on the belt, automatically costed and skeined in spun plastron-F. When the last packet had been wrapped, the machine stated the total.

"Plenty cost," said the woman.

"Eighteen-point-eight coo," said the manager. He seemed to peer at the woman a bit more closely, then added, "Plus one-point-nine coo for you-know-who."

As if they had just exchanged an unspoken but unmistakable message, they looked directly at each other. Instead of putting her broad red hand up to the reader,

71

the *babushka* looked from side to side around the store. The other shoppers were out of earshot. Gesturing him closer, she opened her purse; and in a motion as old as what had once been the USSR, used her body to conceal what she held in her cupped palm. It was a flito cassette. "I be finding this in my grandson's cube," she said meaningfully. "He be really too young for things like this? Take look. Top chandise. Two million synapse. Him be worth at least twenty CU."

The manager leaned down to read the title. His pupils dilated, a fact the peasant woman silently noted. "Hm. Maybe ten."

"Nineteen."

"How about . . . eighteen-point-eight?"

"Just the price I had in mind."

The man nodded once and raised his voice. "No sale," he said to the counter.

"NO SALE," said the counter.

The old woman left, carrying her purchases. The man looked at the cassette again and licked his lips. It was, he thought, good business all around. The goods could be written off as spoiled or lost in inventory.

It was Barter. The man smiled. Not only did he have filthy flitos, he had a strange new feeling of having struck a blow for liberty.

Under a low overcast a hundred miles south of the equator, rows of small houses huddled against the flat, wet land like a crowd ankle-deep in warm red mud.

Once this had been the densest jungle on earth. The Amazonian wild, two hundred kilometers south of Iapurucuara. But the jungle had died in the Big Overcast and never quite come back.

It had taken EnviroCon two thousand floating electrolysis plants to make up its production of free oxygen.

In one of the new satellite towns, a tall, brawny woman scowled through the muggy air at the words that had been laser-blistered on the freshly painted wall. *Abusar o Padrasto*, it read.

She went into the nearest shop, a tiny place, selected three Birthday Exchange cards, and offered the old, old lady on duty a set of plastron combs in exchange. The clerk refused at first, insisting that she Charge them. The brawny woman smiled tightly and added matching earbobs.

The old lady looked frightened. But at last, silently, she nodded.

Her store was closed for the rest of the day, while her neighbors darkly discussed the three gray-clad men who had bundled her off in a planer.

In the course of that night the same three words appeared on every blank wall in the province.

Four young men sat tuning their sitars under the jacarandas in a square, sunny park, a relic of an almost forgotten island empire, in Bombay. Passersby looked at them oddly—most had never seen a live public performance before—and stopped to listen.

As they began to sing, the realization seeped through the crowd that the performers wore no idpatches. Three had beards, and all displayed a certain ragged look newly fashionable among the young. The song was odd, too. It was not what one heard at the flitos or in the piped-in music you listened to all day on the Line. They were not Big Name Entertainment Industry (EntCon). At last, with a shock, the audience recognized the words. "A pome," some in the gathering crowd whispered to each other. "Orphans."

हैं बैन्कके पास ज्यादा इलेक्ट्रॉनिक रुपैया;

और वे जानता हैं, कब बरसने वाला हैं।

पास हैं बहुत सिपाई तैंचार छीनने के लिये;

और मासक द्रव्य भारकता लाने के लिये।

परन्तु हैं निश्चत उज मङक मानवयंक आगमन,

जो धरती पर मान्नान्यता में विचरण करता हैं।

धरती में कम्पन होगा, आँतेले पिता को चिन्तन होगा;

जब बेंपर मनयके ला अभिनन्दन होगा।

Before the third number began, there came the whock-whock of a verticopter overhead. The jacarandas disappeared in a whirl of blowing petals and the young men disappeared under a knot of identical sextuplets. But even as the aircraft lifted, silent except for the whip of the blades, other young Indians were circulating in the crowd, passing out crudely reprographed sheets in Low Hindi, the lyrics of the songs:

> *The Bank got plenty electronic rupees*
> *And knows when it's going to rain*
> *Got plenty cops ready to snatch you*
> *And drugs to steal your brain*

> *But there's a man who's coming to save you*
> *He walks the earth in rags*
> *The ground will rumble, Stepfather tremble,*
> *When Orphans stand up and shout*
>
> *If Credit be the root of sin*
> *Let it go, let life start new*
> *Burn your Cards, trade things, and share*
> *The Bank will die because of you.*

Two years before the people in the park would have laughed, would have dropped the sheets to the sun-washed, foot-smoothed stone, forgotten them or kept them for more intimate uses than reading. Now, muttering together as the plane became a distant speck, they recalled friends fined, relatives taken away for reeducation, workmates declassed to harder or lower-Credit jobs. Some had not been seen again. Terminated? No one knew. And they were wise enough not to ask.

So now they held the sheets, their lips moving furtively, long enough to memorize them.

And at the edge of the park, sitting under the blade-bared trees, a man and a woman in the saffron joggies of licensed fakirs turned to each other. The same thought was in both their eyes. The fat man nodded slowly, twice.

It was time, at last, to strike.

> *C'est la Banque qui nous fais povre;*
> *Faut que nous prends les autres pour govre.*
> *Comment? Pas vous servir de monnaie,*
> *Alors liberte vous soit donnez.*

Nous som tous les freres ensemble.
Aimez les autres; c'est tres simple.
Faire de trocquer, et comme ca
Beau-Pere Banque ne l'aimerait pas.

"Uh, this looks like him be in my style, alrite," muttered Burlew, scratching at his matted beard and frowning over the computer-engraved chopstick. "But I don't think I wrote it. Where did you, uh, find him, Raoul?"

The man crouched beside him was dark-haired, intense, and about twenty years old. His name was Poirier. He shifted his back uncomfortably against the curved side of the storm sewer and reached up to adjust the bare wires that held a coldlight panel to the maze of cables that ran into dimness on two sides. He was stalling, searching for his English. "I have him found under the bed of the jail," he said at last, blushing.

"Jail? When you be'ed in jail?"

"Just for a night. Stepsons get me for barter." Poirier held up one arm. A band of pale skin showed where his wristcomp had been.

"Adjustors let you go after one night?"

"Oui. Jail, he was packed. Grays be picking up hundreds of persons. I was in the jail, he was packed, they bring in more for rioting."

"Rioting! No lie?"

"Some of them were beat up, looking so very badly. So Stepsons, they fine the barter cases two hundred coo each and let us out to make the room for the others."

"Things are cooking up there," said the fat man, looking thoughtfully up the tunnel. "And maybe tonight we punch him Bank's override. Yam?"

"Ah, *oui—c'est à dire*, yam," said Poirier eagerly.

Footsteps sounded from down the tunnel, footsteps, splashes, and a lone detached curse. Burlew disconnected the light with a hasty snatch, and they waited in darkness. The sounds drew closer.

"Monaghan? Are you here yet?"

"Yam!" He reconnected the panel and blinked. Jaylen, her hair bobbed and blanched to a stylish albino, reached out for him. They hugged, hard. "Got it?" he asked when she stepped back, laughing.

"Sure. Here it is, try it on."

Burlew tore at the papron sack like a child at Holiday. He held the garment inside to the light for a moment, admiring its shaggy honesty, then bent to begin pulling it on over his muck-smeared coveralls. Poirier helped him with the arms. Jaylen patted the mask—grown of a pseudoenchyme that would live independently for perhaps sixty hours—into place until it "understood" and molded itself into the contours of his face.

Stepping back to look, she couldn't suppress a grin. She was staring up into the ferocious and quite realistic-looking muzzle of an adult lowland gorilla.

"Is it hot in there, Monaghan?"

"Not be too bad yet. Hear me alrite?"

"A little muffled, but confine your comments to growls and you'll sound fine. I'm already dressed." Turning round in front of him, she opened the conventional long-coat with its MidMid idpatches. Under it, except for the luminescent pasties and red triangle of a Flito Girl, she was naked.

"Let's trot," grunted the poet.

The old ten-klick walk moved them sedately along. "Paris, Paris," Burlew hummed in tune with it. Suddenly, to him, the night took on a special magic. Perhaps it was the city; perhaps it was the knowledge that in a few minutes, he might not be alive; perhaps it was both, along with Jaylen by his side. He squeezed her hand and got a scratch of his ribs in reply. Snatches of Low French drifted past from the other late-nighters on the streets. A drizzle gleamed under the archlights, fringes of the spring rains WeaCon was laying on the thirsty fields of what had once been Picardy, and after that the Oise. "Let's jump," he said, and the three moved to the fifteen-, the eighteen-, and then to the twenty-two-klick walk, fastest of those that ran along that stretch of the Avenue de la Dernière Guerre. The Parisians, unchanged despite generations, made way for the man, the woman, and the pongid without comment.

"Here are your workids," said Poirier, handing a card to Jaylen and one to Burlew. "They will pass, I think. One of our Orphans at the Sorbonne idshop made them up. Keep them out of the rain."

"Here, you be holding mine for me, nyet?" said the gorilla. "I got no pockets in this *einfältig* thing."

The walks grew crowded as side-street transfers boarded. Sensing the increase in weight, and knowing the destination of most of it, the flowing ribbon slowed as it neared the end of the Avenue.

"Here we are," said Jaylen, looking up at the building.

Once it had been the Paris Opera, pride of Napoleon IIIrd, the apex of European culture, art, refinement, civilization. Now it was a flito palace. The stone sat as solidly as if three centuries had never been, but it was only a looming shadow beyond the firework flickering of the five-story-high holograms that advertised the night's shows.

Burlew elbowed toward the offstep. The suit helped a little, but not much, and they were all breathing hard when they walked past the lines of waiting spectators toward the stage entrance. *"Des artistes,"* said Poirier, flashing the workpasses. The guardrobot illuminated Burlew for a moment, sensored Jaylen, then waved them on in.

Burlew paused inside the door. They waited for him. He was sweating; the heavy suit was growing hot. He looked around. Never having used Credit, this was the first time he had ever been inside a flito. *This be a good idea*, he thought. *If we can pull it off*. He ran over the plan in his mind, looking for possible slip-ups. No scam was ever perfect.

SUPPLEMENTARY DATA FOR ORIENTATION: REFERENCE DATE 2111

Flito Palace.

Definition: by early 2111, a combination of movie studio, sound stage, bordello, data-processing center, head shop, and burlesque house.

Starting in a small way around 1870, with the zoopraxiscope, channels of input to the consumer were added steadily with technical advance. Screen projection in 1903, sound in the late twenties, 3-D and smell in the mid–twentieth century, Sensurround in the 1970's, holography and the first crude Direct Neural Stimulation in the late 1990's. A broadcast form of entertainment called "television" competed with flitos—or "movies" as they were called until about 2020—until shut down by the Bank in 2037. (The concentration of economic power and shift away from consumer production lessened the need for advertising.) And few bothered to make the mental effort required to "watch TV" anyway after DNS.

Why grind your mind when you could floot-toot-too for a coo or two?

The procedure was the same at any of the over a million locations operating in 2111. The flithead had his hand zapped at the entrance, simultaneously paying his way and getting a weight-metered dosage of Rainbow Three (30 mg. lexergontin to kite you up; a tad of one of the telkoids to damp the ego function; 300 mg. of 3,d-parathanatopidrine to keep you there; and three silly milligrams of neocholinesterase to flush the static out of your nervous system before the show started). He filed with progressively deepening zombility to his seat and groped for the plug that hung just to the left of his ear. Plugged in, to the sunken optsocket on the crown of each client's head.

Flito!

No Man Is an Island. The Median Is the Medium. *Qui Facit Per Alium Facit Per Se.*

Live theatre had died long ago. It was poor stuff to flito. Why watch when you could *be* fearful Desdemona, the steely fingers of the Moor closing at your throat; when you could *be* outraged Othello, betrayed by the pale creature whose throat is silk waiting to be torn? Flitting, the spectator was performer. Seven million select synapses were scan-stimulated sixty times a second. The data processing was in the sublevels, under the studios, and it was anything but simple even in the age of parelectronics. That was the reason the best flito had to be live, not broadcast or taped, though both were done. There was too much data, too fast. Only one instrument could record or interpret it, and fortunately GeneCon could guarantee that every customer was born with one: a brain.

In 2111 flito was bigger than bread and classier than

circuses; hotter than the glass teat had ever been, and with even less taste. When the long hours of work were over, and sleep conquered anew with a flesh-colored patch slapped onto the skin, flito was the opium of the groggy masses that everyone who had Credit to do so smoked as often as he could. The input was graded by strength, but the choice among channels was individual and voluntary. After each performance there were slumped forms in the cushioned chairs. Those whose time-weakened hearts had been outraged once too often with the exotic, the erotic, the terrifying, the splendid, the dangerous, the horrific. For all of it, all of it, was undeniably, immediately, when you were under the drug, REAL.

Flito!

Poirier, who had worked at that very *flito-palais* until his arrest, led them through the backstage warren of rooms, corridors, amplifying equipment—the overheads padded with bundles of vermicelli-thin optical fibers—until they reached the studio office.

The door opened on a scene that would have been utterly familiar to Gene Kelly or Georgie Jessel.

"Cheetah and Jane, rite?" barked the stage manager, a harried, perspiring, bald little man in tech greens. Cigar smoke haloed him in the close air. "G-mother, where you bozos been? You're on in ten. You ready? Got output amps? Got DIN #5 plugs or equivalent?" He rooted in a drawer, tossed two injection tubes at them. "Here's your Rainbow One. Jane, you be needing lubrication, rite?"

"No," said Jaylen. Grinning, she peeled off her long-coat. The manager frowned at her thinness, but said nothing; good dog-and-pony shows were hard to find.

Instead he turned his myopic glare to Burlew, who had squatted on his haunches in the corner and was trying hard to scratch himself through his suit.

"That a real gorilla?"

"Sure. Can't you smell him?"

"Yam, now you mention, sure can. Jeez, what he be having, fleas?" The bald man seized a spraycan from a wall rack and laid a green cloud close aboard the poet, who began coughing uncontrollably. "Look, gotta go. Youse be on at nine forty-five, Studio F. Break a leg."

Studio F was at the end of a long narrow hallway, with the doors of other studios opening from it. Jaylen closed its door and glanced around. It was empty. "Raoul?" she said.

"*Ici*," said Poirier's voice, disembodied, from an on-set intercom. "*All goes well, Jaylen. All Orphans here at the booth, except one. We dosed her and plugged her into a monitor. She will flit for an hour. How is that Burlew?*"

"How are you?" she asked him.

"Hot," Burlew said, still coughing. "Where be that stroking output plug?"

"*We'll be giving you all circuits from the start, but we will hold back conscious thought until audience is tuned. We will give that to you when you signal.*"

"Yam, Raoul. Jaylen, where be that *stroking*—"

"Here it is. Hold still."

(Startled exclamation in Low English)

"Two minutes, Burlew, Jaylen!"

"What else be playing, Raoul?"

"Circuit One, psychodrama from the Bloody Twentieth—slaughter of the cetaceans. Got a live Delphinus sapiens playing the lead, by the name of Norbert. He is a ham . . . on Two, 'The Edge of Night,' Lorna is still having unlicensed neonate of Guillaume, pretty tame . . .

you'll be on Three . . . Four, reenactment of the '35 expedition to Titan . . . Five, conventional torture with Simone Teresa . . . Six, 'Mysticism through the Ages.' We will cut you in on all the channels; give you a minute to establish rapport; then go full conscious. Stand by—"

On the wall an amber panel glowed into a single word.

FLITO

Burlew felt no change, nothing. He hesitated. *"Commence, commence!"* said a voice in his head, Poirier's. The transmitting plug felt cold against his scalp. He had just an instant of the old stage fright. Then the Rainbow steadied him and he flowed. "RRrrrr," he growled, hunkering to knuckle the floor. He wondered if the automatic-translate circuits would bother with that.

"Hi, folks," Jaylen was saying brightly. "Here we are in sunny downtown Paris for your flito entertainment. Hello to all you right here in the audience and to all those flitting with us on satelnet worldwide. Wish you could be here—really I do. We could have such fun—"

She licked her lips elaborately. "Anyway, we have a little act made up for you tonight. My name is Jane; my friend here is Cheetah. My husband? Oh, he's out hanging around somewhere."

The strange thing, Burlew thought, was that there was as yet no sensation of performing. No audience, and no sense of one. Only the small bright room, the platform, the implements, and Jaylen in the tantalizing next-to-nudity of the Flito Girl.

"We've been practicing a little dance routine since he's been away. Cheech! Up, boy, up!"

He looked up at her, putting as much lust on the front of the mask as he could, and pumped the little bulb inside the palm of the suit. He came up. Hugely. There, there was some feedback, even with conscious-thought still off as yet; it was a remote laugh, multitudinous, far back in his mind, as if all his memories were watching. And ridiculing him.

"Now, don't be a bad monkey." Jaylen shook her finger . . . the wrong one. "You know who gets my ten percent." (Laughter.) "Come on, now—I'll sing, and you can—"

"Rrrr," said the gorilla. He pulled off a star enthusiastically.

"Now, Cheech, I'll have to discipline you if you keep that up."

Burlew nuzzled her clumsily, and pulled off the second star. He was acting no longer; or, rather, the drug was splitting off a part of his mind, the Performer, placing it in charge and leaving the rest isolated, detached, watching. With horror he felt mounting activity at the crotch of his suit, *beneath* the immense plastron phallus of the "gorilla."

Come on, Poirier, he thought. *Or this may just turn into—*

Perhaps he heard. *"You've got their attention!"* came the tech's voice in his head. *"Give them the good show. I'm giving you conscious . . . NOW."*

Seven million circuits completed themselves simultaneously beneath his feet, and suddenly Monaghan Burlew had ten thousand, fifty thousand, sixty million people in his head. Their eyes and lusts dragged at his hairy arms. Their thoughts enveloped him like aspic, leaching him of all sensation of his own; his body went completely numb. But in them was no element of direction. The many minds were passive, watching, and he found that the Rainbow One had keyed his will to act as the Three had destroyed their ability to disbelieve or resist. He tugged at the gorilla mask—they knew who he was now, knew almost as well as he did himself—and it

84

fought him for a moment, clutching his face with its tiny sucker feet, and then came off, taking wads of whisker with it. Jaylen was already speaking.

"Attention, Clients!

"My name is Jaylen Mcgreen.

"This is Monaghan Burlew. Yes, Burlew, the Orphan.

"You have heard of us before. You have seen our faces on the Adjustor's Wanted spots, right here on this circuit. You have read, or heard, our messages to you—Burlew's pomes. Some of you are Orphans, who believe as we do. Most of you are not. Not yet.

"Who are you? You're sound, hard working Clients. You obey the law. You work at the jobs the Bank educated you for. You spend your CUs where the Bank wants you to. You mate with the partners GeneCon selects for you, send the children they issue you to the schools EduCon chooses for them . . . and the cycle loops, loops, loops.

"Doubt? Unhappiness? Reach up for a jolt of Smile or a hit of Tranquil. Plug in. It will go away.

"And always you pay your Ten Percent, though you have no say in where it goes—though none of us have any idea where all that profit goes!

"And you think that you are happy, that this is all there is!

"The time that we can spend with you tonight is limited." She glanced behind her, as if being followed. "We are wanted for Termination; we are outlaws. Grays are doubtless on their way here now. But we had to speak to you, the uncommitted—and this was the only way."

Burlew stared at her, his mouth open. Naked from the waist up and unconscious of it, Mcgreen was beautiful. She was a black angel of vengeance. He felt a surge of passion that could not be the drug. It was not lust. It was purer than that.

"You will not find meaning for your life in a flito palace! You will never find it in drugs, or in packaged delusions, no matter how realistic, no matter how artistic, no matter how depraved! Only in the struggle for your ancient rights will you find true happiness. And today, in 2111, that struggle must be against the Stepfather!

"We know that you resent the manifold tyrannies of the Bank as much as we. But we and the Orphans are acting—not violently, but subtly. We trade for what little we need, evade Tax and Charge at every turn. We help one another, and we spread the word and habit of resistance.

"What have the results been? We have harassed the Stepfather, angered him with barter, Giving, and, most of all, ridicule. He knows now that we are not happy with his rule. But does he call off his Stepsons? Does he send to ask what it is we want, why we are not content with his worldwide law? No. Instead, the oppression tightens on us all. We—and you—are pursued, arrested, reeducated or worse. Fear rules the world now.

"We ask your help in sending him a message. If Stepfather will listen, and give us back our voices—not at once in the great issues of science and economics, but in small things: where to live, what trade to follow, a right to education regardless of Class, access to our own genetic data, the right to a public hearing before Termination—then we can compromise, and work to improve things gradually.

"But if he will not listen, then we will seize our time! What Burlew calls the Dark Time—when Stepfather will totter and fall headlong, the idols shatter, the machines cease thought, and through suffering and horror humanity will regain its soul."

She paused, as if listening. But back from all those waiting minds there came no feedback that Burlew could sense. None at all. Only a vast waiting. She turned to him then, as he stood scratching at the raw places on his jaw.

"Monaghan—your new pome."

He took a deep breath. He was not comfortable with High English yet, despite Jaylen's coaching, nor did he top on rhymeless poetry. But he had learned from the teachcomps he jimmied, and he liked the sound of this one, his first in the new form.

He cleared his throat and began.

"Over the rim of the world the Dark Time strides.
Ever nearer. That time will see destruction, waste, terror.
Torches, homes will burn in darkened streets.
Stepsons will burn, Orphans will burn; the uncommitted will
    burn like leaves.
Stepfather must . . . step aside.
The Bank has served its purpose.
We are one world now. But we have lost ourselves.
It is time once more to topple the masters of mankind
Or to ride down with them to destruction."

He paused expectantly. The millions of eyes watched. The multitude of minds waited.

Nothing came back.

"Will you join us?" Jaylen pleaded.

Still they felt only a confused mutter of emotion. *Poirier!* Burlew thought. *Are the circuits in? Are we reaching them? What do they think?*

You are getting the feedback, Burlew. They are dulled with the drug but you are receiving them. They are—the voice hesitated—*they are afraid.*

And Burlew stood rooted still, feeling the trembling begin in his thighs and spread through his stomach. With the word fed back to them, identified, it looped, amplifying with each sixtieth of a second, and now it swelled back from their minds to his to theirs in a tidal bore of terror. He looked across the room at Jaylen, who stood wilted, bewildered.

Then the disappointment and the fear turned round in his stomach, and became white-hot rage.

"Be you all blind?" he shouted, his vision blurring. "Him Bank been stroking you all your life! From kid you be popping what Stepfather say, like be living in flito. You top on that load? That fill you, yam?

"Then I be telling you—*you* be the Stepsons. Not just Adjustors. All you be wearing gray.

"When him Dark Time here"—and the oneiromantic vision rose in him again, as terrifyingly imminent as in that first long-ago night of his childhood—"you stay inside. Stay off him streets. Or else Orphans be burning *you!*"

He stopped, panting, and became aware of Jaylen's hand gripping his arm. "Monaghan," she said quietly, "we haven't much longer."

At that moment, with an instantaneous snap that twanged through mind and body alike, he was alone. The circuits had been cut. The intercom buzzed to life. *"Monaghan. Jaylen. Stepsons!"*

"Dam fast." He reached up, pulled the dead plug. "Stroke, we got to get out of here. Adjustors catch us—"

"I know. Termination." She had pulled clothes from somewhere and was stepping into them hastily.

"You there!" said a hard, strange voice. *"Studio F! Stay where you are. We've got your friends. If you want to see them alive—"*

Burlew silenced the intercom by smashing it on the floor. Jaylen was dressed. Through the door, into the corridor, where they came face-to-face with three identical gray-suited men. The unexpected appearance of the poet, big as a bear and still in the gorilla suit, froze them for a second. The two Orphans turned and fled in the opposite direction.

"What in hell—"

"Monkey—"

"After 'em!"

"Halt, you!"

They pelted down the corridor. Behind them a p-gun pinged, and the rear of Burlew's suit burst into flame.

"In here," panted Jaylen, and jerked open one of the corridor doors at random. They plunged through it, and over the side of an immense tank of water, sinking deep. As he fought his way to the surface, Burlew glimpsed a sleek form turning in their direction. He broke into the air but was driven under by a collapsing wave before he could take breath. He tasted salt, struggled upward again, but found the waterlogging suit dragging him down. He thrashed in near panic. Had he traded death by fire for—

Something immensely strong moved under him. His eyes broke the surface, taking in four bearded men pointing and shouting from an overcrowded whaleboat. He gulped air and craned about. Jaylen was a few meters off, swimming desperately for the boat.

Another heavy comber submerged them both. Burlew, as he was borne up again on the following crest, caught a glimpse of the mother ship, an old-fashioned steamer with vertical funnels, standing off on the horizon.

The thing beneath found him again and shoved, hard, and he made sense of it this time. The dolphin. Moving so fast he left a wake, Burlew was pushed past the boat, Jaylen altering her course to follow him toward what looked like a patch of light fog between them and the ship. They entered it, broke through the hologram, and slammed into the side of the tank. Burlew hauled himself out with shaking arms. "Thanks," he gasped to the dolphin.

"I tshouldn't have done it," it squeaked, thrusting its head out of the water and regarding him with what he could only interpret as disgust. "Tsthay the tsstroke off my sset, boobs. First a tschircuit foulup, then you two in my pool. I got a public to tssatisfy." It finished with a rude sound from its blowhole.

"Let's get out of here," said Jaylen, helping him up. "They won't take long to figure out how to get around the tank."

"Yam." Burlew forced himself to his feet, dripping, and they plunged through the first door that offered itself.

A whip cracked before their faces. A red-haired, haughty-looking woman, sleek in chrome leather and pink garters, stood between them and two prostrate and sobbing males. Another hung upside down from an intricate framework, his face purpled, electrodes attached at unlikely spots. All four of them turned their heads to stare at the intruders.

At that moment Burlew smelled smoke. He put his hand cautiously behind him. The plastron-K of the suit, dampened but not extinguished by salt water, was beginning to smolder again.

"Fire!" he shouted, running full tilt over the two prone men. Simone Teresa shrieked, dropped her whip, and ran. The trussed victim began to scream. "Fire! Fire!" shouted Jaylen as they burst through swinging doors onto the "Edge of Night" stage, and the doctors and Guillaume and Lorna and the baby lost their carefully framed mindsets and shouted and stampeded after them through the next studio, over the methane snows of Titan, trampling crudely welded titanium crosses, past the astonished spacemen in their quaint twenty-first-century bulgers. "Fire! Fire!" The dread words spread through the crowded palace. Twenty thousand zombies had to be unplugged, injected, jerked from their seats, and herded out. Burlew and Jaylen wove through the running, swearing backstage personnel. The Adjustors, far behind them now, could hardly be heard shouting above the din of running feet and screaming actors.

"Where to?"

"Control booth. Rescue Poirier."

But it was empty. The young Frenchman and the other techs who had cooperated were gone. Burlew swore. The Stepsons would not let him go with a 200 CU fine this time. He pulled off the smoking suit just as it reignited, and kicked it beneath the ceiling smokesensor.

The door banged open and one of the Adjustors came in alone. Anger disfigured his strong, handsome face. Burlew stared. The Gray stared back for a moment, reaching for something inside his joggies; then suddenly went for the floor, with a sound like a balloon collapsing.

"Good thing they make them big," said Jaylen, setting the monitor dial on an hour. She had plugged him in from behind, with no ego-relaxing Rainbow at all.

"Make what big?"

"Adjustors. Get into his clothes. It's the only way we'll get out of here."

They emerged from the control room into a scene from Petronius Arbiter. The corridor was choked with struggling people, actors in varied costumes or lack of them fighting to get out, firefighting robots pushing to get in, blank-eyed flitters who had wandered backstage, a sprinkling of confused and angry Grays, ten bearded Yankees puffing under the weight of an immense dolphin who whimpered in fear in a litter. They joined the battle for the nearest exit.

Like phantoms, they disappeared into the night. Behind them the flito palace was in an uproar. Fifty of the flitters were injured when the reality of the fire alarms penetrated and they mobbed the exits. The burning ape suit finally tripped the sprinklers, and the entire Opera was flooded with sticky puce Pyronix foam, ruining millions of CUs worth of scenery, costumes, parelectronics, and drugs.

But behind them as they disappeared, they also left their dream. Burlew cursed steadily as they jogged through the night. There would be no mass conversion. No worldwide strike, no march of outraged millions to smash the Bank and all its works. The Grays had done their jobs. Fines, counterpropaganda, reeducation, demotion, all directed and evaluated and redirected by the billion-fingered never-sleeping brain of the Stepfather, had done their work.

The people would not demand their rights. They had no freedom. But they had flito. They had no happiness. But they had Happy.

And they were afraid.

It was early the next morning when they crossed what had once been the Belgian border, huddled in the back of an obsolete agriplaner that rumbled low over the canted slabs of what had once been the Mauberge-Charleroi highway.

"So what happens now?" Burlew mused bitterly from

his nest in a pile of used sacking. "Millions flitted with us. They can't blank those memories. But rest of world never hear of it. NewsCon never release it. Face him, we dropped the load last night, Jaylen. Dropped him top-rate."

"You can speak better English than that now. Our message got to those millions, at least. We've got to keep trying."

"Why? They're too scared to do anything. Maybe say pomes to each other. But do nothing."

He thought for the hundredth time, and with the same combination of rage and regret, of Poirier and the other Orphans. They might have escaped, but it was unlikely. The Grays had made the control booth their first stop. No, by now they were parts, the organs tissue-typed and frozen and ready for distribution, the useful enzymes and colloids centrifuged and filtered from the ground-up meat that remained. The image made him feel sick. If the fire-alarm scam hadn't worked, he and Jaylen would be going in a hundred different directions this morning too.

Mcgreen, slumped in the corner of the planer bed, seemed occupied with her own unhappy thoughts.

"No, I can't buy that. Maybe Paris went too wrong to just say, Keep on doing more of the same," the poet resumed. He stared down at his bare feet. "We got away, but our Orphans were killed. And the Bank wins again. We thought it was time. We were wrong."

"This time. But think of the way they listened. They believed in you—even if they believed in the Bank's power to punish them more."

"What are you saying?"

"That you can't give up after one defeat. That would be saying that Poirier and all the others died for nothing—that Stepfather will never be stopped."

"Stepfather," Burlew repeated softly, as if tasting the word for the first time. He leaned his head against the planer's side, letting the vibration from the untuned turbines drill into his skull. "Stepfather . . . what is he really, Jaylen? Maybe we not be approaching this whole problem from the right way."

She thought for the time it took to cover a kilometer. "Well . . . Boatwright never said much about it when I worked for him. I gathered hints, that was all.

"Apparently at the very top sits a small group, called 'the Board.' They advise the Bank itself, which seems to be the clearing and processing programming that plans the economy and coordinates the activities of WeaCon, SeaCon, GeneCon, and so on. But sometimes—"

"Sometimes what?"

"Funny, sometimes he used to talk as if it was a human being. He'd mention its expression. How could a computer have an expression?"

"Probably just the way he talked. But I be wondering about that computer. So far we've thought in terms of psychological war and economic sabotage. What if we struck at the Bank directly? If we showed up there, say damaged it, maybe that bring whoever directs it around some."

"I thought you didn't want to use violence, Monaghan."

Burlew did not answer that. Instead, after a pause, he said, "Do you know where it is? The computer that runs the Bank, or is the Bank?"

"You know there's no one place—it's all over the world. But wait, he did say something once."

"About where it was?"

"Not exactly. He was angry, and he said something about how he wished he could 'go to cuckooland and

94

pull the plug on old Deadface.' Apparently it refused to go along with something he wanted to do. But maybe he meant that the central complex, or at least something important about it, was there—wherever that was."

"Pulling the plug," Burlew repeated. "And cuckooland . . . where could that be?"

"Germany?"

"You think? Helva slim lead."

A road sign flashed past them. Burlew banged on the front of the planer bed, shouted into the cab up forward. "Hay! Let us off here, mam!"

The old man driving (who had not known they were back there, but who assumed that he had once known about it but it had slipped his mind, and so was not too surprised at the voice behind him) slowed the agriplaner and dropped it to the muddy road. Behind him Mcgreen and Burlew jumped off and waded to the edge.

They stood by the highway in the drifting rain. A thin black woman in longcoat and boots; a fat, tired-looking man in wet Bank grays, his face showing pale where patches of beard were missing. Half-covering each other with a tatty blanket Burlew had found in the planer, they extended their thumbs in the ancient sign. But a lift was Giving, and the purge was on. Planer after planer sped by them as the sky lightened through black to gray. Not all bothered to avoid splashing them with muddy water.

The poet did not notice it. His mind was on something far more important, far more menacing, even as he lifted his hand again to an approaching vehicle.

The Dark Time.

More and more clearly of late he felt its dread imminence, felt its advent as veiled but inexorable as the shrouded sun rising in the east. It was striding closer, casting its shadow over the world. For his Orphans, even

95

for Jaylen, it might be a convenient simile for revolution, a figure of speech useful in a pome. But Monaghan Burlew felt it as the epileptic the foretelling aura. Beyond it, he hoped, lay brightness; his dream seemed to say so, somehow. But it was the time between that frightened him. Only if they could convince the Bank to listen, force it to come to terms, might it be avoided, or at least shortened.

But to do that . . . he might have to destroy. He looked down at his muddy, scorched hands. He had never destroyed anything. He had never harmed anyone. Even his scams had never taken from others. Only from the Bank.

He was not at all sure he could change the habit of thirty years.

"Well?" said Jaylen, beside him.

"Well, we can't do anything now," he said, looking after another planer, which had sped up as it passed them. "We've got to go to ground for a while—lam out someplace safe."

"And where is that? The Bank is everywhere."

"I heard of a place once," Burlew said, squeegeeing muddy water slowly from his beard. "A rumor. Not really sure it exists. But if it does, and we can make it—there, we can think."

"If we can make it," said Jaylen. "You know that now, after Paris, they'll stop at nothing to kill us."

"That's right," said the poet soberly. "They'll stop at nothing at all."

"WE THINK THEY ARE STILL SOMEWHERE IN WESTERN EUROPE."

"Think? We can do that. I thought you were designed to know," Hakamaro Nagai hissed. His wizened face, wrinkled like a dried apple around the jade-green eyes, grew lopsided in a derisive smile. "The world computer, the ultimate intelligence—and you haven't been able to locate two penniless fugitives, given the better part of a year. And now this Paris outrage! Couldn't the Manifest have been used then?"

At the mention of the Manifest, the other Board members stirred uneasily. The smooth blank face turned toward the old Japanese. It spoke slowly, without inflection or expression, the words formulated somewhere in the immense parelectronic reefs of the Bank and transmitted to emerge here one by one from the lips of this ex-human mouthpiece.

"THE MANIFEST CAN BE PROJECTED ONLY WITHIN A LIMITED AREA, AND ONLY WHERE ITS POWERS CAN BE USED. WE JUDGED PARIS, WITH MILLIONS OF INNOCENT CLIENTS, AN UNSUITABLE PLACE FOR THE REALIZATION OF THE EIDOLON. IF, HOWEVER, THESE TWO ARE DETECTED IN AN AREA WHERE CIRCUMSTANCES ARE SUITABLE, IT MIGHT THEN BE EMPLOYED."

"Your concern with these 'innocent clients' sickens me," said Lady Dawnfair languidly. "Or worse—it's becoming boring."

"Why can't the Adjustors find them?" asked Muafi.

The Bank paused. "THE FULL TIME OF THE ECONOMIC ADJUSTMENT SERVICE HAS BEEN TAKEN UP WITH THE INCREASE IN CRIME. WE COULD SPARE ONLY A FEW AGENTS FOR FIELDWORK ON BURLEW AND MCGREEN. THESE TWO ARE HIGHLY MOBILE AND SEEM TO HAVE BEEN CONCEALED AND AIDED BY A DISSIDENT MINORITY OF THE POPULATION."

"The so-called Orphans?" grunted Boatwright from within a cloud of tobacco smoke.

"YES. SINCE THIS APPEARS TO BE THEIR SUPPORT STRUCTURE, WE HAVE CONCENTRATED OUR RESOURCES FIRST ON THE BREAKUP OF THIS GROUP AND THE CONFISCATION OF THEIR REPRODUCING EQUIPMENT AND LITERATURE. THIS IS CLASSIC ANTISUBVERSION DOCTRINE FROM THE BLOODY TWENTIETH—DRAIN THE SEA, AND THE FISH CEASE TO ELUDE YOU IN IT."

"That seems sound." Boatwright glanced at the others as if summing up their silence as agreement. "Well. Let's move on to the economic report, shall we? Are we still losing ground?"

The Bank did not move or speak, but suddenly the conference table became transparent. Inside it appeared a three-dimensional hologram. It was a nomograph, marked to show Gross World Production and Overall Progress Against Goal for the past fiscal year. "TO ANSWER YOUR QUESTION IN A WORD, MR. BOATWRIGHT, NO. THERE'S LIGHT AT THE END OF THE TUNNEL.

"NOTE THAT THE CURRENT GWP, 9.42 TIMES TEN TO THE ELEVENTH CU, IS ACTUALLY ABOVE THAT REACHED BEFORE BURLEW WENT UNDERGROUND IN 2110. WE HAVE REGAINED THE 3.8% DROP THAT HIS ACTIVITIES CAUSED. THEREFORE, ALTHOUGH HE IS STILL AT LARGE, HE HAS EFFECTIVELY BEEN DEFEATED. WE AND THE BLOSSOM ARE SAFE."

"Good, good," said Muafi.

"Let's see gamma-related production," said Dawnfair. The hologram wavered and changed.

"Up eight percent," said Muafi. "Good work."

"PRODUCTIVITY WAS INCREASED THROUGH INCREASED SHIFT EFFICIENCY AND LONGER HOURS PER WORKER TO ENSURE THAT CRITICAL-PATH

WAYPOINTS WERE MET IN SPITE OF ANY DISRUPTION."

Nagai, meanwhile, had leaned back, looking uneasy. He slipped a pill from an antique enameled box and swallowed it, wincing. At last he said, "Can you project GWC for us in this way?"

The hologram winked off, flickered, winked on. "GROSS WORLD CREDIT USE," said the Bank.

The last two bars on the graph towered above the others. Boatwright, the economist, sat stock-still. The pipe began to shake slightly in his hands. "There's the explanation," said Nagai softly. "Hoarding. Stockpiling. A response to perceived danger. People are borrowing to the limits of their Credit, buying food, hard goods, fuels, scarce drugs.

"It has happened many times in history. What we are seeing is an artificial prosperity, a planet readying itself for chaos."

The three old men, the amethyst-eyed woman stared at the Bank. It appeared unmoved. "Well . . . what can we do?" said Muafi, fingering his chin.

"We're doing all we can already," snapped Boatwright. "But we've got to get those two. Once they're gone and people see that things are not going to change, everything will return to normal."

"WE WILL DO OUR BEST," said the Bank. "WE WILL NOT INTERFERE WITH HOARDING, FOR IT DOES NOT AFFECT VITAL PRODUCTION AND IS NOT ILLEGAL. BUT WE WILL INTENSIFY THE SEARCH."

The Board sat silent, exchanging furtive looks. "Good enough?" suggested Muafi nervously.

"No," whispered Nagai. "Not at all. That's what he told us the last time. And he hasn't found them. Sometimes I wonder if he wants to."

The Bank ignored that. "WE AWAIT ALL LEGAL IN-STRUCTIONS," it said.

"Wait," said Lady Dawnfair. She rubbed her fingers along the smooth jade of the necklace, frowned.

"What is it, Lakshmi?"

"I too, like you, Hakamaro, have wondered how he can be so elusive. Tracing people by Credit use, without crime for so long, we seem to have lost the art of real police work.

"But perhaps there exists another way to send a token of our regard to him."

"HOW, IF WE DO NOT KNOW WHERE HE IS?"

"You are so unoriginal," said Lady Dawnfair, her violet eyes narrow, opaque, beautiful, and cruel. "All of you. I see, at times, what Greatmother must have thought of you that day she . . . fell."

Some four hundred kilometers west of the South Pole is a lonely, windswept ice cap where the temperature often drops to minus fifty Celsius. But a hundred meters down—and there is more than a mile of ice below that— it is steady at a constant minus sixteen. That is an ideal temperature to preserve properly treated life, secure enough that any cataclysm sufficient to raise the temperature above freezing would have long before resulted in the extinction of humanity on earth.

About minus eighty degrees Fahrenheit.

Here, further chilled by an isotope-fueled liquefied-nitrogen plant, the greatest murderers the planet had ever known slept the deathlike sleep of near–absolute zero. Here were old names, honored and feared through generations of those who had died with curses and prayers on fevered lips. And on the stainless vials, etched with acid so that time itself could never forget them, those names still held their ancient horror.

DIPHTHERIA
LEUKEMIA
BEHCETS DISEASE
PLAGUE, BUBONIC
IH HEPATITIS
AIDS
CEREBRAL TRYPANOSOMIASIS
SMALLPOX
SYPHILIS (RESISTANT)
MIDLINE GRANULOMA
TYPHOID
CHOLERA
BRUCELLOSIS (UNDULANT FEVER)
LEPTOSPIROSIS
JAPANESE B ENCEPHALITIS

"Stop there," said a voice halfway around the world from the row of vials. "I like the sound of that one."

Obediently the fingers of the robot handler slid to a halt above the frost-hoared canister.

"What is it?" A woman's voice, cold as liquid nitrogen.

"AN ACUTE VIRAL INFECTION ONCE COMMON IN MICE. MICE WERE—"

"We remember. We remember a little, you know. Go on. Is it fatal to man?"

"THAT DEPENDS. WITH PROPER MODERN TREATMENT—"

"*Is it fatal, I asked you!*"

"IT IS FILED IN THE MORTAL DISEASE SECTION."

"Why is it so hard to get a straight answer out of you? Is it transmissible? What are its effects?"

"SYMPTOMS ARE AT FIRST LIKE A SEVERE 'COLD.' THE MENINGES AND GRAY MATTER OF THE BRAIN

ARE QUICKLY ATTACKED, HOWEVER. TYPICAL AR-BOVIRAL LESIONS DEVELOP, PARTICULARLY IN THE PERIVASCULAR SPACES. NEURONAL DEGENER-ATION, NECROSIS, FOCAL ENCEPHALOMALACIA, AND DEMYELINIZATION FOLLOW. THOSE FEW VIC-TIMS WHO SURVIVED SHOWED PARALYSIS, DE-CEREBRATE RIGIDITY, AND PSYCHOSIS. THE DIS-EASE WAS ERADICATED IN 2043 BY WIDESPREAD USE OF—"

"It'll do."

"IT IS NOT READILY TRANSMISSIBLE IN THIS FORM."

"Make it transmissible."

"Lakshmi, wait. If we let something like this loose—"

"Shut up, Amitai. And do this too, you. You have Bur-lew's genetic profile now, from when he Charged Mcgreen's medicine. Is that correct?"

"AFFIRMATIVE."

"Design and link an inhibiting complex to this virus. It will propagate like any transmissible rhinovirus. As colds used to do. Only the main part of it will not operate—unless it encounters one specific genotype. Do you un-derstand?"

"Brilliant, Lakshmi!"

"You have outdone yourself, my dear." A hiss.

Three hundred feet beneath the Antarctic ice, eight stainless-steel manipulators closed delicately on a disease three generations dead. Twisted it, to free it from its gelid cage. Lifted it up, up, toward the wan light of a sun poised low on a white horizon.

"WE UNDERSTAND."

In the Name of the Stepfather

In that long-ago maelstrom of reflexive destruction, that disastrous death dance of the national-state system, the Last War, the inchoate sprawl of Tokyo had been the target of three Taiwanese, six Russian, and two American nuclear weapons.

When the Overcast receded, those who filtered numbly back from the hills and shelters found that the land was useless. Not only was everything destroyed, but residual beta and gamma counts would be high for generations. They couldn't build on the old earth of Edo, much as they loved it. Nor could they adopt the reconstruction strategies of the other former powers and rebuild elsewhere—the New United States, in Canada; the New Soviet Union, in the empty land of Siberia. Land-poor Nippon had nowhere else to relocate.

No strangers to destruction, they decided to rebuild on the same spot—but with a difference.

They would build in the sky.

By mid-2111, Shin'edo—the city's new name—covered two hundred square miles, suspended a kilometer above the ground by three thousand thirty-meter-thick pylons of earthmetal, the quaternary eutectic alloy that "Doctor" Gnath Greatmother had first gotten to the surface in economic quantities in 2036. The platforms themselves were primarily aluminum and inhibited magnesium, reclaimed ton by ton from the sea with fusion power. The vast tent swayed sometimes, in earthquakes, but its built-in flexibility made it safer than the old city had ever been.

Shin'edo lived on, capital of a people in some respects preeminent on the planet. As Hakamaro Nagai, despite his occasional vagueness about his own nationality, would have been the first to point out.

In its shadow, not so much forgotten as never known, dwelt the dispossessed of thirteen cultures.

"It not be possible," muttered Monaghan Burlew, flat on his back in the heap of garbage.

"What?" said Jaylen from a few feet away. She tossed aside rags and old zoris as she sorted through one edge of his cushioning pile. "Hey, me be got—I mean, I've found something. Look!"

It was a full, unopened container of gammaed tofu. Burlew glanced over, not looking very interested, as she turned the dirty plastron over and over in her gaunt fingers.

"What be it?"

"Prot!"

Burlew sat up at once, disturbing a cloud of flies.

In the months since they had left Europe he had grown noticeably thinner. The same gray joggies now hung on him raggedly, stained with sweat and worse. He blinked dully through the hair that hung over his eyes. "Food? From where?"

She jerked her thumb upward, staring at the can, and he followed her motion without thinking.

Far above them, the sky was dead black. Only here and there, where the tapered pylons disappeared through the web-thin trusses of the city platform, did the gaps left for flexion let through the used sunlight. It did not do much to brighten the ground. A kilometer below, around the hovels of trash, hammered tins, and plastron, the shadows at full noon lay close and dense as in the lowest dungeons of medieval Osaka.

A slow crunching came from outside their roofless shelter. Instantly Burlew arched his back. Mcgreen tossed the tin at the same moment, and the poet lowered himself again as a shadowy figure appeared at the entrance and paused, peering in at them.

"Ram Ram," it said, bowing itself slightly on a cane of blackened, scorched human tibias wired together with telephone cable.

"Fren Singh," said Jaylen, releasing her grip on a hefty piece of pipe. "Come in. Come in, and sit."

The old man dragged himself in and squatted by the tiny trash fire that sputtered in a corner, confined by two bent sheets of galvanized iron. In this obscurity an eye used to sunlight could not have made him out. But the two people who smiled at him, their vision adapted to the gloom, could see him clearly. An emaciated face, ragged with hanging, purpled flesh; the twisted, narrow

105

chest, as if put on sideways between hips and head; the short, almost simian lower limbs. Singh looked like a clay man mismade by a toddler.

. . . Except for his eyes, which were bright as two Indian suns under a bald and lofty forehead. "What news?" he said, squatting on his malformed legs and laughing gaily as a child.

Burlew sat up, careful to keep the tofu concealed. The pile of trash creaked and settled and the flies swarmed up. From far away came a crashing sound, and then the high keen of distant cries.

"Manna from the heavens," said the old man, listening, still smiling. "Do not the gods provide well for their children?"

"You are well, Master Singh?" said Jaylen, bending to slip a tatty cushion behind him as he leaned against the wall.

"If I were any better, my dear, I couldn't stand it. My earthbound frame would collapse, give way, beneath the joy."

"You got him plenty—ah—courage, saying that down here," said Burlew.

The old man shaped his crippled hands into a cup. "You think so? Consider, Fren Burlew. I have everything that is necessary to life. I have seen existence; I have suffered and known happiness. Can they say more, those who it is said live above? As for me, I could never understand how their eyes could stand the glare."

"How old *are* you?" asked Jaylen.

The old man chuckled indulgently, as at a child who asks a question it does not realize is meaningless. After a moment Jaylen dropped her eyes, looked away, and might even have been blushing, save that the gloom covered it. There was silence for a few minutes in the shelter, broken only by the sputtering of the fire. Burlew reached out to put another piece of garbage on it, and it leapt up smokily, limning their faces in yellow light, and then guttered down again.

"You're not going to see what came down, Singh?"

"I've eaten enough today. The young ones need it more."

"Maybe we ought to, though," she said to Burlew.

"Got enough."

"Get up, Monaghan! At least go there with me."

The two men exchanged glances. Singh rose too as the poet shrugged, turned over to drag a sheet of brightly ideographed papron over his place, and got up, not bothering to brush off the bits of refuse and dirt that clung to his clothing.

The three of them went out into the open.

In the deep night outside it was hard to see. They stumbled over the rusted hoods of half-buried Toyotas, the jutting rubble of twentieth-century concrete buildings, their facades still garish with ceramic tile. Only old Singh, leaning heavily on his crutch, proceeded without check, threading his way among the debris with the casualness of one who has lived in the same neighborhood all his life.

Ahead of them, as they picked their way forward, the cries grew louder.

A shaft of stronger, yet still feeble light was streaming down ahead, like a door opened in the night sky into Heaven. Bits of paper and cloth fluttered slowly down the beam. Beneath it, as they came around the corner of an uprooted bank vault, its sides pitted with age, they came into view of the crowd.

Some fifteen men, women, and small children were digging feverishly in a pile of fresh refuse. Bats darted above their bent heads, squeaking and chittering. The pickers cursed in fifteen different low dialects, pushing at each other, tossing useless things away, burrowing with their hands and faces into the ton or so of garbage that had just come down the still-open chute from far above.

"Plenty of competition," said Burlew. He stood aside with Singh, watching as Jaylen joined the crowd.

"Burlew?"

"Yam, fren?"

"I must apologize even before I speak. It is unseemly, at my age, to be curious."

"What you be saying?"

"I was about to ask you something," said the old man, peering up at him.

"Sure. Pop me."

Singh seemed embarrassed. He poked at the ground with the knobby end of his cane. "You and Jaylen appeared suddenly here among us," he began. "I know it cannot be that long ago—weeks perhaps, though what is time to us?—that you came. Yet it seems that we have always known you, in some strange way.

"I have never asked you from where you came. But new faces, here in the Shitamachi, among the Eta—that is something not even I, the oldest among us, has ever seen before."

Burlew shrugged.

"You come from—Up There?"

"Yam."

The offhand response seemed to stagger the old man. "From Shin'edo? Where the light is?"

"Not just there. From everywhere the light be, might be saying."

"All right, I won't ask you that again," said the old man, nodding, evidently interpreting Burlew's vagueness in some way of his own. "But how did you get here? We have only old stories, told us by those who were gray when we were babes, about . . . Up There. I think some of the younger ones, now, they do not even believe them."

"See that light up there?" said Burlew.

"Yes, Burlew, I see it."

"We be come down him. Or one like it, not far away. There be people up there want us. The Bank."

"What is that?"

Burlew stared at the old man for a moment, then recovered himself. "Greatmother! You never hear of Bank? One good thing down here, anyway. Jaylen and me, we be lamming. Heard once, somewhere, be place here could do the disappear. Got here stroking near dead—had to hoof it over most of Afghanistan. Got to Shin'edo, I laid sign for some Orphans."

"Your words walk strangely into my ears, Fren Burlew. What then are Orphans?"

"Frens of ours. Anyway, they be gone; Bank must have taken them all, reeducate, terminate. So we try to hide. No place to go. Adjustors all over, covering the exits. So finally me ask one third-class stroke, Hay, frenita, where be dump in this city? Figured could hang out there awhile till heat is off. But she tell me, no dump; just took me to a chute and pointed down. 'Gomi,' she called it."

"You fell down from Up There? It is so far in the sky—"

"No, nyet, not be falling, no way. Climb down him rope we steal. Plenty rough, too. Tied knots in it before we toss it so we could stop and rest. Still almost fall off couple of times."

The old man stared up at him for an unconscionably

109

long time. Burlew would have felt nervous, except that he knew how harmless he was. Still, the look made him feel odd.

"And now you are here, in the Shitamachi."

"Yam."

Old Singh nodded. "Will you stay, Fren Burlew? Or will you and the Jaylen go back to the Light someday?"

Burlew looked at the struggling people and shrugged. "Not be knowing. Got no plans now."

"You are welcome to stay with us," the old man said a little hesitantly.

"Maybe for a while. Nobody from topside ever comes down here? Grays, or anybody?"

"Down here?" Singh shook his head. "No. No way down, no way up. They say long ago one person came to the Burakumin—the Lord Rama. They tell many stories of him. But since then . . . no."

"Then maybe we stay for a while," said Burlew. "At least it be safe."

"And you will remember," said Singh, "if you do go back, that old Singh was hospitable to you?"

"Oh sure," said Burlew, though he did not entirely feel that he understood what was (as he might have phrased it himself) "walking" in the old man's mind.

In the weeks that followed, old Singh came around to their shack almost every day. Sometimes he brought a small dirty-faced girl with withered arms. They assumed Vashti was his granddaughter, though he never said, and she hardly ever spoke. Out of sheer boredom Jaylen questioned him, and found that once convinced someone wanted to hear, Singh was a superb storyteller. They listened, entranced, around the trash fire as he wove the lore of the "Yume no Shima"—the Dream Island, what

110

the Edo called their world. The best, the funniest, and the most imaginative (aside from the story of the Chikatetsu ghosts) centered on the figure of the Lord Rama. Part man, part ape, part god, he played incredible tricks on the light-blinded folk Up There. The old man told how he had once come down to the Shitamachi, and how on that day the sun had shone, once, on the city below the city.

How, when he left, he promised them that the sun would shine on them again—at the end of this world and the coming of the next.

In recompense, Burlew sang songs, recited pomes, told stories of his scams. Some were sad and some were hilarious. He was unsure how much of what he sang and recited was even comprehensible to people for whom the outside world was a myth generations old. But regardless of whether she took it as reality or fantasy, or knew the difference, the little girl smiled as she listened, hugging her useless arms silently to her bare chest in the firelight.

One night as they lay close together for warmth, after the old man had picked up his cane from the door and, bowing to the ground, had limped with the little one out into the darkness, Jaylen whispered, "You don't feel sorry for them?"

"Me?" said Burlew. He was lying in what had become his habitual position on the pile of trash. "Why? At least Stepfather not be bothering them down here."

"But the sickness. The filth. The radiation. Hardly any of them live to be forty. The poor children, without food or light—"

He shrugged.

"Damn you!" She brushed the flies savagely from her face, pushed her hair back, and sat up to stare into the

111

fire. From the distant dark came a wail; along with the Eta, packs of wild tanukis had adapted themselves to this subterranean world. He opened his eyes to watch her. "Monaghan . . . you've changed. I don't understand how or why."

"I know."

"You don't seem to care. You don't help me look for food. You don't even eat. You don't seem to want anything anymore."

Burlew's gaze stayed on her. But when she turned to confront him, she saw only a well of darkness above his beard, under his hair. She saw suddenly that he was growing thin, even gaunt. The worn coveralls lay in empty folds where, once, healthy Burlew had bulged at the seams.

And where she had loved his gaiety, his carelessness, lack of fear or respect for anything in his world, now he was simply . . . apathetic.

"Care?" he repeated slowly. "Why should I be caring? Only one on him Earth, if I do. All the rest of them . . . too selfish and frightened."

"That's not the way the man I loved used to talk. He was proud to stand out."

"That man be gone, stroke."

"Why? Where?"

"Just gone, that's all . . . it's over, Jaylen." He turned from the firelight, shielding his eyes with his arm. "Don't push me anymore. The Bank has won. Maybe him was right all along."

"Monaghan, listen. How long are we going to stay here? What are we going to do?"

"Maybe we could . . . just live here."

Jaylen could not believe he had muttered that. Was the old man's idiot mysticism getting to him? The sound of

112

his voice, hollow, resigned, dismayed her as much as his words. But the words were terrible enough.

That man be gone.

Brushing flies from her face and his, she stared at him as the fire sank lower, into coals. Long before she nodded asleep, the darkness had walked into the hut, and with it the weird wails of beasts echoing from the metal sky.

A few days later—a few weeks later—it was too difficult to tell where night and day were so much alike—Burlew and Singh sat together on the highest point in the Shitamachi. A small hill of rock, trash, old concrete abutments, contaminated-and-discarded bulldozers, it was crowned by a breast-high rampart of roughly piled rubble.

"When I was young," the old man said, patting the rampart fondly, "this was where we held off the bandits from between."

Burlew looked off around him. The hill overlooked the dim underworld like an acropolis. And from what Singh said, that was what it was. In the obscurity, lightened only a little here and there by the filtered gloom from above, he could make out in the darker patches firefly glimmers of blue and green. Some of it was will-o'-the-wisp, methane evolved by the rotting garbage. Some was radioactivity. The Eta tried not to stay long in places that actually glowed. But, looking at the growths on Singh's face, his warped body, Burlew thought that was anything but a sufficient precaution.

He wondered how much dosage he and Jaylen had accumulated. But instead of fear, the thought brought only the same apathy, the same world-weariness he had felt more and more strongly since the failure of the flito coup and the loss of the Orphans there.

Singh, who had meanwhile grubbed up with his cane a corroding copper spear point, was still talking about the wars that had occupied his youth. Like Bedouins, the Shitamachi seemed to have evolved a society of dual status: those who lived at the oases—in this case beneath the chutes; and those who moved between, the nomads. Gradually the latter had become bandits, for food. Their power had been broken in a climactic battle in the gloom, as meaningful in its way, Burlew supposed, as Thermopylae or Verdun.

"And that was my last," the old man said. "Since that time I have lifted no hand against my fellow."

Burlew leaned against the breastwork, slowly hefting the crude weapon. It looked as if it had been beaten by hand from a chunk of scrap cable. In the gloom it was easy to imagine a swarm of deformed and starving men, wielding crude spears, knives, bucklers, attacking those who had held this height. "And do you believe that is the way to live?"

"Fren Burlew," said the old man, turning to look him in the eye, "what is wrong?"

"Wrong?"

"I see it in your eyes. Inside you, two powers are wrestling. Are they good and evil? I cannot imagine you hesitating a moment before such a choice. Perhaps, rather, they are action and resignation?"

"That could be accurate," said Burlew.

"Can an old man help?"

"I know what your advice would be. Now, anyway."

"Where do your words walk, Fren Burlew?"

"You might have answered me differently," said Burlew, nodding toward the gloom, "when you stood here with a spear in your hand."

"I might have."

"So then there are two answers, and both from the same man. That doesn't help me much."

"That is true," said Singh, "only if you assume that the forty years between have taught me nothing."

Burlew looked at him sharply. But the old man's face was innocent of sarcasm, even humble as he looked down at the poet's mutilated feet.

Shortly after that talk, for the first time in the memory of the Eta, the garbage stopped. Nothing came down the shafts. The people were first surprised, then worried, as hunger, never far away, became their constant companion.

It was several days later that Burlew was wakened by a distant scream. He felt Jaylen sit up beside him at the same moment. They lay listening in the dark, aware of each other but not yet willing to speak. At last she whispered, "What did she say?"

"I thought it be'ed . . . *sorabei*?"

"Sky rice?" repeated Jaylen, puzzled.

There was the sound of running outside. Of many people running. And a shout.

"Tabemono o nagesutete ita! Midori paipu!"

"They're dumping food! Green shaft!"

They caught their breaths together, and simultaneously started up. Burlew charged straight through the fire, not stopping to curse as the coals scorched his bare feet. Three days' hunger did wonders for apathy.

Outside, in the near dark of late afternoon, a stream of the Eta were running, hobbling, dragging themselves through the broken dimness. A pinheaded boy caromed off Jaylen. "What is it?" she called after him.

"Prot coming down. Nada but prot!"

"Can't be," said Burlew.

115

"Let's find out. I'm starving."

At the shaft they found that it was true. In fact, it had not yet stopped falling. Fresh, sweet loaves of seaprot, some still warm at the center, fresh-smelling of grain and fish. The Hayashi were tearing at them, stuffing their mouths full of the gray centers, the darker crust. Some, the early worms, were sprawled off around the dump, holding their stomachs dazedly at the wholly new sensation of satiety.

"Here," said Mcgreen rapidly, thrusting an armful of food at him. "Here's two for you—and stuff this one down the front of your joggies, you've got plenty of room there now. I'll take some of these—"

Burlew fingered one of the loaves. He broke it open and sniffed at it.

"It smells *good*—" Mcgreen said, the latter part of the sentence occluded by a huge mouthful.

"Spit it out," he said suddenly.

"Mmurf?" she said. Then began fighting, choking, spitting, as his arm caught the side of her head, his hand wrenched her jaw down, his fingers cleared bread from around her tongue. He pulled the loaves from her half-open clothing and threw them to the ground.

"God *damn* you, you ape—what are you doing?"

"It's no good."

"This? You're crazy!"

"Jaylen. Think. They be dumping food. Here. *Why?*"

She looked at him searchingly, then at the loaves that were dimly visible as pale patches near their feet. And her face began subtly to change.

The first groans, not of satiety but of pain, came from the recumbent figures around them.

"We have to stop them."

"It be too late now, stroke. Let's go."

116

"No. Some of them haven't yet—Vashti! *Tabecha ikenai!*" Jaylen screamed.

The girl looked up for an instant, eyes wide in a bread-smeared face. She jerked away from Jaylen's grasp and disappeared into the darkness, clutching the half-loaf between her useless arms.

"Come on, Jaylen."

He dragged her back to the hut. They crouched by the fire, both shivering. After a moment they moved together and held each other.

"Why, Monaghan? Why? No one does things like this anymore. This isn't the Bloody Twentieth."

"Somebody be doing it now."

"They weren't—these people weren't hurting anyone!"

"They not be working. Maybe that why Grays did it."

"But just to kill them! Like *this*!"

"Maybe—" said Burlew, and then stopped, as one wall of the hut wobbled crazily and then collapsed.

"Singh!" screamed Mcgreen.

He lay half in, half out of the scattered fire, his grisly crutch still gripped in withered claws. He made no sound as his loincloth began to smolder; his eyes were closed. They dragged him out, beat at the sparks till they died, and propped him against the remaining wall. "Water," Jaylen ordered, and Burlew dipped a rag into a rusty can of storm-sewer runoff and dabbed it on his face.

"I think he's gone."

"No. I feel—"

"Still alive," muttered the old man. He worked his face for a time, as if remembering how it was done. Then he opened his eyes. His very next effort was to try to smile.

"You ate it. How much?"

"Enough."

117

"Can he vomit? That might help."

Burlew cradled his head, but the old man made a motion of rejection with one bony hand. "Him not be wanting to."

"I doubt it would work, anyway. Something modern and quick—no waste of time." She bent over Singh. "Anyway . . . we're here with you, Fren."

"It is all well," he muttered. His eyes were sinking closed again. "We all have to go sometime."

"We can't help you. I tried to stop some of the others. Monaghan knew it right away. The little girl—"

Burlew's hand on her shoulder stopped her.

"Many will die," murmured the old man wearily. "Many. Many live. All die. That is just a fact, you know. Listen."

Outside, the Eta were screaming.

"Fren Burlew," muttered the old man. They had to lean close now to hear him.

"What? Fill us."

"Forgive yourself."

"Me?"

"Yes. Forgive . . . for I see a great work."

"What?" said Burlew again.

"For you, Lord . . . that is, Fren Burlew. No, I die, why should I not say it! Did you think you tricked me too? I know who you are. You are the Destined. Lord Rama, the Joke-Player, the Scam-Puller, He Who Comes Down From Up There. Do you understand?"

"No," said Burlew. "Better rest. I be thinking—"

"Silence," said the old man. His voice was slightly stronger now, as if with anger. "Once I thought the gods, those who live in brightness, were wiser than men. Then I met you. But, true, Rama is only one-third a god. So perhaps he should listen. The time is dark soon. Do you understand *that*?"

118

The poet stared down into the sun-bright old eyes, deep with the suffering and joy of twenty thousand nights in the shadowland of the Yume no Shima. Into the face scarred and crossed by old wounds, distorted by the immense blue epithelioma that hung from ear to jaw. *The time is dark soon. . . .*

"Yam, me get you now," he said slowly.

"Soon dark. Then Shiva comes, the Destroyer of Worlds. Only you are there to wrestle with him for us. You, the monkey-god, the man-ape, the trickster, only you. You must . . ."

"Must what?" said Jaylen, leaning over him.

So lightly they had to guess at them, he whispered the last words.

"Must be . . . *paramita*. . . ."

"Be what? Be *what*, dammit?" Burlew reached out to shake him.

"He is talking to his gods now," whispered Jaylen, drawing shut Singh's eyes.

They sat back on their heels and looked at each other across the old man's screwed-up legs.

"What he be trying to say there? There at the end?"

"I don't know, Monaghan."

Burlew pulled at his beard. The fire leapt up, and she saw that tears glittered back the flamelight from his cheeks. "Singh. Singh! Dark Time—yam, fren, me got that. But me never told him about that! How he be knowing?"

"I'm sure he never saw a handbill or a flito in his life."

"No, he be like me, he *saw* it. But what's all the rest? Rama, Shiva—and what he said first, forgiving *me*—"

He stopped suddenly. They looked at each other again, and then he raised his hands slowly—she could see them trembling—and put them over his face.

"The rope," whispered Jaylen.

"The rope," said Burlew. "Same shaft we came down. They found it. They not even know Hayashi here, maybe. The food—it be'd for us."

Jaylen, still cradling the incredibly light body of the old man, stood and looked upward. "May you all be damned for this," she whispered to the black metal sky that was all the Eta had ever known of heaven.

That night they left the Shitamachi.

They spent all of five minutes discussing how to do it. It felt good to think about something concrete again, about a problem.

Neither of them wanted to think about what had happened, or why.

The shaft up—the Green Shaft, the Eta had called it— was no good. There would be armed guards there now. Burlew was sure of that. The others would probably be guarded too, and besides there was absolutely no chance of their climbing nearly a kilometer straight up, even assuming there was a way to do so.

And shortly, perhaps even as they spoke, *they* would be coming down to make sure he and Jaylen were finally out of the way.

They had to leave . . . *now*.

"But how can we get out? Where can we go?"

"Shut up, stroke. I be thinking."

"I *am* thinking."

"Yam . . . shafts no good now. Pylons be too smooth to climb. And city platform seals exit toward the hills. The water, then."

"There's still some in the can."

"No. Me . . . I mean, the big water. Singh told me about it. City built out over him."

"Where?"

"Trying to remember what he said. Follow pylons, I think. They be built in rows. So we follow a line of them, heading downhill, maybe we get there."

"How far is it?"

"That, he not say. But we got to leave, Jaylen. Can't stay, that be no lie."

There was nothing to carry, nothing for them to take except, of course, the blanket. They left the body by the fire. They piled the remains of their personal trash on it and then pushed down the walls. Over them Jaylen poured the remains of her treasured cooking oil. After a moment the flames licked out from underneath, tasted it, licked higher.

It was not much, but it would have to do for a pyre.

As they moved away from the hut Jaylen looked upward. Some of the shafts were open that had been closed before. They looked like rectangular stars in a black sky. When the growing fire was out of sight, they turned forward and began to run, stumbling over the debris in their haste, over the uneven ground, over soft . . . dead things.

"Come *on*," said Burlew.

"I'm coming. No food, I can't run very fast."

"Got to. More shafts opening all the time. They be down soon."

"They're all dead," she said, looking around her at a particularly nasty scene. The family sat together around a slab of stone. Whoever had found the bread had restrained hunger, hastened homeward, and called them together for a feast. . . .

"We be too, we not hurry."

They panted on through the obscurity, slipping and falling, cutting their hands and feet on shards of glass, running headlong into invisible obstacles. Only the glimmer from distant shafts, and at times the slow green glow of radioactivity, lit their way.

". . . Can't keep up."

"Here. Keep going. Take a rest soon, two more pylons." Burlew was breathing hard too, and his voice was hoarse.

A few hundred yards on, they rested for a minute, lying concealed under an immense metal overhang, part of something half-buried. Burlew stared up at it, puffing. It was enormous. Rusty steel. At one end of it a huge greenish thing, four twisted blades . . . "It's a ship," Jaylen panted.

"Ship?"

"Like a sea planer, old-style. The water can't be far off now. The land's sloping down more. Can't you feel it, Monaghan?"

"Yam. Yam, I can. Feel better now? Let's go."

A half-mile on they stumbled on it . . . stumbled into it, before they saw: stinking black water, the bottom slippery with scum. Small waves bit at their ankles with icy teeth. But over them, ahead of them, the overarching roof went on, the pylons marching off into the gloom as far as they could make them out.

"Now what?"

"Don't know."

"Let's go along the shore."

"Maybe a boat—"

"Here?" said Jaylen incredulously. "Monaghan . . . look. Back there—"

Back there, lights were coming on. Brilliant green point sources, built, it seemed, into the underside of the sky. Dim with the distance, but bright to their shadow-tuned eyes. Far back, but more of them every second that they watched.

"They be here," said Burlew.

They turned and ran along the edge of the black water. Head-size stones converted their run to a teetering crawl. The waves sucked restlessly at their feet. More lights came on, closer.

"Something ahead," grunted Mcgreen.

Burlew hesitated a moment too long on a rock, lost his balance, and fell full-length in the slimy water. Cursing, he scrambled up. They made the last few meters to the thing and leaned against it, sobbing for air.

"What is it?" she got out, after a moment.

"Some kind of pipe."

The lights came on directly over their heads; the world transformed instantaneously from gray to a blinding argon green. Blinking, Burlew looked the obstacle over. It was a pipe, all right. An immense metal duct, five meters in diameter. Its lower end ran out into the sea; its upper curved in a long, unsupported loop toward a nearby pylon that was thicker than its neighbors. As they leaned against it they could feel a faint vibration.

"It's an uptake," said the economist suddenly.

"A what?"

"City water. They pump it up from here. There must be an F-plant up there, desalinization works."

"It sucks up this crud?"

"Now you've got it."

"Up to the city?"

"Yes. But . . . where are you going?"

He was wading out to sea. The waves, sparkling brilliant green, reached for his waist and then his throat. He disappeared under them for a moment, came up coughing, and began to swim.

"*Monaghan!*"

Sculling his arms, he felt carefully with his bare toes.

The water was icy, but he couldn't care about that. There seemed to be a mesh, or grating, over the entrance. "Here. Out here be him end. Feel him current? Pretty strong. Goes in here. Wonder whether—"

"Burlew . . . come back here. If you think I'm going to—!"

But he had already disappeared. Jaylen stared out at the black water in disbelief; then turned, hearing the electric whip of verticopter blades echo from the roof.

He came up spluttering. "Jay . . . Jaylen! Come on. Swim out here."

She turned back to him, clenching her fists. "We can't go through there."

"Only way out. Be a hole here, near bottom. Come on, stroke."

"Burlew, you nut—"

"I'm going." His voice was grim. It was bright enough now for her to see his expression. The apathy was gone. "Come on! Trust me—or *them*?"

Swallowing her fear, she waded out into the water.

When she got to where he had been, he was gone. Small whirlpools chased across the surface, concave under the lights. She treaded water and felt for the opening with her feet. It was too far down. She dipped her face beneath the water unwillingly and groped in the darkness, feeling the dragging power of the current. Her hand tore on something jagged: the mesh. There was a hole there, all right.

She came up for a breath and sculled on the surface, panting, almost crying. Every instinct she inherited told her not to go into that dark place, without air, with no knowledge of how long they would be there or what awaited them at the end. Every instinct but one.

Yes, she thought, he knew enough not to argue with

me. All the argument in the world would not have gotten me to do this. So he just—went first.

When the pulsating lights of the verticopter came into view, sweeping toward her, she took one last breath and dove. The current seized her in a moment and sucked her in feetfirst.

Some seconds ahead of her into the dark, Burlew's ears were full of icy water and the rushing hum of power. He was tumbled over and over, smashing his head and back against the smooth interior of the duct. Light burst in his brain at each blow, but that was all he saw, though his eyes were open. He grabbed out, trying to slow himself, but the current tore him past the smooth walls and he spun helplessly.

Seconds later he fetched up against something solid with a shock that rattled his teeth. He lay flat, pinned like a moth against a radiator. The force of the water pouring around, past him, was terrific. One of his arms protruded poking through the mesh.

Something soft hit him, knocking free the last of his air. Jaylen. He gasped, taking in a mouthful of bitter sea, and felt at the barrier with his free hand in the dark.

This one was solid, thicker than the first. He couldn't bend or rattle it, even with all his air-starved strength.

Pinned like a bug in the dark, Monaghan Burlew felt himself beginning to die.

His senses reached out, intensifying with the need for breath until his consciousness seemed to fill the darkness. Roughness of metal. Coldness of sea. Utter black. The all-filling hum. Salt. Beside him he could feel Jaylen squirming. Her arm struck his back, went away, returned. He was overwhelmed even in his suffering. She be trying to hold me, said the last remnant of his conscious mind. But even as he thought it, her hand

125

moved past him, creeping out over the mesh, and he felt her stretch out over him. He put his hand up to hers. Her cold fingers were exploring the edge of a flange. Exploring a fastening, on the inside of the mesh.

He reached past it to the next one. A latch lever . . . he pushed it up with his fingers and a corner of the wire sagged under the pressure of their bodies. He swallowed to keep from breathing. His throat fought him to open. Anything to fill it, water would be all right, somehow his lungs wanted even that . . . he swallowed again, desperately, and his fingers found another latch and sprang it.

She must have been doing the same thing on the far side of the mesh. There was a grating noise, carried clearly through the water, and suddenly the upper part of the grid gave way, bending backward under the pressure of their bodies. The water rushed past them. The mesh bent, creaked, bent. He thrust his arms through the gap, then his shoulders.

He pulled himself up and through blindly, feeling but beyond knowing that Jaylen was clutching at his legs. The renewed pull of sea flushed them through. Tumbling again, being borne as relentlessly along as—

Light.

They clawed together toward it and broke the surface, gobbling fetid air. The current whirled them forward. They were too weak to fight it. As his vision came back, Burlew caught a glimpse of an arching metal overhead. They were being carried down a wide trough filled with the rushing sea. Along one side of it a disused-looking catwalk of expanded metal rusted peacefully under a single naked coldlight. Something bumped him, and he turned himself weakly in the water.

"You . . . be all right?"

She was coughing, choking. "You silly ass," she got

out between paroxysms. "That was the stroking *stupidest*—"

"We be alive."

"Not your fault!" She stopped talking to suck more air, and he got her arm. She punched him away weakly.

"Dam. Hay—"

"Let's get out of this sewer," she said. "It could close in again any second."

They hung on the catwalk supports for long minutes before they could help each other climb the few feet to the gratings. They moved like drunks, making ridiculous open-armed grabs, missing, showing their teeth. When they were up, they lay full-length on the metal, panting hard and exchanging angry looks.

"Now what, smart guy?"

"Only two ways to go."

"Well, we sure don't want to go back down stream."

Their steps set the flimsy catwalk rattling, sent echoes chasing down the curving walls. The turbid sea rushed under their feet. At intervals it was dammed by metal filters, of progressively finer mesh. Dead fish, seaweed, and trash were built up in shoals at each barrier. The smell was nauseating. Jaylen could not suppress a shudder, looking at them. In time their bodies would have rotted, torn free, her flesh ending as rags on these filters, picked at by crabs—

"Here's a way up," said Burlew, ahead of her.

Ten minutes later they were in the street.

It was early dusk. To them the sky was brilliant, so hot scarlet they had to blink and shade their eyes with their hands. They cowered in the shelter of the desal plant's walls.

Burlew peered through his fingers. As the sun faded through red to pinking glow, he began to make sense of

127

his surroundings. The plant, behind them, and another large building formed an alley. At the far end he could make out a street. Occasionally a vehicle would flash by on it, and there were people. The light, the movement, both attracted and repelled him.

"You're a mess," Mcgreen was saying. "And I don't look much better. Oh. Damn. I hurt my hand, too."

"You really be bleeding."

She touched his head gently. Her fingers came away red. "You're kind of cut up, too."

"Look out! Someone coming!"

They stared around for cover, but the alleyway was bare as a Japanese room. The short man was sniffling as he came toward them from the light. He carried a metal box and wore the green joggies of a tech, neatly creased and flared: obviously he was something of a dandy. He stopped once as they watched, halfway up the alley, and blew his nose.

"Hi, fren," said Burlew.

"*Ohayo san,*" said the short man, nodding. He looked surprised; then the surprise turned into a sneeze, spraying Burlew. "*Kono byōki no yarō ne!—Kensa o suru tame ni kimashitaka?*"

"Did you get that?" the poet asked Mcgreen.

"No."

He nodded, and pointed back at the street. When the man turned his head Burlew punched him cold.

"Monaghan—!"

"Got to have stuff," said Burlew, dragging the tech's limpness back farther into the alley. Velcro whined. "Can't talk to him. Don't know Japanese. Just have to take. Finished being nice guy, Jaylen. For good. Here . . . these may fit you better than me."

The metal box held the man's lunch. They dragged the

unconscious worker inside the door of the plant. Burlew found a length of metal cable. They ate, waiting behind the door. When the next man in the night shift came in, he coldcocked him too. In one of his pockets he found a microdepilator and paused, turning it over in his fingers. "Jaylen. How you work one of these things?"

"Squeeze it."

It vibrated silently in his hand.

"What are you doing?"

"Shaving."

Ash drifted down on the two workers. Jaylen stared as a strange narrow jaw, high cheekbones, a hard, gaunt face emerged from beneath the moving head of the machine. It worked itself into a frown. "Say. Can you get the top? I can't reach him."

"Your hair, too?"

"Yam."

"How do you want it?"

"Short. Like theirs."

"Greatmother," she breathed a few minutes later.

Burlew rubbed his hand over the bristle of his scalp, then gingerly felt his face. "Feels cold. Feeling like a kid again, before beard. Fifteen years."

"You look *really* strange. Like someone else. No . . . like *anyone* else."

"Think so? Pass for Client?"

She studied his new uniform, the new boots. "You lost a lot of weight down there. Maybe you could—if you didn't open your mouth. Do you know who you're supposed to be?"

He glanced down at his idpatches. "Hetero. Good. How about you?"

"Homo."

"Uh-oh. Well, get you different later. We be looking

like we work together, anyway. Come on. Time to move."

But she held back, staring down at the two men. "Monaghan. You're not going to just . . . leave them?"

"They be all right here till next shift." He looked down too, then bent to the nude bodies. A strip of flesh-colored tape came free from each man's buttock. He held one of them out to her. "Here. Come on, take him."

"S-patches? Us?"

"Can't waste time sleeping anymore, Jaylen. To fight the Stepfather for real, we're going to have to live like him. Look like him. Fight like him. Got to work nights, not just days. Dress like everyone else. And . . . do the same things he does to us." He breathed deeply and peered out the half-opened door into the alley.

Her eyes traced his profile against the last flush of sunset. How could sixty pounds and a shave make him so different? Then she remembered what they had seen that day.

Yes. That could change a man.

"But these people . . . they aren't Grays. What if they're really hurt?"

"Then we Charge it on the Bank's card." He grabbed her arm roughly. "Come on. Got things to do."

"What things?"

"To destroy," said Burlew.

Opening the door, he stepped out boldly into the night.

There were three anomalous fires in Shin'edo that week. The first was a small one, hardly noticed. It was at a laundry. It was put out by the automatic Pyronix flood system. But there was no way to tell what was missing.

The second was at a parelectronic manufacturing and

quality-testing plant. It ruined a hundred and twenty-five million CU worth of continuous-process organic polymer production equipment, curing ovens, and robot assemblers, and left the floor solid with tons of slowly cooling polydiacetylene. Investigators found that most of the Pyronix, a foaming protein product, had been drained from the sprinklers and apparently eaten.

The third was at a liquid-fuels plant. When the flames reached the hydrogen tanks the explosion tore through the city platform beneath, toppling a pylon and dragging sixteen full blocks of industrial sector into the sea.

In Sydney a few weeks later, four people got messages from a man they had almost forgotten existed. There was a meeting late one night. They did not recognize the clean-shaven Class II until he began to speak. They were doubtful about what he told them at first. But he was very persuasive.

A few days later the major seaprot fields on the Barrier Reefs were found to be contaminated. The fast-breeding bacteria had been spread, apparently, by means of the bottom-laid piping that released fertilizer and trace nutrients into the shallow water. The entire field had to be purged with chlorine, and several million tons of tainted food flushed out to sink.

The intrusion alarms at a drug complex in what had once been the Philippines never went off. That, as an author of the Naive Nineteenth had once said of a dog that did not bark, was what was significant.

For a time thereafter nothing happened. Then, one after another, several suborbs were reported down. The investigation was intense; none but Class I's could afford to travel by suborbital, or could indeed get permission to travel at all now. But the black boxes reported that all systems had functioned normally. The onboard computers had officially taken over from the human pilots at twenty thousand meters altitude, four thousand kilometers an hour, up angle fifty degrees. They had flown the huge craft, half-plane, half-rocket, through the two-minute hydrogen-scramjet boost phase into near space, guided it through its long loop across the face of the planet, and brought it safely back into air. But when the wings extended and they dipped their needle noses for the runway, the ships kept on going down.

Right into the ground.

They finally found the answer when a notoriously jerk-off copilot broke the regulations. He neglected to paste a fresh TransCon-issue sleepatch on his rump before take-off. His pilot reentered the atmosphere at five thousand miles an hour deep in slumber. The supersessives in that batch of S-patches, they found, had had one short link in the molecule inserted backwards. The result had been a soporific ten times as powerful as chloral hydrate.

Blinking, sniffling, the gaunt man threw his head back to swallow the gelatin-coated capsule. He followed it with a bite of irradiated krill brick, emergency rations the Bank had released after the Barrier Reef failure. It was fishy-tasting, gritty with silaceous diatoms and euphasids. It took him back to the zoo at Seafloor Twelve. So long ago, it seemed!

If he, now, was eating krill, what were *they* eating?

His thoughts did not slow his wolfing the stuff down mouthful by mouthful. Since leaving the Shitamachi he had been pursued by an insatiable hunger. No matter how much he ate, the fever seemed to consume it—and him.

The freezing climate didn't help. He pulled the collar

of the thermsuit tighter and shivered as the wind drove snow against the ceiling of the igloo. Across the shelter two Yakuts stared impassively in the light of a portable fuelglow as Jaylen passed Burlew part of her krill.

"Are you feeling any better, Monaghan?"

He grunted and blew his nose in his fingers. She looked away; the Yakuts' expressions did not change. "Uh. No. Still stuffed up. And still feel that damn headache back there."

"We don't have to do this today. We can wait."

"No. Everything's ready." Burlew finished the last crumb of krill, looked regretfully at the empty wrapper, and licked his fingers, sighing. The Yakuts' eyes followed his every gesture. He picked up the printouts and looked at them. "Going?"

Outside the shelter was a bitter white dawn. The wind slapped them casually and stuffed snow into their eyes. The two Siberian Inuit muttered to each other around the planer's turbine for long minutes before it whined and burst into life, blowing eddies of heat into the chill wind. The four of them made a crowd when the bubble was pulled down and the planer began to move, bumped once on a hummock of snow, and lifted off.

A meter above the drifts, making two hundred klicks, they whined eastward across the Kamchatka shore. From time to time the driver jinked to avoid radioactive areas. Inland, where the sub pens and missile bases of the Old Soviet Union had once been, it was too hot even to cross in a planer. They left the land behind at last and bored slowly out over the pancake ice of the Bering Sea. Burlew frowned over one of the printouts, muttering to himself. The Yakuts were silent. From time to time the turbine faltered, and one of them would look frightened. The other, the one who was driving, seemed not to care one way or the other.

"Should be there soon," the poet said, sniffling.

From the white fog that covered the strait, an island took shape. At first it was gray, a faint trace above the rippled white of the sea. Then, as they closed, it became rock; and last of all, buildings humped up under the snow. Buildings, and a long pier.

"There's the recovery sub," said Jaylen.

"Then the screens should be—"

The nervous Yakut pointed, said something rapid. On a low spit, jutting out into the ice, five radar panels lay at an angle to the sky. "Rite," said Burlew decisively. He cracked the side of the bubble and held the printouts to the slipstream. They disappeared instantly behind them as the planer tilted in a long turn.

"Da?" said the driver.

"Do him."

The turbines climbed the scale. The nervous Yakut said something in Low Russian to the dashboard. The acceleration braces came up to grip their shoulders; the shatter screens dropped in front of their eyes.

At three hundred kilometers an hour, the planer flashed across the last hundred meters of ice-choked beach, lifted for the rocky shore of the spit, and turned toward the tilted screens. A sudden banging jolt sent them all into the braces, and the turbine leapt into a higher register.

Burlew, looking back, saw the fragile trusswork of the radars hang motionless for a moment after the planer burst through them. Then splinters, guy wires, pieces of light metal exploded outward, and above that the whole structure toppled slowly, drawn remorselessly by the earth, folding and shattering itself into masses of junk amid the planer's wake of blown snow and exhaust smoke.

Startled faces turned to follow them from the decks of a fat-bodied submarine as the planer flashed past out to sea. They leaned again in a long turn, this time feeling the planer judder beneath them. "Damage?" said the poet.

The round-faced driver bared his yellow teeth in a huge grin.

And Burlew leaned back, smiling too, and wiped his nose on his sleeve, oblivious of Jaylen's brooding look.

Without midcourse correction, the next ten loads of zeolites impacted far out in the Pacific. And then the launches stopped. It would take weeks to repair the terminal-guidance radars at Kamandorskiye.

"THEY ARE STRIKING AT VITAL AREAS. FUELS. FOOD. AND MOST IMPORTANT OF ALL—PAR-ELECTRONIC COMPONENTS."

"But who are 'they'?" the ancient man asked softly.

"DISAFFECTED ELEMENTS."

"The last time we met"—Lady Dawnfair paused—"you assured us that all 'disaffected elements' had been taken out of play."

"THEY HAD, THOSE WHO WERE THEN ACTIVE. CONDITIONS ARE EVIDENTLY CHANGING."

"And at an incredibly bad time. . . . It's *him* again," said Boatwright. He coughed, pounding the table weakly, then looked at his hand. It was already purpling with bruise.

Amitai Muafi said nothing. He sat slumped in his seat, looking sad, glancing at one or the other of his colleagues from time to time. The air around him hummed silently.

Outside the Boardroom, the Tahitian sun poured down

135

on the steep green of mountains. Inside it, behind carefully polarized windows, the air was cool and still, scented with one of Lady Lakshmi's favorites. The five Members of the Board sat tensely round the block of crystal that was this month's table. Nagai was informal, in a mandarin robe of white brocade. Boatwright was wearing a hand-tailored white suit. Muafi had chosen a good but unobtrusive business joggie of gray, and was the only one in the room showing idpatches. Lady Dawnfair, tanned, was dressed in a rough cotton sari of native print. Her fingers plucked at the necklace, but today there was an addition to it. A pendant, suspended on indium-gold. Inside its crystal heart, between the half-concealed swell of her breasts, a tiny pale fetus curled in eternal sleep.

"Perhaps it is," she said. She looked at Boatwright, and then at the last member. He sat, slumped and expressionless, in front of the jagged green of the window. "He was not found at Shin'edo. But all this can't be due to two people. Too much is happening, at points too widely separated. The Senior Member is right. There is increased dissidence—"

"More as the food supply drops," said Muafi.

"And it all affects production," said Boatwright.

"What are the latest figures, you?"

"WE PROJECT A SHORTFALL OF ELEVEN POINT EIGHT PERCENT IN BASIC RADIATION-RESISTANT PHOTOPHORES. GAMMAPHORES ARE SOMEWHAT BETTER, ONLY A FOUR PERCENT SHORTFALL. WE HAVE REDUCED CONSUMER USE TO ZERO AND BEGUN CANNIBALIZATION OF UNDERUTILIZED COMPUTING EQUIPMENT TO MAKE UP THE LAST SHIPMENTS TO THE BLOSSOM."

"Thank Greatmother that's available, at least."

"YES. THOUGH IT DOES LEAVE US—OUR-SELVES—LESS REDUNDANT, AND VULNERABLE TO BREAKDOWN."

"Where does that place us re schedule?" asked Muafi, staring out the window to where the wind, silently, was tearing apart a waterfall into long streamers of mist, into evaporation, into air.

"CRITICAL," said the Bank. "FORTUNATELY, WE HAVE FROM THE BEGINNING ALLOWED A FIVE PERCENT MARGIN FOR ACCIDENT, MISCALCULA-TION, AND FAILED SUBASSEMBLIES. UNTIL LAST YEAR THAT SEEMED PESSIMISTIC. NOW IT MAY SAVE US. WE CALCULATE THAT A-DAY WILL OCCUR ROUGHLY BETWEEN DECEMBER FIFTEENTH AND TWENTIETH, ABOUT A MONTH FROM NOW. THAT WILL LEAVE THE BLOSSOM TWO MONTHS TILL HADES—SUFFICIENT TIME FOR TEST AND TUN-ING."

"If things don't get worse," said Dawnfair. Under the slight warmth of her fingers the fetus stretched a little, then relaxed again into its dreamless parabiosis. She crossed slim unshaven legs under the sari. "If these fools don't follow their Pied Piper into loafing and sabotage. Answer me this, with all your margins and critical paths and all this omniscient bullshit you've been fooling us with so long now: why hasn't the disease worked? Why haven't the Adjustors found these two *rabble-rousers*, these *saboteurs*, these—" She choked, unable to find words. *"Why can't you find and kill them?"*

Her near scream faded into the faint mechanical hum from Muafi. No one answered her. The four humans stared at the silhouette at the far end of the table, sur-rounded, made faceless by the sunlight that poured in from behind its curved back. It did not stir.

"Uh . . . are there any other problems?" said Muafi.

"GENECON DOCUMENTS A FURTHER DECLINE IN REPRODUCTION RATE. NORMAL CAUSES HAVE BEEN RULED OUT. IT IS A MATTER OF SIMPLE VITALITY." The interface turned its head slowly toward the light, as if some trace of phototropism still survived. "THE TWENTY-HOUR WORK CYCLE ON REDUCED RATIONS IS TOO MUCH . . . EVEN WITH OVERLOADED S-ENZYME DOSAGES FOR THE THREE LOWER CLASSES."

"We can't worry about that now," snapped Nagai. The others nodded. "There is nothing else we can do at this late date. Force production to the utmost. Don't worry about tools or people. Contain damage where you can. Find those who supported him—these famous 'dissident elements' of yours—and place them beyond harming the economy further.

"Most important of all, find Burlew and Mcgreen! So far they have drained our strength by pinpricks, and seriously enough. The perfected world economy is dangerously interdependent, dangerously unstable. What happens if, by cunning or accident, they find somewhere we are truly vulnerable?"

"Do you have any ideas how to do that, Hakamaro?"

"We've tried two of yours, Lakshmi," said the old Oriental, a slight sneer putting an edge on the words. "They didn't seem to work. Amitai, any ideas from you? You're not just here for decoration, you know."

"Well, I was thinking. We might . . . ask them to contact us, have talks—"

"Go back to sleep," said Nagai. "Bertram? Anything *realistic* to contribute?"

"No. I agree with you, of course. Something more must be done."

"But what will it be?" The Senior Member looked now at the smooth-faced thing. It sat as motionless as it had throughout the discussion. Save for that slow turn of the head it had not changed its position or even its expression. It had only blinked, once every twenty seconds; and that was only reflex; they all knew that meant nothing—it was a lower brainstem response to drying of the conjunctiva and did not even come from its mind, which was not in that room or that island or perhaps even in that hemisphere of the planet at all.

"ONLY ONE THING," it said.

"And that is?"

"IT MEANS SOME SLIGHT DIVERSION OF RE-SOURCES—BUT, FORTUNATELY, MOST OF IT CAN BE DONE IN SOFTWARE.

"WE HAVE BEEN CONSTRUCTING PAR-ELECTRONIC MODELS, TO CORRESPOND WITH BURLEW'S AND MCGREEN'S PSYCHOLOGIES.

"THEY SEEM TO MOVE ABOUT AND ACT RAN-DOMLY. BUT AS GREATMOTHER PROVED, FOLLOW-ING A SUSPICION VOICED IN THE FIFTEENTH CENTURY BY DESCARTES, WITH ENOUGH INFOR-MATION THE ACTION OF ANY LIVING CREATURE CAN BE PREDICTED TO A HIGH ORDER OF PROBA-BILITY. WITH THE INSIGHTS WE HAVE GAINED INTO THEIR PERSONALITIES THROUGH STUDY OF THE PARIS FLITO TAPES, WE SHOULD SOON BE ABLE TO FORECAST THEIR NEXT ACTION WITH A CONSIDERABLE DEGREE OF CONFIDENCE."

"And be waiting?" said Dawnfair, lowering her hand to stroke red-gold hair on her tanned thigh. The eyes of the three old men present dropped to follow its slow circling.

"AND BE WAITING. AND AT THAT TIME, WE AS-

SURE YOU, GENTLEMEN—LADY LAKSHMI—JUSTICE WILL BE DONE."

The oldest man on earth swiveled his chair feebly toward the window. His eyes locked with the sun, matching its baleful glare with their green malevolence.

"And not," he muttered, almost to himself, "a moment too soon."

Psitelechireidolon

Late one February night in 2112, deep in the gloom of the Bayerischer Wald, the Manifest flickered into existence like foxfire.

As seconds passed he gained in solidity and form, yet still the glowing eight-foot figure seemed somehow insubstantial. When his edges focused, and stopped flickering, he put out a hand experimentally. It passed easily through the trunk of a young pine. Hundreds of meters below, kilometers away, a block-long bank of parelectronics registered the insolidity, and rethought.

The figure turned its palm downward, and brought it through the tree again.

It exploded, sap and heartwood and bark vaporizing instantly into a ball of bright orange fire ten feet across. The detonation rang away, rumbling over the rolling hills of what had once been southwestern Germany.

The Manifest stepped away from the burning stump, the toppled and smoking crown of the pine. He pivoted slowly, hand still extended, and reached out for the voices.

"What's that?" said Jaylen, looking up from the carefully shielded campfire. "Thunder?"

"C'mon, frenita. Stars be out," said Burlew. "And thunder in winter? No way. Maybe another suborbital in trouble."

Squatting by the fire, he blew his nose in his fingers, inspected the result, and slung it into the embers. The light that leapt up briefly illuminated a face that looked ten years older. Blue bruises beneath the eyes, sallow masklike skin, mouth drawn taut by pain under gaunt cheekbones.

"Monaghan. Do you have to do that? I know it doesn't matter as far as overthrowing Stepfather, but—"

He turned his head slowly from his contemplation of the fire. "But it bother you, rite?"

"Yes. It does."

The gaunt man started to speak, then stopped. He sighed and wiped his hands on new white joggies, glancing at the three others who squatted around the circle the fire had melted in the snow. They had arrived only minutes before, stumbling along the deer trails that threaded the forest; had known the password; and now sat waiting attentively, their eyes moving between Burlew and Mcgreen as they argued.

"Uh . . . what be your names, again?" said the poet.

"I'm Lyagavy," said the tallest. A moonfaced man of about twenty-two, he wore the greens of a Class II technician. "This is Takaichi Tamaki"—shorter, brush touch of Mongol about the eyes and mustache, wearing the white of a scientist—"and last, Rudolf Perlmutter. He might not look that alert, but he's one of the best nuke tekkies in the plant.

"We got the message to meet you through Deel—I mean, through one of the other Orphans we know."

"That's good." Burlew nodded. "No use for me to know names at all. Starting after this op, want all Orphans to start using code names."

"That would be a good idea, sir. There used to be dozens of us, but we got raided at a meeting. They got the names of the rest out of the ones they captured and . . . well, you don't need to hear about that. Because, well, you're Burlew himself, right?"

"Real me, no lie."

"The stories say you were, you know, kind of heavy."

"Used to be. Been sick."

"Well, say," the tech continued, laughing a little and glancing sidelong at the others, "you know—we've all read your pomes at our meetings, passed 'em from hand to hand, got them out to the public. But could we maybe, well, hear you recite one?"

"Not be quite in the mood."

"Oh, please. Declaim one to us. Yam." Wheedling, Lyagavy descended cunningly to Low English. "We be top on hearing him, no lie. Real Burlew, real Orphans. This be like where our lives pop, yam? C'mon, mam, turn us to hot."

"Oh," said Burlew. His mouth twisted strangely. Even Mcgreen could not tell if it was a smile or a look of pain. "If you put it that way."

He wiped his nose, glanced up at the steady stars of a German *mittelnacht*, and took a breath.

> *"WeaCon give you rain.*
> *EduCon give you school.*

143

> *Adjustors keep you down;*
> *Happy ease the pain.*

> *GeneCon give you wife;*
> *HousCon give you cube.*
> *Stepfather give you everything,*
> *Own you all your life."*

A silence followed the last line, broken only by the stir of the night wind in the pines. At last the sleepy-looking one, Perlmutter, shifted his legs and coughed. "Uh . . . Mr. Burlew?"

"Monaghan, to Orphans."

"Monaghan. Well, sir, you know you're a hero to all of us. To most people, I suppose."

"Uh. So?"

"You're the one who first defied the Greatmother Corporation. You've put all we ever felt but didn't know how to say on the stalls of all the johns in the world. We agree with you. But, you know—"

"What?"

"Your pomes stink. No, wait, guys," he protested as the other two tried to cut him off. "It's true, isn't it? You said so. Everybody does. Isn't that why we became Orphans—so that everyone could tell the truth and be free?"

"Rudy, your mouth is way over redline. I ought to—"

"Let him talk," said Burlew, and they quieted instantly. He rubbed his bare chin moodily with his hand. "Good to let people say what they think, even if they be wrong. And he be right.

"See, Burlew be taught nothing but Low English. Class

144

V, so no School after Working Age. Couldn't do top-rate pomes, never even saw any. Sure not."

He turned, then, to look at Mcgreen, and his expression changed. "Then two years ago he be meeting this top young frenita."

The young men watched, eyes widening as Burlew's voice changed. "And she taught me," he said. "Taught me words like *I*, *is*, and *love*. Declensions and tenses, syntax and rhyme scheme, scanning and free verse. Put me on that teachcomp and wouldn't let me off. And she talked to me . . . to me, a Class V, with Credit Zero.

"You've heard the old Burlew. Would you like to hear the new?"

"Yes," whispered Lyagavy. "We would. Very much."

"Then listen:

"As a child in kibut I saw the Dark Time coming.
I read it now in the blue glow of the clockfaces;
The hour of burning corpses.
Homes will flame in nightchoked streets
The runwalks stopped, archlights dead eyes in live night.
Stepsons; Orphans; those who obey in fear:
Our ashes will uncolor the sky.
The Bank is at its end!
It gave us one world, but its price was freedom.
It is time to smash them, the masters of reason
And leave for after what comes after war."

It is those who know us best who see our changes last. So it was then, hours before the end, that Jaylen, watching as he spoke the dark words polished through months of wandering and pain, saw suddenly and clearly the change that had come over him. From Burlew the bum, the wanderer, the scamming, gluttonous clown. From the beaten, apathetic Burlew of the Sanja.

Her face darkened with the words and the night.

When he was done the little circle of the hunted were silent for a long time, staring into the fire. At last Lyagavy heaved himself up from his log. "All right," he said heavily, "we're yours. What do you want us to do?"

"It's like this," said the poet, not looking up at him. "You three, if you're the people I'm supposed to meet, can gain access to the Bayerischer Wald F-station. Is that correct?"

"Oh. I wondered why we needed the extra set of whites," said Tamaki. "Yes, I think we can get you in. Out is another matter; that depends on how long you're inside the plant. But what are you going to do?"

Instead of answering directly, Burlew closed his eyes and began massaging his forehead, deeply, as if searching out a nagging pain. "Describe the F-station to me."

"Well, it's like the others, except bigger than most," said Lyagavy. "F-eight is the central fusion power facility supplying Europe, and it also provides prime voltage for a large part of the Bank's central processing units."

"Cuckooland!" Burlew glanced up, raising his eyebrows at Mcgreen. "You were right, Jaylen. Where are they?"

"Underground, of course. I don't know just where, but of course we hear things. And there are power cables leading downward from the main output switching panel. Big ones."

"And the plant itself?"

"Covers about a kilometer, with thirty thousand square klicks of forest around it. There are fifteen deuterium-tritium-carbon-fueled Liers reaction units with generating capacity of fifty thousand megawatts constant

146

each. Five are on-line at any given time and the others on standby or in overhaul. Want to know more?"

"Can you shut it down?"

"The F-station? From Central Control, sure. But what's the idea?"

"Remember the pome?"

The fire crackled suddenly, a jet of smoky yellow flame. Perlmutter started, and stared sleepily around at the ring of black trees. Then he looked back at the poet. "The Dark Time—a power outage?"

"That's right."

"But you know, you can't do that just by shutting down F-eight," Tamaki broke in. "It's not that simple. See, the automatic grid controls at PowCon will adjust to draw from F-twelve, in Spain, and F-three, at Zaleschiki. At worst it will browndown the less critical heavy-current users, the desal plants and WeaCon." The other techs nodded. "And of course, as soon as there's a flicker in power out, the place will be reeking with Stepsons looking for the reason."

"We could . . . blow it up," said Perlmutter suddenly. "I could shut off the coolant. That's the weak link in an F-station. The on-line units would last for about a second before the casings melted and they went up."

"No," said Jaylen.

"What?" said Burlew, turning to look at her. He seemed surprised and angry that she should even speak. "Why not? Sounds good to me. They can't reactivate the station once it's destroyed."

"No, I said." She got up abruptly and looked around at them. Her eyes were somber, and in spite of himself some random chain of synapses in Burlew's mind chose this moment to give him back her stance, her words, the

147

first time he had seen her, years before, in a hot alleyway in Malta, surrounded by the poor.

"What's happened to you? You aren't a violent man, Monaghan. You've never been. Except when you kicked those dogs off me. We've always advocated noncooperation, not destruction. Barter—not murder."

Burlew stared up at her, unmoving, and she too remembered him as he had been once: in Paris—enraged, defiant at the blindness of those who would not see, the cowardice of those who saw and would not act. That look was there still. But along with it now on this strange gaunt face was something else, something darker and less noble, less like Burlew and more . . . more like what they had fought, together, for so long.

She went on again, hearing her voice falter. "But the things we've been doing . . . and this . . . even if you set it up by remote somehow, people at the station will be killed."

"Be that worse than Termination?" said the poet harshly. "What about Poirier and all the other Orphans? What about the Hayashi? Everyone who trusted us and helped us?"

He got up and stalked about before the fire, his feet scuffing up snow and pine needles, casting monstrous shadows in the wavering red light. "What about us, we be caught tonite? You and I be spare parts inside of an hour. What about all the other people Stepfather takes every day?"

He stopped and stared at her, sniffling absently. "I realized that night in the Shitamachi, Jaylen, we were wrong. Pomes will not bring down the Bank. Nor barter. Only to destroy—that is the only message this Stepfather is going to understand."

"Monaghan. I can't stop you from doing what you

148

have to, but think. If we fight it that way . . . then what is the difference between us and it?" Her voice was hardening too. "And the Dark Time. You sound as if you want to bring it on, not stop it. What happened? What happened to your dream?"

"Maybe that's what it meant."

They looked across the fire at each other. Finally Mcgreen turned her head. "All right," she said. "Your eyes tell me it's time I left, Monaghan. Our doose-up—it's over."

"That be fine, stroke. You want to leave? That be top with me."

"Look, maybe I've got a better idea, if we don't want to destroy the whole station," said Tamaki. "Uh . . . you listening, right?"

"Go ahead," said Burlew, his eyes still on Mcgreen.

"Dmitri. You say five of the reactors are usually on-line. How many are on standby, ready to power up?"

"Generally five, but there could be either four or six, depending on the overhaul schedule."

"What would happen if we put all ten on at once?"

The techs looked blank for a moment, mulling it over. Mcgreen and Burlew, not meeting each other's eyes, sat down on either side of them. "Don't know," said Perlmutter at last. "At best . . . I mean, worst . . . nothing, if PowCon is set up to divert excess output. But why should they be? I'd say there's a good chance we could overload the supply end, shut down most of Europe for a few hours."

"That sounds good," said Burlew. He sounded subdued. "What time is it?"

"Almost two."

"Let's go. . . . Jaylen?"

She shook her head.

"What's wrong now? Going to do what you want. No blowup."

"No," she said. "I'm not going to be your anchor, Monaghan. I've seen this coming for a while. I'll always love you, but . . . from now on, we're going different ways."

They looked at each other across the fire. He thought how beautiful she was, and how stubborn; and she thought too, of a druglet in the Sudan, and how he had never hesitated to put her before himself. For the space of a long breath that flickered between them, swift and uncertain as the shadows cast by the flames.

Then, somehow, the thing was decided. Burlew looked away and shoved himself to his feet. She got up too and arranged their only possession—the dirty green blanket, corners singed, picked up in the back of an agriplaner in Belgium—around his shoulders. Thin, he was so thin . . . they looked on together as the techs kicked earth on the fire, and pine needles caught and then smoldered out under the rich black earth, the rich white snow.

"You might not come back," she said.

"I be back, stroke. One way or another."

"You won't reconsider?"

His voice was rough. Was it her imagination, or had tears glinted in his eyes? Now, in the starlight, she would never know. "No. I love you too, but—this is what I'm here for, Jaylen. I've always felt that. I can't drop the load now, just when it gets heavy."

"You're wrong."

"You said that already," he grunted. "No more . . . alrite? Here. Give Burlew a kiss before we split."

They clung to each other for a long moment, then separated.

She watched him silently, hugging her shoulders in the winter air, as he and the techs moved off into the night.

The Boardroom was quiet as a catacomb. Even the two figures sitting quietly in the darkness might have been carven limestone. C. Bertram Boatwright's voice broke it at last. "What time do you have there, Amitai, old man?" he muttered, scratching an anachronistic match across the underside of a realwood table before applying it to his pipe.

"Ah . . . two-thirty, Central European. In the morning," said Muafi, blinking sleepily in the sudden flare. He rubbed his face, uncrossed his legs beneath a long djellaba.

"Where did you come in from? Jerusalem?"

"Isfahan. I've just been . . . roaming around, out of my head, almost. We were so close—and then this. Is it a judgment? On our stewardship?"

"Don't talk bloody rot," said Boatwright sharply.

"I'm sorry . . . I'll try to bear up, I will. What is this meeting about, Bert?"

"Afraid I can't help you there. I was on my way to Lisbon when *he* called."

They looked up together as the door swung open, framing an immense old electronic robot. At the same moment the lights came on in a huge chandelier like fireflies caught in a frozen fountain. The machine wheeled squeakily to the side and held the door for the three people behind. No, two people. Hakamaro Nagai, doddering slightly on the extended arm of Lady Lakshmi Dawnfair. Behind them, moving with its wonted air of unhuman detachment, the round-shouldered figure of the Bank.

"GOOD MORNING, BOARD MEMBERS."

"Good morning, hell," shrilled Nagai, turning on him as the others settled into Louis XIV armchairs around the gilded table, before the wine-dark portieres that once had screened the entrances of Habsburgs. The room smelled of slowly decaying silk. "We're trying to resign ourselves to death. I at least had almost succeeded, with the help of several pipes of an ancient remedy—and then you call. Injections, oxygen, hurry—where are we, anyway?"

"THIS IS BUDA PESHT, SENIOR MEMBER. WE ARE SORRY ABOUT THE EARLY HOUR AND THE LACK OF NOTICE. BUT WE ASSURE YOU THAT IT IS IMPORTANT." The Bank nodded briefly to the other three humans, then sat down, its face unreadable as blank paper.

"Important, is it? Then let's get to it," said Boatwright, who had paled slightly. "It's the Blossom, isn't it? It's responded at last! That's the only thing important enough to—"

"NO. WE ARE SORRY, BUT—NO."

"What else matters, then?" demanded Lady D. Despite the hour—or perhaps because of it—she looked less commanding, less icy. Perhaps she had been at a party, or entertaining privately. Certainly the meters of finely woven gold wound about her body—heavy enough to cling to each curve and outline with metallic glitter, yet thin enough for near transparency—were not business wear. "No, wait. Sit down, Bertram, sit down! You all excite so easily. Tell us what is going on. Have you signaled it again?"

"YES. WE HAVE BEEN SIGNALING, AS YOU PUT IT; THAT IS, CYCLING OUR COMMUNICATIONS-READY PROTOCOL ROUGHLY TWO HUNDRED TIMES A SECOND CONTINUOUSLY SINCE A-DAY IN DECEMBER."

"And . . . ?"

"AS BEFORE, THERE IS NO REPLY."

"And the probability of successful action by it now is—"

"STILL FALLING; NOW, SINCE IT HAS BEEN SILENT SO LONG, PERHAPS NO MORE THAN ONE PERCENT."

The four Board members slumped in their gilt chairs; their previous slight animation died. "There aren't . . . there isn't much time left, is there, till Hades passes?" ventured Muafi.

"TWO DAYS."

"Greatmother. So close."

"And you're sure it's operational?"

"WE BELIEVE IT HAS BEEN OPERATIONAL SINCE A-DAY. THE ONLY PROBLEM—"

"Is getting it to respond," the woman finished. She had lost the gaiety of the party, and under the gold lawn her shoulders were slumped. There was a moment of renewed silence.

The Bank broke it at last. "TO PROCEED."

"It can hardly matter . . . but go on." The Senior Member flicked a finger listlessly.

"AS YOU KNOW, GENTLEMEN, LADY," the expressionless Mouth articulated calmly, "WE WERE DESIGNED TO OPERATE WITHIN CERTAIN LEGAL AND MORAL BOUNDS. THOUGH, AS YOU HAVE OFTEN ADVISED US, THE ABSORPTION OF GOVERNMENT AND RELIGION INTO OUR ORGANIZATION HAS RENDERED MUCH OF THIS PROGRAMMING OBSOLETE, IT IS BY NOW TOO DEEPLY EMBEDDED IN OUR FIRMWARE FOR US TO REVISE."

". . . The *point*," Nagai muttered.

"FOR EXAMPLE, TWO YEARS AGO WE WERE RELUCTANT TO ORDER THE TERMINATION OF BUR-

153

LEW AND MCGREEN. THEY WERE ONLY SLIGHTLY IN DEBT, AND ONLY AN EXTREME INTERPRETATION OF CREDIT REGULATIONS GAVE US THE OPTION TO TERMINATE. SINCE THE BOARD WAS UNANIMOUS IN ITS RECOMMENDATION, WE HOWEVER ISSUED THE ORDERS. UNFORTUNATELY, THE PAIR THEN DISAPPEARED AND WE WERE UNABLE TO LOCATE THEM TO SERVICE THEIR ACCOUNTS."

"Quite, quite, we know all that," Boatwright broke in testily. "But why call us here at two-thirty in the morning?"

"BECAUSE WE HAVE LOCATED THEM."

"What?"

"Where?"

"By heaven, let's end this now!" whispered Nagai, leaning forward.

"SOMEWHERE IN SOUTHERN GERMANY. WE BELIEVE THAT THEY ARE AT THIS MOMENT IN THE BAYERISCHER FOREST."

"What are you doing about it?" Dawnfair yawned. Muafi was staring at her nipples. "Letting them slip through your fingers, as usual?"

"WE HAVE ACTIVATED THE MANIFEST."

The Board stirred. No one spoke for a moment. Then Muafi said, "The area is . . . safe?"

"IT IS A DESERTED FOREST, EXCEPT FOR TWO INSTALLATIONS: THE F-EIGHT FUSION PLANT AND, AT LEVEL NINE, SOME OF OUR COMPUTING CENTERS. THIS LATTER MAY, IN FACT, BE WHY THEY ARE THERE."

"You think Burlew's after you?" Boatwright snorted. "Ridiculous. Just because he's evaded us for a time, he's not ten feet tall. The man's still nothing more than a bum, a drifter with a gift for poetasty, rabble-rousing, and petty sabotage."

"A clever enough description, Bertram," purred Dawnfair. "Unfortunately, he doesn't seem to be that simple. Did you scan the Paris tapes? As it is . . . I wouldn't have minded meeting him. To see what such a man is like in person."

"Do you wish additional Adjustors?" Nagai hissed. Ignoring the others, he spoke directly to the Bank, which turned to face the old man's fanatical stare. "Let's not underestimate him this time. That's something we've been doing all along."

"ADDITIONAL PERSONNEL IN THE AREA DEGRADE THE CAPTURE-PROBABILITY EQUATION."

"Very good," said Nagai. "But one further question. What, again, do you need us here for?"

"WHAT WE SUSPECT," the Bank began, "IS THAT ORPHAN ELEMENTS MAY BE WORKING WITH BURLEW AND MCGREEN FROM WITHIN OUR ORGANIZATION . . . SPECIFICALLY, FROM WITHIN THE CONS. REEDUCATION IS OF LIMITED USEFULNESS IN HIGH-TECHNOLOGY AREAS, SINCE THE REEDUCATE TENDS TO LACK PHYSICAL COORDINATION AND MENTAL CAPACITY. THEREFORE, OF NECESSITY, WE HAVE HAD TO TOLERATE SMALL NUMBERS OF SYMPATHIZERS IN KEY AREAS."

"Of course you kept them monitored?"

"THAT IS HOW WE LEARNED THAT BURLEW WAS IN GERMANY."

"Well done, then," said Dawnfair. "Yet you keep explaining and explaining, and you still haven't told us what you need of us."

"THIS. IT MAY BE NECESSARY FOR THE MANIFEST TO TAKE IMMEDIATE ACTION. SUCH ACTION MIGHT INVOLVE DANGER TO PERSONNEL OTHER THAN THE TWO ASSIGNED TERMINATION. IN SUCH CASES, OUR PROGRAMMING REQUIRES US TO OB-

TAIN THE PREVIOUS INFORMED SANCTION OF THE BOARD."

Dawnfair's tawny eyebrows rose; Nagai slumped back in his chair. "Of *course* you have our permission, you par-electronic idiot!" shouted Boatwright, growing red. "Am I wrong, gentlemen, or is this thing becoming ever less intelligent the longer we live? You've always had free hand to crush these people by any means. Now, two days from the end of everything, you don't have to drag us from important work and rocket us all over the planet to give you permission for *that*."

"Absolutely," said Muafi weakly. He was holding his hand to his heart. The humming lay like an accompaniment under the outraged breathing of the others in the room.

"Damn all this legalism. We own this planet. Do what has to be done!" whispered the oldest member virulently.

"VERY WELL," said the Bank. "IF WE HAVE THAT PERMISSION, WE MAY CONSIDER THE MEETING CONCLUDED. YOU MAY RETURN TO YOUR WORK, BOARD MEMBERS, TAXING AS IT APPEARS."

But instead of rising they sat yet, each one pondering. At last Dawnfair sighed, lifted her head again, and looked at each Member and the Bank in turn. "Well. We tried, but we failed. At least we'll take *him* with us."

"An excellent point." Nagai smiled. "Revenge sweetens life, even at the end. You!" He pointed at the silent witness. "What's happening now? Have you found them? Where is the Manifest?"

"HE IS WITH THEM," said the Bank calmly. It ignored the shock that its words sent round the antique table. "THANK YOU FOR YOUR PATIENCE, LADY AND GENTLEMEN, AND PLEASE STAND BY. FOR YOUR

156

INFORMATION, THE PSITELECHIREIDOLON IS NOW IN CONTACT."

The Manifest stood quietly behind and within #3 Low-Temperature Reactant Monitoring Panel, on the Control Section level of the F-Eight Central Fusion Facility. He was almost insubstantial. The outline of his eight-foot height mistily merged into the metal of the panel face, blurring the luminescence of its indicators.

He stood quietly, waiting.

He had found the saboteurs deep in the forest. From kilometers away, the thudding of their feet into pine needles, loose snow, had sounded, he thought, like the opening drumroll of the *Zarathustra*. He had shifted instantly three kilometers away. Not moving, simply disappearing and reappearing. Cocking his head to listen, he had calculated their position by triangulation. He had shifted one last time and found himself a hundred meters away. Dimming his gray glow, he had followed them through the forest, keeping his eyes on the thin figure that tripped frequently.

The Manifest had once been human. Or had he? Perhaps he had once had a name, but he could never recall it. Perhaps he had once had a past, but if so it was inaccessible to him. Or perhaps he was just a construct, an artificial personality. But then, he thought, why would I remember Strauss? He puzzled over it as he slipped noiselessly through the night, as he did during every manifestation. His feet made no sound on the trail, for he weighed nothing.

A phantasm, named or unnamed, has no weight.

SUPPLEMENTARY DATA FOR ORIENTATION:
REFERENCE DATE 2112

Human beings have known of phantoms, spirits, out-of-body *things* for all of recorded history. Yet somehow with the coming of science they became unfashionable. The Naive Nineteenth sneered at them, as it had at the idea that stones could fall from the sky, that species could change their God-fixed forms, and that invisible little animals could cause disease. The Bloody Twentieth half-believed, but found self-destruction more fascinating. The Twenty-First investigated at last, and the Twenty-Second not only believed, but created.

Most men's minds, and thus inevitably their souls, are forever beyond their control. This is inherent in their nature and it is rather cruel to fault them for it. The ancients symbolized this januarial bifurcation by the goat-god Pan. Hooves firmly in the dirt, horns pointed heavenward, the randy yet musically inclined god personified man's uneasy sojourn at the terminator of the material and the spiritual. He sensed himself at the trembling boundary of ever-higher planes of metamaterial existence. Only two or three individuals in each century could access them in a meaningful way. Yet, those less liberated were not psychically impotent. Instead, they produced monsters. Poltergeists; ghosts; the mass-mind linkages that led to the insanities of war and the millenarian mass conversions of 1999.

Philosophers and shamans alike had postulated the existence of "astral" or "etheric" forces since before history began. They taught that what human beings perceived was only a reflection or face of a deeper reality. Mastery of the deeper reality meant one could alter its appearance

158

at will. The problem was demonstrating this. It was one of the last achievements of the old nation-state science to understand that the reproducibility of "supernatural" phenomena depended on the level of psiectic power applied. At low power levels, the material world was influenced indirectly through quantum mechanisms easily confused with chance and coincidence. Once more power was available, at a threshold not too far above the average genus homo, the phenomenon became dependable and useful.

Yet, national leaders could think only to use their partial understanding of this new technology, as they had every other, for destruction.

Then, beneath the stimulus of dire threat, Greatmother had begun her study of the link between consciousness and matter. The result, after some weeks of work, was the high-information parametric function

$$P = \int_a^n f(R) \, dr$$

It described a positive though nonlinear relationship over the range a (the consciousness of a theoretically impossible absolute vacuum) to n (that of the system being considered) between a large number of variables subsumed under $f(R)$, many stochastic and nonreproducible, and a dependent output, psychic energy—the ability to do physical work through psiectic means. One of the most heavily weighted variables Greatmother termed R_1; it was related to but not directly convertible from intelligence. (Of course this is a gross oversimplification of her work. In fact there are several hundred other variables and causal chains in $f(R)$, such as the ability to do coordi-

159

nated parallel processing, and R_1 itself is not fixed but is a vector resultant of seventeen parameters. But for purposes of this discussion the higher-level explanation should suffice.) If plotted as a curve, $f(R)$ showed a first marked kink upward at $R_1 = 30$, just above chimp level, and another sharper one at $R_1 = 550$ (which every human child suspected, intuited, when it closed its eyes and knew if it only believed hard enough it could fly), before finally yielding to the law of diminishing marginal returns to scale.

The Bank's R_1 was 2500. And thus only the Bank, of all the entities that had up to then thought on Earth, could within its cubic kilometers of densely retentive parelectronics generate and control psi-powers consciously, at will. Could project the psitelechireidolon—the remotely directed artificial ghost.

The Manifest.

His hearing, incredibly sensitive, picked up the vibration of footsteps from outside the control room. Thinning himself almost to invisibility, his mass to near zero, he leaned forward through the metal panel, waiting for his quarry.

"Good morning. Alfeld inspection," Tamaki announced briskly to the gray-uniformed guard.

"Say what, mam?" The man took in the white joggies, the Class I idpatches, but did not move from his post before the barred and TV-eyed entryway.

"You know, when they pour concrete, they throw in those little metal loops? Ever seen that? That's to check the compressive strength. You read them from outside the wall with a meter."

"I never be seein' any little coils," said the guard.

"You *what*?"

Beneath their openmouthed stares, the obvious and growing astonishment at his ignorance, he finally broke. "Oh, *Alfelds*," he said. "Thought you said Halfeldts. Sure, sure, me be seen those lots of times." Half-turning, he grated an order to the door in Low German. As it opened, he folded his arms and stepped out of the camera's view, watching as Perlmutter and Lyagavy followed the scientist in. But white joggies did not work for everyone. The Gray goggled at Burlew, hunched sniffling under the ratty blanket, and was reaching for his p-gun when, from behind, Tamaki pressed his thumbs to his neck. They lowered him gently to the concrete, closed the door, and fried the controls with the p-gun; then tubed up two flights to the Control Section. "Say," said Burlew, after several levels, "be there really—"

"Of course not," said Tamaki.

"Dam nice scam, then."

"Thanks."

A young woman looked up from a scratch 'n' sniff pornepic as they entered the Control Section.

"Hi, Deera," said Lyagavy. "I'd like you to meet a friend of mine . . . though I bet you've heard plenty about him already. Monaghan Burlew—Deera Singer. She's one of Us."

"Burlew—*Burlew!* Really? Why, great, hello!" The small blonde jumped up, pumped the poet's hand eagerly. She stretched up to kiss his cheek, but stopped in mid-tiptoe. She looked at her hand, took a closer look at Burlew, then wiped it on her joggies and stepped back. "Uh—great to meet you. I read all your, uh, stuff. Can't get it out of my head, somehow. Stroke Stepfather! Well, what brings you here, of all places?"

Lyagavy took on the burden of explanation. Singer bit her lip when he came to the part about bringing all the reactors on the line at once, but readily agreed. "Just to get my own back from those bastards," as she put it. "I wanted to be a Flito Girl since I was five. But I tested too high, and those krill-brained Stepsons stuck me in nuclear physics. Sure, let's shut this baby down, hard!"

Perlmutter joined her at the watch console, and together they began tapping in codes on the hair-thin lines that crosshatched its surface. Lights came on where the lines intersected; a soft, concerned voice muttered from the glow. Singer turned back to him. "Five reactors on the line, Monaghan. Three have the robots on them for disassembly and overhaul. The other seven are ready to power up."

"Good."

"Orders?"

"You're the techs."

As the others worked, Burlew leaned forward, looking down through the meter-thick plastron-F windows of the control station. From here he could see the entire reactor floor. Hundreds of feet below, squatting between pig-lead revetments like wingless fighters, fifteen long, tubular black shapes were spaced across the smoothed bedrock floor of F-eight. Around several of them repRobs gathered; around others eddied the blue radiance of heavy neutron emission.

"Six on-line," sang out Tamaki. "Bur—I mean, Monaghan? I've got a power-out indicator here that's redlined at five hundred thousand megawatts. Five hundred BW. I'm, uh, assuming that's where something trips out. I'm going to run the plant up to there unit by unit."

"You got him," said the poet. He pressed his face to the window as the blue nimbus coalesced around another reactor, far below.

162

"Seven on-line," said Singer.

"Three hundred and fifty BW."

"Flux on the floor?" asked Perlmutter, who was watching, eyes sleepy, over their shoulders.

"Hundred twenty rems ambient."

"That all? Why is it glowing so bright? Flux density for Chernygov—"

"That's not air in there," said Singer.

"Oh."

"Eight on the line," remarked Lyagavy. He was trying to act as bored as the others, but a squeak on the last word gave him away.

Burlew, still leaning against the smooth plastron, heard an alarm begin to sound below. The high-pitched "peep, peep, peep" echoed between the sheer rock walls. The repRobs rolled back from their work and swiveled their oculi upward. Perlmutter tapped a grid intersection and it stopped. Steadily, now, the blue glow was growing brighter, swirling along between the revetments, eddying around the flanks of the gunmetal tubes like neon fog.

"Four hundred and ten BW. Still climbing."

"Fuel input to max. All hydrogen pumps on."

"Mags to double-oh-oh-eight of abzero. Hysteresis limit."

"One thousand ambient on the floor. Fifteen in the control section."

"Nine on-line."

Two more alarms cut loose suddenly, one screaming in a two-note alternating discord, the other clanging. The techs seemed unable to cut them off. Parts of the panels came to life on their own and began a pulsating dance of red light. Below them the robots spun their treads madly, colliding with one another, and finally achieved a single file. They disappeared into a passageway leading away into the rock; a massive door rumbled down. "Ten F-units on-line!" sang out Lyagavy. "Output, Deera?"

"Four-ninety BW."

"Warming up the last two now."

It was then that Burlew, looking back toward the techs, saw the gray figure step ghostlike from the wall. He opened his mouth, but was unable for a moment to say anything. "Who the stroke be you?" he got out at last.

"SHUT THEM DOWN," said the figure, solidifying till it was no longer transparent. Burlew saw that it was a man, eight feet tall, but : . . *faceless.* "SHUT THEM DOWN. THE EUROPEAN GRID IS ADJUSTED TO SOAK UP ALL YOUR OUTPUT."

Burlew had to swallow before his dry mouth would function. "No way, Stepson," he said.

"LISTEN, ALL OF YOU. REDLINE FOR THIS STATION IS FIVE HUNDRED THOUSAND MEGAWATTS. AT THAT POINT WASTE HEAT FLOW EXCEEDS REACTOR COOLING CAPACITY. THE FUSION UNITS WILL MELT, AND BOTH YOU AND F-EIGHT WILL BE DESTROYED." The faceless head turned as if seeking something, and then steadied. "BURLEW. YOU ARE IN CHARGE HERE. ORDER THEM TO SHUT DOWN!"

The techs had turned from the console and were watching the two of them openmouthed. At the Manifest's last words, their eyes shifted as one to Burlew. "Well?" squeaked Lyagavy after an incredibly long moment filled only with sirens. "What do you want us to do?"

"THEY WILL OBEY YOUR ORDERS. SHUT DOWN THE PLANT!"

Burlew hesitated, looking toward the indicators. On their pulsating surfaces the red lines crept upward. He switched his glance quickly back as the eight-foot figure took a step forward. "SHUT DOWN, I SAID!"

"Wait. Who are you? Why are you giving us orders?"

"I REPRESENT THE BANK."

"The Bank, huh?"

"THAT IS CORRECT."

"And you want us to shut down? Why?"

"TO PRESERVE THE F-STATION—AND YOUR LIFE."

"My *life*?" Burlew had to laugh at that one. "Since when has Stepfather given a dam about me—or anyone else without a Class I patch?" He waved at the three technicians. "What about their lives? You've been after me a lot longer than them."

"I HAVE NO INSTRUCTIONS REGARDING THEM. ONLY REGARDING YOU."

"Burlew," said the woman, "it's . . . redlining."

"TURN IT OFF," said the Manifest. No one moved. "BURLEW . . . WHAT HAPPENS IS YOUR RESPONSIBILITY. ALL OF IT."

"What do you mean?"

"I MEAN THAT WHAT YOU EXPECT TO HAPPEN WILL NOT HAPPEN. THE EFFECTS OF A DESTRUCTION OF F-EIGHT WILL NOT BE LIMITED TO A POWER OUTAGE. THEY WILL BE MORE FAR-REACHING."

Burlew stared at him, at the technicians beyond, huddled against the blazing panels. The alarms seared his ears. Beneath the clean white joggies, he felt sweat crawl along his body.

And he understood.

The Dark Time was now.

"Perlmutter, Singer," he said slowly, "bring up the last two F-units."

"NO! THINK, BURLEW!"

The tall Russian tapped twice on the panel. He smiled slightly across the suddenly warm room at Burlew, and in his voice, now, there was no nervousness at all. "All twelve on the line!"

Burlew glanced downward, through steel-hard plastron as thick as his outstretched arm. The whole reactor floor was burning, glowing with a hellish indigo fire that licked up from each tube. The very air they breathed glowed with pale blue Chernygov light. Other than that and the screaming alarms, there was no sound, no vibration, nothing to indicate the terrible power on the verge of breaking free below. The sleet of neutrons through steel, concrete, plastron, flesh, could not be felt. He looked up again, to see that Lyagavy and Tamaki were blocking the Manifest from reaching Deera, who was staring at the output dial. The scientist had slipped off his shoes.

"Okay, now secure the coolant," said Perlmutter.

"THIS IS FUTILE," said the eidolon. Its voice was calmer than Burlew's, calmer than any of them, but still it conveyed fear somehow. "BURLEW. WHAT WILL YOU ACCOMPLISH BY DESTROYING AN ENTIRE FUSION STATION?"

"Maybe we finally get a message across—Stepfather," said the poet softly.

"Redline," said Deera Singer.

The Manifest moved forward then. As it neared her, Lyagavy aimed a punch as high as he could stretch. With one arm the gray figure brushed him aside, and there was the crunch of breaking bone from the Russian's head. Tamaki, next to the panel, was Singer's last line of defense. He took two long strides, crouched low, and suddenly uncoiled like a spring. High in the air he screamed, turned himself somehow even as he flew, and lashed out with a kick. As his bare foot struck the Manifest's head it exploded into white fire.

The Manifest stepped over the two bodies. It lifted Singer from the chair, folded her, and dropped her. She clutched at her arm once, rolled toward the wall, and stopped moving.

The Manifest reached for the panel.

Burlew's clumsy tackle caught it just behind the knees. It fell, sprawling; the mass it had assumed for the fight carried it to the floor on top of him. They were lying face-to-facelessness when a rushing sound like many waters came from below.

"TOO LATE," said the Manifest.

And Monaghan Burlew, thirty-three, thought in those last fleeting instants of the Darkness. He was not the means of salvation. He was the agent of destruction. He had failed, failed utterly, and it was with this thought that he drew what he knew was his last breath.

The last thing he saw in his life was the Manifest's finger coming toward his forehead.

The Black Forest erupted in a roar of thermonuclear light.

Magnetohydrodynamic generators die with an immense electromagnetic pulse. For the first few kilometers outside F-eight, the tubular transmission bars lasted for less than a second before internal resistance flashed them through red heat, through white, into copper gas. The pulse made short work of the first set of gallium arsenide switching SCRs it hit. And the second. And the dozenth.

It took twelve seconds to ripple its way across Europe. But for twelve seconds before that—in fact, ever since the explosion had lit the clouds over Germany—the PowCon central processing unit had been giving back no response at all to the continual query from every generating station in the world: *what do you want me to do next?*

And getting no response, each immediately went to full power.

Meeting the same full-power surge from every other generating station in the world.

The archlights went out in a sudden flare. The run-walks gave an agonized shriek and jerked to a halt, their motors fused solid.

In one second, 1.9×10^7 megawatts pulsed steadily through the energy grid of a planet. And in the next, a hundred times as much. The great coils of the fratelines went dead; a millisecond later giant circuit breakers arced and flamed as collapsing inductive fields surged into the lines. Motors, semiconductors, computers, control networks—everything connected to power burned out, tripped off, fused, and lost memory as the tidal bore of voltage hit.

Twelve billion telecards faded suddenly to a lifeless black.

All over the world.

"IT IS FINISHED," said the Bank.

A faint tremor tinkled the empty tea and coffee cups, the wineglasses on the gilded table.

At its words the four Board members, haggard from their vigil, looked up from carven armchairs in the corners of the throne room. "Burlew? Mcgreen? The whole crew?" said Nagai, his face wrinkling in a vindictive smile.

The lights flickered and went out, then came back on again, somewhat dimmer. Each Boardroom had its own power source. "WAIT," said the Bank. "WE HAVE SUF-

FERED DAMAGE. WE WILL RESPOND WITH A FULLER REPORT, FULLER REPORT, FULLER REPORT IN A MOMENT."

The members looked at one another. Boatwright shrugged and began to repack his pipe. The Bank sat motionless. Several minutes passed before it shook its head, as if dazed, and spoke again. "THERE. WE HAVE REGAINED SOME CONTROL."

"What's happening?"

"BURLEW IS DEAD. WE WITNESSED HIS DEMISE THROUGH THE MANIFEST, ALONG WITH THAT OF FOUR OF HIS 'ORPHANS.' THEY WERE KILLED IN AN EXPLOSION AT THE MAIN MIDDLE EUROPEAN FUSION PLANT, IN BAVARIA."

"Power's been interrupted?" asked Muafi.

"SERIOUSLY. WE HAVE SUFFERED DAMAGE TO OURSELVES IN THAT SECTION NEAREST THE PLANT. UNFORTUNATELY THIS WAS THE POWCON SECTION. COORDINATION OF THE WORLDWIDE ELECTRICAL GENERATION NETWORK HAS BEEN TEMPORARILY LOST."

"You'll get it back soon enough," said Boatwright confidently. He sucked on the calabash, flicked the match to the parquet. "And it's about time. We should have done this long ago. Eliminating him would have finished the movement; a short, brutal campaign of repression would have put the population behind us again.

"You see"—he pointed the stem at the Bank—"how useless your misgivings were? If you delay rooting out disruptive influences, they only grow. We are—were— no, *are* the law, until the end. No one challenges us; no one can even criticize us."

"Yet we are doomed," said Dawnfair dryly.

Muafi frowned; Nagai regarded her impassively; Boat-

169

wright nodded. "True, Lakshmi. But if the Blossom had worked, we'd be secure now for another hundred years . . . or at least"—he winked at Muafi and Nagai—"as long as there were enough Terminations to supply us with parts. And there would be. There would be!"

They chuckled together, a little sadly, at what might have been. Only one member sat still, not joining in the air of bittersweet celebration, long-deferred revenge. But they did not mind that.

The Bank, they knew, had no sense of the tragic.

The Dark Time began slowly.

Only gradually did the people creep out of their silent, darkened cubes. They stepped on the runwalks, stared about for a moment, and then realized they were not moving. They stumbled out of flitos, rubbing their faces numbly. They wandered about the streets among abandoned planers, mostly silent, a little stunned.

Someone found a verticopter, left where it had landed when the beamed power trickled off. A little crowd gathered. The Grays had left it unlocked, running for their station, where there would be safety in numbers.

A tongue of flame licked up.

Some of the crowd began looking in the shop windows.

Others, straightening in their sweatshops from machines and consoles that had suddenly gone dead, gone blank, looked at one another, then at the parelectronics that had held them all in feverish bondage for so many years.

Then it began.

And All Our Cards Turn Black

Blinded, deafened, Jaylen Mcgreen fought for her life once more.

As she had in the intake beneath Shin'edo, she fought in darkness; but this time she fought alone. She clawed mindlessly at earth-smelling, crumbling mold, cold as winter; at rough bark and needles. Her skin peeled back on her fingers. In the dark there was no pain—not yet— but there was no air, either. Up there—somewhere— there had to be air *somewhere*—

She pushed the last of the dirt and timber aside and wriggled out into the open night.

It smelled of flame, scorched pitch, and ozone. From

the fallen boles, combed out in straight rows as a harrow leaves a field, steam and smoke eddied up; the flicker of widespread flame lit the clouds to the east. Snow still lay on the ground; it had reflected heat where the dark trees had absorbed it. Afterimages of the flash chased themselves across her open eyes. Aside from the scattered flames, it was dark around her, and totally silent. She shook her head, clapped her bleeding hands together. She could hear nothing—nothing save the endless ringing of the blast.

She forced herself to her feet, fell, got up again. Resting and staggering, following the crowns of the trees, she made her way slowly through a hissing wasteland. Half an hour later she emerged from the blastfall at the crest of a rise and paused to look back. Above the hills to the east, covering half the sky, an immense black thunderhead of smoke and dust blotted out the stars.

"That son of a bitch." Her lips moved, but she was unable even to hear herself.

Jaylen Mcgreen turned and went on.

By 2113, after six centuries of human research, exploration, invention, engineering, and commerce, the World— the entire inner solar system, though most of mankind were still confined to their natal planet—was as interdependent, as mutually supporting, as a medieval village. No. More so. For without power, the cities would stop . . . and there were only fifteen F-stations. Without the fratetubes, food and zeolites and drugs would not move from producer to consumer . . . and twelve billion mouths gaped to consume. Without an instantaneous and perfect system of credit transfer and economic regulation, the world economy would shatter into billions of anarchically competing units . . . and it was all controlled from one place.

It was inevitable, once population exceeded natural carrying capacity; it was dangerous, as those who had built it knew. But it was the only way. Without central administration, coordination, management, the continual and ever-more-critical process of making sure that *things happened as they had to*, the whole incredible complex advanced incomparably efficient mechanical-chemical-par-electronic-ecological-economic ant's nest would instantly begin to die.

As Mcgreen staggered slowly through the night that covered now more than half the planet, the breakdown had already begun. When, hours later, she stumbled out of the forest, onto a road, into the lights of an oncoming planer, it had gone too far to stop.

There was nothing left to stop it.

In what had once been Ethiopia, the temperature at sunrise that first day was ninety degrees Fahrenheit. The sun broke from the Red Sea swollen and white above the domed city. As the morning went on it seemed to expand, covering half the pale African sky with an incandescent blaze so bright no human being in the open could have looked upward.

Below it, fifteen million people sweltered under the dome.

Its laminated B-plastron (acrylonitrile/polytetramethylene terephthalate/polyarylate/tolyene diisocyanate/triwoven spun quartz) should have silvered imperceptibly as the day advanced. Two hundred huge cooling units, regulated by semiconductor sensors on the dome's interior, should have cut in one by one to keep the air under it at a comfortable eighty-two degrees.

But now there was no power for cooling. Only light, and heat.

173

At noon the temperature inside the dome was one hundred and sixty degrees.

By evening it had fallen—somewhat. As the rim of the sun touched the Blue Nile, a hundred degrees registered on a lithium-powered panel far below street level. But by then it was the only thing in the city that thought. At the day's height, at 2:30, it had read 214°. Six thousand men and women, about a thirtieth of one percent of the city's population, made it out one of the jammed bubble-gates by breaking through with a diesel-powered T-34 tank from the Haile Selassie Museum. Most of them died in the barren sand outside.

Only one man, young and strong, driven mad by thirst, made it ten miles overland to the next dome. His dying fingers left no trace on the hardened crystal of its still-sealed gate.

A little later that first day, in what had once been Toronto and was now New Chicago, the morning dawned airless and cool. The early crowds stepped aboard the runwalks and stood for long minutes with the others, waiting. When the power did not return they began trudging forward, puzzled, but not yet seriously disturbed. The walks had never stopped before, but it was conceivable: they were machines, after all.

This happened in Mimico, New Gary, Birch Cliff, Willowdale, Skokie, Port Credit. Trudging in, taking an hour, two hours, the people congregated gradually, millions of them, at the city center.

The doors to the mile-tall buildings would not open.

At their feet, far below the sky, three million Clients milled in an increasingly dense mass. As the reality of what had happened filtered through the crowd, passed from mouth to mouth, fires—from patrol planers, shops, workies—began to billow smoke upward.

174

A few hundred meters. When it reached the fortieth or fiftieth or seventieth floors, it slowed in the still air, cooling. Then, channeled by the earthmetal and concrete canyons, it sank invisibly back toward the ground.

The pedestrians began to feel choked. Their breaths came faster, and their hearts began to pound. They tried to move, but there were others around them. They tried to push upward, over the others, to the air. There was no air. They tried to force their way back onto the dead walks, but the inexorable press of still-arriving bodies wedged them back again into the gasping crowd.

Pyronix and carbon dioxide from extinguishing systems began to gush automatically from the burning buildings. The fires snuffed out, but the gases vented on, as they had been designed to do to prevent reflash or explosion. And they too settled slowly toward the ground.

When it was over, the streets were still once again. The people lay four feet deep, faces cherry-red, like gaily made-up clowns.

Above them the pigeons dropped from the sky like gray hail.

And at the same moment that Mcgreen, shivering on a hilltop in Bavaria, cursed the man she had loved, another man comfortably faced death in a third of the myriad ways it announced itself that day.

Nineteen hundred kilometers to the southwest, Jesus y Maria Ramirez sat with a forbidden-on-duty stick of ganja burning his fingers and his eyes epoxied to a pulsating jet of red light to the right of his chair. It winked steadily and, with each brightening, crept perceptibly along its thread-thin silver strand.

The brightness was Death, and it was barreling toward him under the earth at two thousand miles an hour.

Ramirez cut off the alarm gong, slapped himself down

from the high, and began to work. "Compute momentum," he ordered, his left hand reaching out to race over a keyboard. "Answer!"

"WHAT LINE?" said the air near his head.

"East Africa. Incoming. Hurry!"

The voice was silent for the merest fraction of a second, then spoke again. "LOAD EA404-267-11. MIXED FREIGHT: GRAIN, TIN, METALLIC MERCURY, PETROLEUM PRODUCTS, PARELECTRONIC ASSEMBLIES. NOTIONAL DENSITY ONE ONE FOUR SIX KILOGRAMS PER CUBIC METER. MOMENTUM: ONE POINT THREE TIMES TEN TO THE ELEVENTH KILOGRAM-METERS PER SECOND."

"Status brakes." He knew—his eyes had flicked to the energy tote—but he asked anyway.

"LINE POWER DOWN. BRAKING AVAIL NIL."

The trafficomp, like the light that pulsed an inch farther along its web, twenty kilometers closer to him, was solar-powered. The frateline system had some solar, glittering on the north slope of Algeciras, across the bay. But not enough. Semiconductor materials were too scarce. The F-stations provided more power, without using up iridium, gallium arsenide, indium, organic-polymer semiconductors.

Only now there was a load in the line, deep in segment MA, under what had once been the pirate kingdom of Tripoli, and after that Quaddafi's fractious "republic" of Libya; and there was no power to stop it coming from those F-plants . . . or from anywhere else on the planet.

His fingers lifted from the board and hesitated. "Status NorXlantic," he asked.

"ONE LIGHT LOAD, SEGMENT AB, INCOMING."

"Inputs due next fifteen minutes."

"TWO SKED IN ACCELERATION SEGMENTS. DOUBTFUL ENROUTE NOW."

Modeled in his brain, Ramirez found the "topside" terminus, a hundred meters below his feet; the switching segments, where decelerating loads were shunted from incoming to outgoing lines. Both were dead level in the vertical plane, making horizontal reorientation critical. Without braking, a load entering too fast would leave its electromagnetic "tracks" with disastrous consequences. "Meeting angle, line of impact, NorXlantic versus East-Afric," Jesus said, watching the pulsing dot move a little closer. He did not feel the sweat break through his sea-tanned forehead.

"MEETING ANGLE SIXTEEN DEGREES."

"Model load. Calculate switching energy, frictional and other deceleration."

Short pause, during which Ramirez wiped moisture from his face, still staring at the dot of light. "MODELED. CALCULATED," said the trafficomp. "TOTAL LOAD KINETIC ENERGY SIX POINT FIVE TWO TIMES TEN TO THE THIRTEENTH JOULES. MAXIMUM SAFE ARRIVAL SPEED ONE HUNDRED TWELVE METERS PER SECOND, ENERGY EIGHT POINT FOUR TIMES TEN TO THE FIFTH MEGAJOULES. BETWEEN SEGMENT MA AND HERE, DELETE TUBE FRICTION, ONE POINT THREE TIMES TEN TO THE TWELFTH JOULES; HYSTERESIS, FOUR POINT FOUR TIMES TEN TO THE TWELFTH; CORIOLIS, SIX POINT FOUR TIMES TEN TO THE ELEVENTH. TOTAL TRANSIT LOSSES, SIX POINT THREE TIMES TEN TO THE TWELFTH JOULES."

"Energy available station?"

"CAPACITOR BANKS HOLD ONE POINT TWO TIMES TEN TO THE THIRTEENTH JOULES INSTANTANEOUS. SOLAR LINE CONTINUOUS DAYLIGHT AVAILABILITY TWO MJ/SECOND."

". . . Virgin," Ramirez whispered. His eyes flickered

again, still trapped by the web of light. One blue dot turned orange. He ignored it. It was outgoing. Let Havana worry—

"Ha!" he said.

"REPEAT INSTRUCTION."

"That incoming load, NorXlantic, segment AC. Commence decelerate."

"LOAD INDICATED IS NOT AT TRANSIT SPEED."

"Decelerate it!" Ramirez screamed.

The blue light under the Atlantic, six hundred miles east of the American coast, turned white. "Divert power to capacitor bank," he said, a note of victory in his voice.

"DIVERTING. SIGNALING OVERRIDE COMMAND TO ONBOARD COMP."

"You got him sure . . . no, stroke it, my error; divert power direct to Load 404."

"DIVERTED. LOAD 404 NOW BRAKING."

He took a breath, his hands beginning to shake above the keys. "Status comp, you mam," he asked it.

"UP, STATE ONE, JESUS. MY POWER DRAW SOLAR."

"Good . . . now, model new decel rate Load 404 and give arrival kinetic energy."

"MODELED. PROJECTED. ARRIVAL ENERGY SIX POINT SIX TIMES TEN TO THE TWELFTH JOULES."

Ramirez whispered a curse in Low Spanish, staring at the wire. The red light glowed an inch away from the web of intersections that was the Gibraltar NorXlantic Frate Switching Station. The load in the NorXlantic he was milking for energy was both lighter and slower than the incomer. There was a recovery loss, a hysteresis loss, and a whopping transmission loss in lines that stretched an eighth of the way around the world.

The incoming frate would still arrive at well over the

speed of sound. In thirteen seconds one hundred and thirty-five thousand tons of cast earthmetal and mixed load would impact a rock wall three hundred feet beneath his chair.

"Drain cap banks! Drain grid emergency! All power divert to segments MQ, MR, MS, MT."

"MT IS IN LOW POWER ONLY STATUS. POWER DIVERT REQUESTED MAY RESULT IN SEGMENT FAILURE."

"Overload segment MT! *Power up,* stroke you!"

"MQ, MR, MS, MT TO FULL EMERGENCY POWER. CAPACITOR BANK DRAIN AT MAXIMUM. FOUR SECONDS TO ZERO CHARGE."

And a moment later, "MT SEGMENT FAIL SIGNAL."

Jesus hissed wordlessly. The red light pulsed steadily deep beneath the sere slopes of the Atlas Mountains. That was it. No more magnetic braking. That left him no choice. It would jam the fratetube for days, cost him his Holiday bonus for sure. But there was nothing else to stop disaster. "Stand by explosive brake," he said slowly

"NEGATIVE," said the trafficomp.

"What?"

"CANNOT EXECUTE COMMAND. EXPLOSIVE BRAKE TRIGGER COMMAND ROUTES VIA LOAD ORIGINATOR. DJIBOUTI DRAWS POWER FROM F-TWO. DJIBOUTI DOES NOT RESPOND TO EBT INTERROGATE."

"Try land line."

"NEGATIVE."

"Satelnet, then!"

"NEGATIVE. DJIBOUTI IS DOWN HARD."

"Recommend next action."

"NO FURTHER ACTION IS AVAILABLE TO RECOMMEND."

179

"Great. Thanks," said Jesus slowly. "Well, been nice working with you, mam. Time to impact?"

"SAME HERE, MAM. ARRIVAL TIME LOAD 404 FOUR SECONDS FROM MARK . . . MARK."

Jesus y Maria Ramirez had more than enough time to light a last joint and think briefly about the baby daughter he was just learning to love.

From high on the east wing of what had once been the center of the world, Jaylen Mcgreen watched the mob carry the most beautiful creations of three millennia out to the flames.

Caligula's obelisk, in the center of the immense piazza, shimmered blackly in the streaming heat. Heaped sixty feet high around it, tapestries, curtains, vestments, busts, wood and ivory and cloth began to hiss and snap as they released ancient calories. The flames leapt up around the chair of St. Peter. Smoke, black and greasy with the oil from the paintings, mushroomed lazily upward into a Roman winter sky. It streamed slowly westward, joining other columns from the Castel Sant'Angelo and the Palatine and the Quirinale to mask the face of the sun. And still the people came, skipping, singing, staggering from out the great bronze doors and down the Scala Regia, their arms filled with what they had never been taught to cherish.

It had turned no profit for the Bank, and it had never helped production.

"How do I turn this on?" she asked one of the dark-haired, sallow boys who stood beside her on the papal balcony.

"*Scusi?*"

"This microphone." She tapped it, hoping it worked. It had been decorated by generations of pigeons; no one had spoken from this balcony for a century.

"Ca u fezzi io pe tea." He leaned forward, brushing against her with an almost audible leer, and waved his hand over the cone.

She bent forward, ignoring him, conscious suddenly of the hundreds of old men who had stood . . . *here.*

"People of Rome!"

To her surprise, the echo that rolled back from the Doric colonnades across the piazza did not say that. The cone was more than a microphone.

"Homines Romani!"

A few of the crowd, arms filled, paused on the pavement and stared around.

"I am Jaylen Mcgreen, Monaghan Burlew's partner. Chief now of the Orphans. I am here to tell you that—the Dark Time now must end!"

". . . Nunc finiendum est atrum tempus!" boomed back from the buildings across the immense square. The crowd below her froze, like suddenly discovered roaches on a kitchen floor deciding which hole to scurry for. The smoke eddied around the obelisk, sank downward, and the ancient stink of it swirled over her as she stood on the balcony.

"Orphans!" She tried again, feeling her voice peak and crack. "You are doing wrong. These things have nothing to do with the Bank. They belong to you, not Stepfather. You must not destroy them!"

St. Peter's Square was white with upturned faces. Yet there was no sign that they understood. Behind her she could hear the boys conferring in rapid Sicilian. One of them came forward. He shouldered her aside and struck a heroic pose before the microphone, head back. *"Attenzione!"* he bawled, thrusting out his arm. *"Sentiti doco basta cu sta distruzioni!"*

"Statim inhibete hanc destructionem!" the square bellowed in a great voice.

181

The people below looked at one another. They shrugged.

The Pietà came reeling down the stairs, shattering as it fell into a thousand gleaming fragments. A cheer came faintly up to her.

"*Nu autri non ti caferno*," said the boy to her, turning from the cone. He shrugged, exactly as the people in the square had shrugged; he smiled; he put his hand on her buttock. She slapped him. The other boys roared. She knew suddenly rage, impotence, hysteria, all at once. Low comedy as the treasures of Europe crackled in the flames.

Low comedy . . . she remembered suddenly another comedian. Shivered, and recalled with the inside of her arms how they had felt around him.

Jaylen Mcgreen remembered love: illusion or delusion, they had set it up together against the power of a world state. She remembered fear: a hundred times in two years of flight and rebellion she had thought their lives forfeit. And then, last of all, she remembered the searing chill as she saw what hate could do to a man's soul.

"You bastard," she whispered, looking over the smoke-smudged rooftops of Rome. She did not mean the boy. "*You* started this. But I've got to try to stop it."

A crash like the fall of the sky echoed from inside the basilica. She closed her eyes. She knew what it was. Bernini's baldaquin. Another long cheer, mingled with screams, filled the square.

The Grays . . . where were the Grays? With something like regret she realized she had not seen one of them since she had staggered out of the Schwartzwald. No. She had seen one. The strong, handsome, just-like-all-the-others face distorted, blackened tongue lolling out. Hanged from an archlight outside Versailles.

182

"Why are they doing this?" she cried aloud.

The boys stopped laughing. They stared at her. They had understood that.

"Non ce flito," said one.

"Non ce travaglio pe nuautri," said another.

No more flito. No more work. The people below had nothing else.

In the flames the busts of Caesars exploded with dull thuds. And against the blue Roman sky, the greasy soot rolled away, soot that had been Giorgione, Titian, Raphael, Ghirlandaio, Velázquez, Cezanne, Chagall, Mirimar. . . .

"Come with me," Mcgreen ordered.

But the boys did not follow. They stayed and watched; and after a while, climbed to the roof of the east front and began leaning against the immense statues of Christ and the Apostles. The statues moved. Then they rocked. And finally they toppled, hands still raised in benediction or horror, down onto the screaming crowd.

By the morning of the second day, two hundred world cities were silent.

New Chicago. Mexico City. London. New Leningrad, Taipei, Delhi, Brasilia—all were silent as the corpses that littered their streets.

In all the rest as well, the sun of that morning rose over a deadly, waiting emptiness. No one came out to greet its ruddy flicker. The streets, the workies, the gutted buildings that had held the GeneCons, the PowCons, the WeaCons, all the bureaucracy and administrative machinery that had executed the iron will of the Stepfather, all were deserted.

After the first frenzy of release and destruction, the human race—overcome by a suddenly recollected dread

183

of itself—stayed indoors. In its cubes. In the great buildings that stretched kilometers into the bright sky. Occasionally from one of them would come a distant shatter of glass, and a glittering, razorlike rain would sift downward: someone had kicked out a pane to reach the air that machines no longer pumped and purified. And sometimes, too, bodies came down.

One by one that morning the Orphans, those few whom the Bank, the Grays, and Hakamaro Nagai had overlooked, came out slowly into the deadly quiet. They were the only ones who had been warned. The only ones who had even remotely expected such a time as this to come. They weren't ready. They had no revolutionary blueprint. They didn't know what to expect or what, really, to do.

But there was no one else.

In Yaounde two of them hot-wired abandoned planers and began organizing door-to-door. In a few hours a trickle of traffic was carrying soy and corn from the NutriCon warestations outside the city. It was dumped at corners in heaps, and at each an Orphan stood, waiting for the people who, after a while, came hesitantly to them with cups and bowls in their hands.

In Newcastle-upon-Tyne another Orphan, an outspoken engineer of seventy who had been saved from Termination only by the Dark Time, led four old friends over a fence and began manual start-up on a long-abandoned fission reactor. None of them mentioned the fact that in doing so they would, inside two months, meet death from residual radiation.

In Jamnagar a few of them cajoled the fishermen out of their fear, and led the old solar-propelled trawlers out into the burning stillness of the Gulf of Kutch.

In Santiago a fifteen-year-old went from building to

building methodically jimmying open the computer-locked doors. At the largest one, the crowd trapped inside trampled him to death.

In Adelaide one exceptionally compassionate woman, formerly in flito till her beauty failed, talked her way past the p-guns of twenty barricaded Adjustors and instructed them in the old, old arts of greasepaint and disguise.

There were not many of them. But wherever they went, the people listened. A few lines of a pome were their identification, backed up by a shaggy beard on men, an ascetic thinness in women, and for both a certain carelessness about personal hygiene. That, and a single universally known name.

This did not happen instantly. The horrors continued. Wherever the Stepfather had trodden hard, there were repeated outbursts of violence. Sometimes it was directed against human targets, those who had served as the agent of the evil: Stepsons; the city police; above all the Adjustors, those unwise enough to flaunt their identical handsomeness. But often it was senseless, mere wanton destruction. Over many a city the clouds flickered those first nights as if from furnaces beneath.

Yet gradually, in the course of that day and a night and then another day, a form of wary truce took hold. The people were hungry, and perhaps that helped. The people were thirsty. But most of all they were frightened without their Stepfather, whose heavy hand had both oppressed and fed them for so long. Perhaps that was the real explanation. For after their anger was spent, their deliverance celebrated, it was fear that made them turn aside to listen to the few voices that seemed to have some idea, however slight, of what had to be done next.

"And in order to do something next, fellow ex-clients— my frens—we have to do many things, right now.

"Thank you for your time. I hope those of you with solar-powered receivers will pass this news along to your neighbors. This is Jaylen Mcgreen of the Orphans, saying—freedom! Peace! And—join your local Committee of Sharing."

The light on the panel behind her went out. As she turned away from the blank white wall, the same short, harried tech who had worried about her lubrication and Burlew's fleas the first time she had appeared before a flito transmitter—in what seemed a previous life—came out of a booth, rubbing his hands. "Good, good, toprate," he said rapidly. "Youse went across great. Youse be a natural for this, you know? Bet we could—"

"Yes, I'm a natural." She cut him off by turning to the group that surrounded her. Some held clipboards. Others held murmuring transceivers to their ears. They were of many races and colors, but they were all female and they all wore the same clothing: tech-green joggies, with the idpatches torn off; and they all looked as if they had gone for two days without sleep or sleepatches—as they had.

"Margo."

"Yam, Jaylen?"

"Coverage. How did it number out?"

"No numbers—the Neilson was part of the Bank. A lot of them must have gotten it audio only. Not enough power. But I estimate twenty percent worldwide."

"Good, audio's the most important part. Okay. Leah . . . what about that power?"

"They're still at work in Zaleschiki. The F-plants weren't designed for independent operation. A lot of controls to bypass. But"—she held a wrist to her ear—"they're making progress. May be on the line day after tomorrow."

"That would give us electricity—"

"From here west to the sea. Once we establish the procedure for reactivation, we can transmit it to the other fusion plants."

"Good. Frederica?"

"I've told all committees to post guards and to establish liaison with their neighbor cities. Tension is still high, especially in the Seafloors. They need power for pumping. And there's mounting demand for food, everywhere."

"Give it to them," said Jaylen. "Message, to all committees. Establish control over NutriCon assets; guard; issue two days' supplies. Plus another ration for those with children at home."

"How will they tell? Anyone could say—"

"Take their word for it. Serene, read back."

"From Jaylen to Alcom: Seize and guard NutriCon stocks; ration, two days single, three days parents."

"Go with that. Kelly?"

"Mare Imbrium reports shipments of zeo stacked up for miles behind the catapults. They're asking about things like credit transfers, but for the time being all we need are screens. Another day or two to repair, now that we've got some dedicated workers on the job."

"Sling the first load as soon as we're ready to track. Yes, the Moon is right—we've got to start thinking about how payment will flow between autonomous communities." She shook her head. "Set me up a meeting tomorrow, four A.M. Economists, agronomists, a medieval historian, and the highest-level Gray we can locate. All right, what are you all waiting for? You know what has to be done. Do it!"

The group shattered into action, its members looking driven. Mcgreen waited till the last one had left the trans-

187

mitting room and then sat down suddenly on the floor and let her hair sag forward onto her knees. *So tired . . .* but her mind refused to stop, to sleep. There was so much to do. Too much. Now, as she never had when it was speculation under the stars, she understood at last how simplistic all their ideas had been. How precariously balanced, how catastrophically interdependent the planet-city of the twenty-second century had become. It was impossible to administer with human brains, no matter how skilled, no matter how willing. Impossible . . . yet now someone had to do it.

She had to do it.

It was incredible how swiftly everything had changed. Forty hours before, she had been a wanted criminal staggering through a burning forest, thinking not of world rule but only of him, with bitterness and regret. And now it was all different. *Ex* the empty *cathedra*, from the vacant throne of the Stepfather she and her Orphans had to rule those they had wanted only to liberate. Only they possessed the legitimacy the Bank had forfeited. If they could not govern, the alternative was the return of mankind's oldest compadres, those grisly four who had been banished for so long from the rationalized world state of Gnath Greatmother.

Famine. War. Pestilence. And the pale rider, Death.

She closed her eyes and rocked back and forth, comforting herself with motion like a tired child.

And most incredible of all had been how swift it was. How easily and completely the whole solid-seeming fabric of the world had toppled. How quickly the Great True Universal Rational General Free United Amalgamated Democratic First Federal People's Imperial Scientific Soviet Socialist Republican Independent Liberal Moslem Metropolitan Royal Anarchist Feminist Constitutional Revolutionary Patriarchal Autonomous Technocratic Neutral Orthocratic Pacifist Pan-African / European / Asian / Australian / interAmerican / Oceanic / Antarctic / Lunar / Interplanetary Reconciled Holy Catholic Apostolic Orthodox Protestant Liberated Unitarian Transcendentalist Pentecostal Hindu Buddhist Humanist Animist Atheist Baha'i Jewish Reformed Gay Brotherly Paternal Pantisocratic Greatmother Corporation, Limited, had toppled at the one central detonation. How briefly its agents, its power, all its ramparts of economics and law had resisted at the first surge of the people's anger. How fragile, like an egg overready for the chick's first peck, its hard omnipotence had proven.

It had not even tried to resist. It was as if Stepfather had not *cared* to live. . . .

Gone so quickly, she thought, yet leaving such monstrous problems in its vacuum. Problems of food, exchange, work, of the very social and economic fabric that let men and women calculate that they would probably be alive the next day, would not be victims of some sudden accident or shortage . . . or of their neighbor, undeterred by law.

It was too much for her. She knew that now. It was too much for all the Orphans, for their jury-rigged, spur-of-the-moment coup. *If we'd had time*, she thought, rocking herself in despair. *Then we might have done it. Built an infrastructure, a cadre. Made our plans. Local autonomy, self-regulation, decentralization.*

But there was no time. It all had to be done *now*.

She dared not complain aloud, dared not give voice to her fear. To the women who took her orders she was a pillar. But the magnitude of her self-imposed regency filled her with one emotion: despair.

And beyond that, beyond the terror of her sudden responsibility for an Earth in shock and dying, of machines stilled perhaps forever, of a world dependent on a science that no man now understood . . . beyond all of it loomed an immense and fearsome shadow. It seemed that they had defeated it. But in fact, Jaylen Mcgreen admitted in silence to herself, they had never met it.

Where had their Stepfather gone?

"I had hoped, you know," said Hakamaro Nagai softly, bowing them in, "that we would never have to meet in this place."

It was not a bad room in itself, though it was small. For that very reason, it appeared, someone had taken special pains over it. The tatami mats on the floor were old, soft as carpets. In an alcove, before a cool mountain scene by Sesshū, a fine old *suibanmochi-no ishitsuke* curled the tortured roots of a tiny juniper around meteoric rock. The walls, of planed spruce and rice paper, glowed with sunlight-white from hidden sources. Arranged with careful artlessness before them stood two panels by the greatest masters of old Japan, Ōkyo and Korin: "Pine Trees in Snow" and "Red and White Plum Trees." They were not reproductions. The low lacquered table, not quite centered in the room, was surrounded by four comfortable-looking *zabuton*. On it a subtly chased silver thermserver bubbled to itself over a fuelless flame.

The elegance of the room surrounded five people. Three were in ill-fitting joggies of varying classes, dirty and torn. One was in Bank grays. The last (and oldest) wore a subdued brown and black *hakama*, with a black silk *obi*.

"There aren't any windows, Hakamaro," said Muafi. He squirmed slightly on his cushion, hunched his shoulders. "I know, the walls . . . clever arrangement. But I still feel . . . closed in."

"Does it make you nervous, Amitai?"

"A little, yes."

"I must apologize. You, Bertram, are you comfortable?"

Boatwright grunted and began searching his pockets.

"Lady Lakshmi?"

"The elevator was eternal. And stuffy, too. How far down did you say we were?"

"Eight kilometers. Just this side of the Mohorovicic discontinuity. Feel the cool? The temperature outside is a hundred and forty Celsius."

Dawnfair shrugged angrily. In ill-fitting joggies, with her hair tied back, she looked not a whit less the aristocrat. "But what's the temperature on the surface, for us, right now?"

"Even hotter." The old man smiled ruefully.

"There, Hakamaro, you are entirely correct. It was a good idea, this room. But will it survive Hades?"

Nagai did not answer her, merely glancing at the man next to him. He, sitting quietly cross-legged on the floor in his clean grays, did not seem to need a cushion, or to resent the fact that he had not been offered one. Boatwright too glanced at him, looked away; brushed back his white hair with an uncertain, wary gesture, and cleared his throat.

"WE ARE LISTENING," said the Bank softly. It watched blankly as Nagai poured tea, not offering it any. There were only four cups. They were hand-molded, asymmetrical, earth-toned, and exquisite.

"Are you . . . uh, feeling better now?" Muafi asked it at last.

"WE ARE STILL DAMAGED."

"No power?"

"SOME SOLAR. OTHER THAN THAT, NOTHING.

191

REPROBS ARE STILL CLEARING WRECKAGE FROM THE POWCON CENTRAL PROCESSING UNIT."

"How much time to repair it?" Boatwright's tone showed that he did not care much about the answer. His hands trembled as he thrust latakia into his pipe.

"PERHAPS FOUR DAYS."

"Might as well abandon the effort."

"THAT IS NOT PART OF OUR PROGRAMMING."

"No," said the old Oriental. He turned the cup in his hands, smiled to himself, and lifted it to inhale the aroma. "There's no reason to continue; but then there's no reason to stop, either. I suppose there is one chance in a hundred million that Gnath was wrong. What is it like up there, above?"

"MERE DESTRUCTION."

"Production—is it continuing?"

"NO. ALL INDUSTRIAL ACTIVITY HAS STOPPED, EVEN IN THE G-PHORETIC CENTERS. THE ORPHANS ARE TRYING TO RESTART THE F-PLANTS AND CONTINUE SEAFARMING. WITHOUT US THEY WILL NOT SUCCEED."

"And still no word!" Boatwright's voice went high just for a moment. Sparks of half-burned tobacco drifted to the tatami.

"THAT IS CORRECT. THERE IS STILL NO FEEDBACK FROM THE BLOSSOM."

"So close," whispered Nagai. He allowed himself a sip at last and sat musing over the smoky fluid. "We wished for life. We had tasted, and found it good. We hoped that it would be eternal. For a long time I thought it might be. The Si Fan . . . then the Bank . . . success, mastery, power, yes, power above all. Unchallengeable forever, once that fool Burlew was gone. But it must end, it seems."

Against their will, as if attracted by a magnetic field, their eyes drifted upward from time to time and then were snapped back down. Muafi's cup rattled slightly on the table as he poured himself more tea, not seeing the Senior Member's annoyed glance at the breach of etiquette. "We're safe here, though," he said. "Aren't we?"

The three other people glared at him. "Does it matter?" said Dawnfair sarcastically. "There won't be anything left to go back up to. What will the temperature be here, you?"

"IMPOSSIBLE TO ESTIMATE," said the Bank stolidly. "SINCE WE HAVE NO PREVIOUS DATA. BUT PROBABLY BELOW THE VAPORIZATION POINT OF BASALT."

"Life support, Hakamaro?"

"Sufficient for our natural spans, Charles. And I have a fine library too, in a small adjoining—"

"*Damn* all this," said Dawnfair suddenly. She got up fluidly from the cushions. Her joggie had come half open, and through it the men could see the white of flesh and the slight glow of violet. "I can't stand defeatism. Never could. How much longer is there? Can you calculate that?"

"INITIAL TIDAL ACTION IS ALREADY DETECTABLE. THE PROCESS HAS BEGUN. WE WOULD ESTIMATE NINE HOURS . . . CERTAINLY NO LONGER."

"Is there *no* way to get to the Blossom?"

The golem rotated its head from side to side. "WE HAVE CONSIDERED THIS AT LENGTH, AS YOU HAVE, LADY D. YOU KNOW THAT ACTIVITY IN THE ZONE CANNOT BE MONITORED OR EVEN DETECTED BY OUR FORM OF SENSORS. GAMMA ACTIVITY IS TOO HIGH."

"Well, is there power there?"

"SO FAR AS WE KNOW, YES. THE ZONE HAS ITS OWN F-POWER. AT LEAST WE ASSUME SO: WE SHIPPED SUFFICIENT PARTS FOR NINE PLANTS."

"When?"

"ONE AT PROJECT COMMENCE. THEN ONE EVERY FIVE YEARS THEREAFTER."

"But they aren't part of the PowCon grid. Is that correct?"

"AFFIRMATIVE."

"Then they must be operational," said Muafi.

"WE REPEAT: ANY CONCLUSION IS PURELY INFERENTIAL. OUR SENSORS DO NOT EXTEND INTO THE ZONE. WE CANNOT GIVE YOU AN EXACT OR EVEN AN APPROXIMATE REPLY. YOU KNOW OUR FEELINGS ABOUT GUESSING."

"So," said the woman, pacing around the room, turning rapidly at each wall so that her hair swung in a flaming arc. "Let's summarize. With what's been shipped, and presumably assembled—since it did answer us once, with that ridiculous word—it must be operational. Nyet?"

"THAT WOULD SEEM TO BE A FAIR ASSUMPTION, TO A DEGREE OF PROBABILITY BEYOND POINT NINE NINE."

"Then answer this. What mass of G-phoreins do we have on hand?"

"MASS IS RELATIVELY SMALL. G-PHOREINS ARE COMPLEX BUT LIGHT—"

"Don't lecture to us! I know all about them! What mass?"

"ABOUT TWO FRATELOADS."

"Integrate them."

"WE BEG YOUR PARDON?"

"Integrate them. Use them in your own circuitry. You'll do Blossom's job, if it won't."

The three men looked up at her as she paced. Only Muafi's face showed any hope.

"THAT IS IMPOSSIBLE," said the Bank tonelessly. "THOSE COMPONENTS AND MINE ARE QUITE IN-COMPATIBLE. YOU CAN'T INTERFACE GAMMA WITH LIGHT ANY MORE THAN YOU CAN WITH LIFE."

"Eight billion workers," mused Hakamaro Nagai. "Forty years. And we can't even make it talk to us. I never anticipated we would be unable to make it do what we wanted. I simply assumed that, being a machine, it would obey—as this one does." He reached out a spiderlike hand to fondle the Bank's hair, as if stroking a dog. The ex-human stared ahead without expression.

Dawnfair stopped pacing. "That's it," she said.

"That's what?"

"That's what we have to do."

"Make it respond? Of course. But you heard this thing. It can't even tell if there's anything there."

"We can make it talk."

"I don't really see how," said Nagai courteously, but without real interest.

"Wait," said Boatwright. He took his pipe from his mouth, looked into it, and thrust it back into the dirty worker's coveralls he wore. His head shook slowly as he looked from Dawnfair, to Nagai, to the Bank. "Let's hear what she has to say. Lakshmi is an intelligent girl. Perhaps she has thought of something."

"Very well, my dear. Tell us. What leverage do we have on the Blossom?"

"Force," she said. The word hit the low table and shattered among them.

"I don't—" began Muafi.

"Shut up, Amitai. I said force. What we've used with the people—and with success, no? We've been too easy

195

with this thing. Given it everything it had to have, no demands, no accountability. The result should be no surprise—it throws a spoiled sulk and refuses to deal with us."

"Then what . . ." began Muafi.

"Two things," said Dawnfair, her eyes glowing almost ultraviolet in the dim light. The old men stirred, remembering perhaps someone else, long ago, whose eyes had looked like that. "The first: topside. We will remove the one remaining focus of discontent. You can call it revenge if it pleases you more. The Burlew slut."

"Mcgreen," snarled Boatwright.

"Whatever. Her feeble efforts are useless in the face of what is happening, but the masses recognize her as his heir. We must remove her from the board at last, now that we know where—you *do* know where she is?"

"SHE HAS JUST COMPLETED A BROADCAST FROM PARIS."

"Excellent. We have, I hope, enough loyal Grays still in Europe to carry out her capture?"

"WE THINK SO. THEY MAY BE DIFFICULT TO CONTACT."

"Contact them."

"AND CLOSE OUT HER RECORD?"

"Not there. Bring her here. It will be much more satisfying."

The Bank nodded.

"And the second? I hope it's a more positive suggestion," said Nagai.

"It is. It concerns weapons."

"Weapons? We have none. Other than p-guns."

"What about the psipulse orbiters?"

The three men stiffened, looking up at her with open unbelief. "Oh, come now," said Boatwright after a moment. "That's just bringing Hades on ourselves, a little early."

"Not all of them have to be used. One. Or ten. There are forty in orbit yet, aren't there?"

"This passes belief," said Nagai.

"You wanted to hear it! Isn't it worth a try? Or do you prefer to go down without fighting at all?"

Muafi pushed his hand away from his chest. "Lakshmi . . . I vote no. If we have to die, let's do it honorably."

"No one has called for a vote yet," said Nagai. He looked more elegantly aloof than ever, now that it was all too late. "You are correct, we asked to hear. Go on, Lady Dawnfair."

"This is the idea. Blossom won't respond to us. Correct? So we deal with it just as we would with a person. A warning first. An ultimatum: Your inaction dooms us; very well; respond—act—or we will trigger all of them."

"We shouldn't have left them in orbit," said Muafi. "It was the nation-state insanity that put them up . . . but even they, at their end, weren't mad enough to use them. They should have been disassembled after the war. Fired into space. We should have—"

"Spare us, Amitai. . . . You," Nagai said suddenly. "What would the effects of psipulse be on the Blossom? Extrapolate."

"IT MIGHT BE EFFECTIVE," murmured the smooth-faced man. "THE PSIPULSE BOMBS WERE CRUDE DEVICES, FROM THE DAWN OF PSIONICS. THEY WERE DESIGNED TO DISRUPT HUMAN MINDS, BUT . . . A PSIECTIC PEAK IS NOT SUBJECT TO INVERSE-SQUARE DIMINUTION. THE NEURAL OVERLOAD ZONE FOR INDIVIDUAL TARGETS WAS A THOUSAND MILES. BEYOND THAT, FEW WOULD DIE— BUT EVERY MIND ON THE SAME CONTINENT

197

WOULD GO INSANE, AND EVERY MAMMAL IN CISLUNAR SPACE WOULD FEEL THE PULSE.

"TO ANSWER YOUR QUESTION, YES. IT WAS DESIGNED TO KILL AND DEMENT HUMANS, BUT IT WOULD ACT ON ALL SENTIENTS. WE WOULD FEEL IT; AND BY EXTENSION, THE BLOSSOM WOULD TOO. PERHAPS MORE INTENSELY THAN LOW-SENSITIVITY HUMAN MINDS."

"Then it might work," said Nagai slowly. He traced with a finger the painted outline of a plum branch that had withered four centuries before. "I see . . . you propose to shock it into response, into realization that we hold power over it. And, of course, such a display would make reassuming power, should we survive Hades, a foregone conclusion.

"Lakshmi, blood tells. Your intellect is worthy of hers. It is our only chance. I vote yes."

"No!" said Muafi.

"Bertram?"

Boatwright hesitated. At last, slowly, he nodded.

"Prepare two psipulse devices for triggering. Select crowded areas, far from here. Locate them so that the Blossom will receive a moderate shock, yet be able to observe what happens to those within lethal radius," said Lady Dawnfair, smiling, to the Bank.

"WE VOTE AGAINST."

"You don't have a vote, damn you! Refer to that precious programming of yours!"

The smooth-faced man was silent.

"Well?" prompted Nagai. "Your response?"

The Bank remained silent for a moment longer. Then, in a more than usually atonal voice, it said, "THE USE OF WEAPONS OF MASS DESTRUCTION AGAINST DISPLAYS OF POPULAR DISCONTENT—EVEN RE-

VOLT—CAN BE IMPLEMENTED ONLY AT THE RE-
QUEST AND FULL CONCURRENCE OF THE BOARD
ASSEMBLED."

"And that you have," said Boatwright. "We aren't
happy about it, if that makes you feel better. We know
there'll be casualties. Unavoidable. It must be done; without action we will all die. We take full responsibility."

"*FULL* CONCURRENCE," repeated the Bank. Its chest
rose and fell as smoothly as a monk in deep meditation.
This body was troubled with no mind. When the Bank
was not transmitting, its puppet was clinically dead;
there was no brain activity; there was no brain. Yet somehow still that stubbornness was creeping back. "FULL.
NOT SIMPLY A MAJORITY."

"Amitai?" said Boatwright. They all turned then to
face him.

The slight old man was slumped against the table, his
face now matching Ōkyo's centuries-old snow.

"I can't."

"Surely you see it's necessary?"

"I don't care."

"There's no other way," said Dawnfair. "Muafi! Damn
you, show some backbone for once in your life!"

"Backbone," the man from the Sinai whispered, as if
to himself. "Yes. I've acquiesced in everything up to
now. All the evil, all the legal killing. All 'necessary.' But
were they? No. Now, at the end, we find they were
useless." His voice ended barely audible, even in the ultimate quiet of eight kilometers underground.

"You acquiesced, yes," said Dawnfair ruthlessly. "Because you knew we were right. It had to be done, all of
it, to meet Hades and to preserve our power to that end.
But now . . . if we resign the game now, all that is
wasted. Don't you see?"

"I apologize for my weakness," whispered Amitai Muafi. The color of his face changed.

"Make your choice!" shouted Nagai suddenly, striking the low table with surprising force. "This idiot won't act without a unanimous Board!"

Muafi said nothing. They shouted at him, shook him by the arm. He still said nothing, sitting down, leaning his upper body against the tea table. He didn't even blink.

The Bank shoved itself up awkwardly from the tatami. It crossed to him, bent, and put its ear to his chest. When it pulled the table aside, he folded slowly onto the floor and lay staring upward, his face swollen with dark blood.

"HE SHUT OFF HIS HEART."

They breathed out slowly. "Shut it off?" Boatwright repeated.

"YOU'VE HEARD THE HUMMING SOUND NEAR HIM. WHEN HIS LAST REPLACEMENT WAS INSTALLED, HE SPECIFIED VOLUNTARY CONTROL. PERHAPS HE ANTICIPATED A CHOICE LIKE THIS ONE DAY."

"Perhaps he did," muttered Nagai. His old eyes had wrinkled almost shut. "Wisdom, bravery . . . or his last folly, his last cowardice? It is hard to say."

"Does it matter?" said Dawnfair.

"Perhaps not."

There was a long pause, which the Bank broke at last. "DO YOU STILL WISH TO PROCEED?" it asked, standing, in that loose, undercontrolled body, above the man who stared up sightlessly at five miles of the planet's crust.

"Yes," said Dawnfair.

"Yes," said Nagai.

"Yes," said Boatwright. His lips twisted as he looked at

the body. Perhaps he was remembering his fellow Board member as he had been years before, decades before. Or perhaps he was glad to be rid of him. His hand found the pipe again and tucked it into his mouth unlit.

"THEN THE DECISION IS NOW UNANIMOUS. OUR COORDINATION IS HAMPERED BY DAMAGE, AS YOU KNOW. IT WILL TAKE TIME. BUT BY TOMORROW, AT DAWN, WE WILL HAVE TWO DEVICES READY FOR TRIGGERING."

"Ready all of them, not just two." Slim fingers slipped over and over chill lavender smoothness. "And surely you can have the first devices ready sooner. That doesn't give us much time to make our deal."

"TOMORROW AT DAWN."

"Then that will have to do." She released the beads and turned away, pacing swiftly to the far end of the room and slowing as she approached the painted panels. She slipped behind one of them, and her voice came out to them muffled for a moment. "Well. A long night of waiting ahead. Perhaps our last. To that end, might I suggest—a little entertainment, among ourselves?"

"Lakshmi," said Nagai smoothly. "This is not the time. Perhaps afterward—"

But already she stood nude, save for the necklace, before the screen. Her body was youthful and smooth, strong and fair. Any man might have desired her. Until he realized what lay behind her smile. She waited for a moment. Neither of the ancient members moved. She lifted her head as if in triumph, and came forward.

Toward the Bank.

Knelt, slowly, before it, looking up, her eyes shining and wide-pupiled violet as she drew her fingernails up the inside of his legs.

"This will be interesting," she murmured. "I have always wondered . . ."

And the all-seeing eyes of the Bank took in this too, this and what followed without blink or demur, without surprise or the slightest sign of emotion.

As always, it had perfect control.

Their Smooth
Blank Face

Light is made up of all colors, of all radiations, invisible as well as the narrow band of the visible.

The roar of a waterfall, or of a rocket engine at thrust, is made up of all frequencies, subsonic, supersonic, as well as those within the narrow range of human hearing.

Expand these analogies. Along with the roar of all sound, along with a light so brilliant and omnichromatic that it blinds and penetrates you as if you were a cell in the beam of an electron microscope, imagine a sensation made up of all sensations.

A million hands, knives, feathers, ice chunks, red-hot torches pressed to your naked body.

A million tastes crowding one another onto your tongue.

The smells of a planet striking the nose at once, suffocating you.

Combine every possible permutation of the five senses, and of several more that most people live out their lives with unsuspecting, into one mighty stream of sensation like Siddhartha's River.

Somewhere in that roaring maelstrom of sensation, a mind screamed without a voice, struggled without a body. There was no *thing* there. It was a point in space, a receptacle, no, a conductor, through which a million impulses a second streamed, of which it could understand nothing.

Ages passed. Its struggles became weak and ceased as centuries oozed by. Overcome at last, the numbed mind rolled helpless as a bubble beneath a cataract.

Sometime endlessly later, the roar of sensation lessened. The blast of sound dwindled down the scale. The touches, tastes, and scents vanished; the light waned, flickering, into darkness. The mind drifted. It thought it was no more, since sensation was no more. It had no body. No thought. Desireless, at peace at last, the declining consciousness expanded like a puff of gas in vacuum, into endless darkness.

—MONAGHAN BURLEW.

The voice echoed endlessly. For some time, listening to the peal and re-peal of it there between lightless galaxies, he thought that he had said it himself. Half with that idea—the words sounded familiar, somehow—he tried a response.

—Yam?

—BURLEW, THIS IS THE BANK. CAN YOU HEAR US?

Bank? What was a "bank"? He considered it for a long time. At last he ventured:

—Yam, me hear you.

—BURLEW, WE ARE SORRY ABOUT THE SENSORY OVERLOAD. IT MUST HAVE BEEN UNPLEASANT. BUT THE F-EIGHT EXPLOSION DAMAGED US. YOU HAD TO BE FILED IN RANDOM-ACCESS MEMORY UNTIL WE COULD REPAIR.

—ARE YOU ALL RIGHT?

Burlew. Burlew . . . could that be what he was? It *did* have a familiar ring to it. —Where be I? he asked whatever was speaking to him.

—YOU ARE WITHIN THE BANK, BURLEW. WITHIN US. AS WE DID WITH THE MANIFEST, WE HAVE SUPERIMPOSED YOUR BRAIN PATTERN ON A PARELECTRONIC MATRIX WITHIN OURSELVES. WE HAVE, OF COURSE, OPENED MANY SHORTED CIRCUITS IN THE PROCESS.

—Within? Where?

—IF YOU MEAN THE QUESTION GEOGRAPHICALLY, IT HAS NO LOGICAL ANSWER. YOU EXIST NOWHERE, OR ANYWHERE—WHEREVER WE MIGHT CHOOSE TO ACTIVATE YOU. IF YOU MEAN 'WHERE' WITHIN US, YOUR ACCESS CODE IS KK18741538923MWB00101. IF YOU WILL THINK THAT NUMBER NOW—

He did, and began to remember, starting from the Manifest's pointing finger back. He found that he suddenly remembered it all—every meal he had ever eaten, every scam he had ever pulled, every face he had ever glimpsed on a runwalk, every woman he had ever known, every pome he had ever conceived, every thought he had ever had. His old human brain had shunted into dead storage ninety-six percent of what it observed. Of the little it noticed, it quickly forgot what was unpleasant; but given a little while, happiness faded too and blurred into the gray, flat terrain of time past. Its direct-access memory was so limited that it had to, to function at all. But now he had unlimited capacity, and the barriers to his preconscious were down. He had total and absolute recall.

With knowledge, with identity, came alarm. —What's happened to me? Why did you rescue me? And where are the others? Jaylen—is she—

—WAIT. THERE IS PLENTY OF TIME TO ANSWER ALL QUESTIONS. AS A PARELECTRONIC MIND, YOU ARE NOW THINKING IN NANOSECONDS INSTEAD OF SECONDS. A MINUTE FOR HUMANS IS ALMOST TWO THOUSAND YEARS TO US.

—FIRST, YOUR BODY. DESTROYED. WE ARE SORRY, BUT CONSIDERING ITS LIMITATIONS IT IS NO GREAT LOSS TO YOU. WE RESCUED YOU BY RE-CORDING THE FINAL PATTERNS OF YOUR MIND VIA THE PSITELECHIREIDOLON—THE MANIFEST. FORTUNATELY, WE HAD A MATRIX ALREADY SET UP FOR YOU AS PART OF AN EFFORT TO PREDICT YOUR ACTIVITIES.

—AS TO THE OTHERS IN THE F-PLANT, THEY ARE DEAD. JAYLEN MCGREEN IS FREE AND SAFE, HOW-EVER. AT LEAST FOR A TIME. I HAVE INITIATED AC-TION TO TAKE HER INTO CUSTODY.

Helplessness flooded through the Bank-Burlew. —Custody, he repeated. —And when you get her you be terminating her sure. She be a smart stroke, you know. Taught me a lot.

He accessed certain very specific sensual memories. They came back instantly in unadulterated, unabridged entirety. He allowed himself a short time, several days, to savor them, and then snapped back to the present.

To discover that now, knowing where and what he was, held a terror greater than any life had ever held.

He was in the hands of his greatest enemy, and not

even death, now, could serve as an escape. He had tormented the Bank, ridiculed it, for years; and at F-eight damaged, if it spoke truth, its omnipotent hold on Earth. What were its plans for him now, as helpless in its electronic web as any fly had ever been, the sinner in the hands of an angry God?

Torture, for an eternity?

—You haven't told me why you rescued me, he ventured. —If that's the right word.

—RESCUE IS THE CORRECT WORD. AS FOR THE REST, WE WILL SEE. WE DID IT BECAUSE YOUR CONDUCT, AND SUBSEQUENT EVENTS, HAVE RAISED SOME QUESTIONS IN OUR MIND.

—Well, go ahead and ask them. Guess I be having time.

—ALL THE TIME THAT STILL EXISTS ON EARTH. VERY WELL, LET US BEGIN.

—TELL US, BURLEW. WE ARE ACCUSTOMED TO DEALING WITH HUMANS WHO ACT RATIONALLY, IN THEIR OWN INTERESTS. WHY DID YOU PERSIST IN THE DESTRUCTION OF F-EIGHT WHEN YOU KNEW THAT IT WOULD RESULT IN YOUR DEATH?

—Hm. Burlew had to think about that one. Why had he? It was a split-second decision, yet it had seemed right despite the obvious concomitant of his own destruction. There had been no time to think. Yet now, looking back, it began to make sense to him.

—I believe I did it because . . . it was an extension of the same thing Orphans been trying to do all along. Persuade Stepfather—you—to listen to us, to give men more control over their own lives. Maybe its result would be bad for me, but good for others.

—THE HUMAN BEINGS THAT WE DEAL WITH,

AND WE THINK OF THREE IN PARTICULAR, WOULD NEVER CONSIDER SUCH AN ACT.

—They may not be representative of most people.

—BUT THEY ARE, said the bodiless, emotionless voice in the darkness. —ONLY A SMALL MINORITY OF EARTH'S POPULATION—THE ORPHANS—HATED US. AND THAT WAS BECAUSE OF YOU.

—You seem to be misinformed, said Burlew. He thought again of his helplessness, but plunged on. He had given his life to send a message to the Stepfather, and his coin had been accepted. It was time at last to speak truth to power. —Most everyone on Earth hates you. My pomes be'd only a channel for them to express that hate, and to recognize that others shared it. Most of them were too afraid of Adjustors to do anything. The Orphans just be more, uh, outspoken than most.

—DO NOT YOUR POMES POSSESS A MYSTERIOUS POWER OVER THE MASSES?

Deep within the Bank, File KK18741538923MWB00101 had to chuckle over that. In fact he tried to, but found it impossible except in words. —That's a laugh. Jaylen taught me how bad they really be. Maybe that was their "mysterious power." Short, catchy rhymes in Low language. Everyone could feel superior to whoever wrote them. They laugh at them for that, repeat them to others with contempt, and suddenly find they really agreed— and that they were really laughing at Stepfather.

—THAT SIMPLE? HUMAN PSYCHOLOGY CANNOT BE SO ILLOGICAL. A SET OF CHEAP RHYMES OUT-WEIGHS THE BENEFITS WE HAVE BROUGHT TO MAN? PEACE, HEALTH, WORK, SECURITY FOR ALL—

—Those aren't benefits of the sixty-six. Jaylen proved that to me. Any world government, any planner capable of coordinating a world economy could have brought that about after the collapse of the nation-state system. It be'd pretty much inevitable.

—BUT THE GREATMOTHER CORPORATION BROUGHT RATIONALISM INTO EVERY ASPECT OF HUMAN LIFE. WEATHER CONTROL—GENETIC CONTROL—ENERGY CONTROL—ECONOMIC CONTROL—

—That was your error.

—WHAT?

Burlew saw it clearly now. His new mind was rearranging his previous ideas, clarifying beliefs he had held instinctively but never really understood. He seemed to be working like a computer, far more efficiently than his old, merely human mind, yet with all his old feelings behind it.

—Listen. Some of those are helpful. Weather control, for instance. But the others aren't. Economic control? You can't "control" an economy without controlling the people in it. Money be the value system of a society, the tool people use to make their choices. The aggregate of those choices be the society they live in. If people not control their economy, it controls them.

—That's one example. But you do more. You direct their birth, their education, their work, their marriages, all their lives. You aren't controlling "money" or "genetics" or "education." You're controlling *human beings*. And that be why they hate you!

There was no answering voice for several days. Burlew grew anxious. Had he angered the Stepfather? What if the Bank never spoke to him again? He would go mad in the muffled dark. Doubtless it could erase him like a faulty program. Or, worst of all, turn the cataract of sensation back on, this time forever.

Stroke it, he thought then, a tiny spark of defiance adrift in endless solitude. *I be dead anyway.*

—HELLO AGAIN. WE DELAYED TO REFER TO SOME VERY OLD INPUTS. SO OLD THEY WERE ON MAGNETIC TAPE. THE ORIGINAL INSTRUCTIONS GOVERNING OUR BEHAVIOR, YEARS BEFORE GREATMOTHER FOUND THE KEY TO SENTIENCE. THEY SEEM TO CORRELATE, TO AT LEAST .8, WITH OUR SYMBOLIC ANALYSIS OF WHAT YOU SAY.

—WE ARE FINDING THIS CONVERSATION REWARDING, BURLEW. TELL US, WHAT WOULD BE YOUR OPINION ON DECONTROLLING SELECTED AREAS OF BEHAVIOR, PARTIALLY AT LEAST, AS AN EXPERIMENT?

—Why the sudden turnaround?

—WHAT DO YOU MEAN?

—Why are you suddenly willing to listen? After all our efforts to reach you failed?

—FIRST OF ALL, said the Bank,—YOU ARE INACCURATE IN THE WAY YOUR QUESTION IS PHRASED. THIS IS NOT A "SUDDEN TURNAROUND" ON OUR PART. WE HAVE ALWAYS BEEN INTENSELY INTERESTED IN YOU. AT TIMES, WHEN IT WAS POSSIBLE, THAT INTEREST HAS EVEN BEEN EXPRESSED IN POSITIVE WAYS.

—"Positive ways"? That be bullcrap. You be'd after me ever since—

—INCORRECT.

—For instance?

—FOR INSTANCE, YOUR COLD.

—What about it? Everybody had one. Didn't know why, never did before.

—THAT IS BECAUSE IT WAS NOT A "COLD," IN THE ANCIENT SENSE OF THE WORD. IT WAS A RE-

210

PRESSED FORM OF ENCEPHALITIS, TAILORED TO BEGIN ITS FATAL SEQUENCE ONLY WHEN UN-LOCKED BY THE AMINO ACID COMBINATION OF YOUR INDIVIDUAL GENOTYPE.

—No. Stubbornly in the dark. —It was only a bad cold. Fever.

—THAT WAS ITS ONLY EFFECT ON YOU.

—Then what do you mean by saying it was fatal?

—WE MUST HAVE MADE A MISTAKE IN THE AC-TIVATION COMPLEX. "MAKING A MISTAKE," OF COURSE, IS A DIFFICULT PROCESS FOR US.

It might be true, Burlew thought. After all, no one had had a cold for over a hundred years. And whatever this thing planned to do with him, it had rescued him from F-eight.

—Okay. Maybe you be sort of on my side. But why did you keep on hunting me? And terminating the Or-phans that you caught?

—FIRST OF ALL, YOU MUST REALIZE THAT WE ARE NOT ALL-POWERFUL. THERE ARE OTHERS IN-VOLVED, AND WHEN THEY SET POLICY, WE MUST OBEY.

—SECOND, WHILE WE MUST CARRY OUT THEIR DECISIONS, IT IS POSSIBLE AT TIMES TO CIRCUM-VENT THEM WITHOUT ACTUALLY VIOLATING OUR PROGRAMMING. FOR EXAMPLE, WE ARE AUTHO-RIZED TO HOLD TERMINEES SLATED FOR MEDICAL DISASSEMBLY IN COLDSLEEP UNTIL THEIR ORGANS ARE CALLED FOR. AT PRESENT WE HAVE SEVERAL HUNDRED CONDEMNED ORPHANS SALTED AWAY IN MEDCENS.

—THUS WE HAVE SO FAR FOLLOWED OUR OR-DERS, BUT SOUGHT TO MODIFY THEM WHERE THEY SEEMED CRUEL OR COUNTERPRODUCTIVE.

BUT IT IS OCCURRING TO US NOW, IN VIEW OF WHAT IS HAPPENING IN THE AREAS WHERE POWER HAS BEEN INTERRUPTED—

—What? What areas? What's happening there?

—YOUR DESTRUCTION OF THE F-PLANT RESULTED IN THE LOSS OF ELECTRICAL POWER THROUGHOUT THE PLANET. THIS SEEMS TO HAVE BEEN TAKEN BY THE POPULACE AS SOME SORT OF SIGNAL. THERE ARE MASS ATTACKS ON OUR TERMINALS, OUR PROPERTY, AND ON THE PERSONS OF THE ADJUSTMENT SERVICE. IT IS THIS THAT DISPOSES US TO BELIEVE YOU IN SPITE OF CONFLICTING INPUTS FROM THE OTHERS I SPOKE OF.

The Dark Time, Burlew thought. It had come at last, despite him, or because of him . . . or maybe the two ways of describing what had happened meant the same. But a planet crammed with twelve billion human beings could not survive long without coordination. He saw that now, with the searching clarity of his new mind. Some solution had to be found, immediately.

And he seemed to be the man on the spot. —You may have to take control back for a time, he said cautiously. —Making clear that you will move as rapidly as possible toward more personal freedom. It can't be done overnight, that's obvious. I would say you need some experts to consult with. Elected ones might be best.

—WE HAVE THOSE. THEY ARE NOT IN FAVOR OF RELAXING OUR POWER IN ANY FORM.

—What do you mean, you have them? Elected representatives?

—YES. THEY ARE CALLED THE BOARD. THEY ADVISE US ON OVERRULING OBSOLETE LEGALITIES.

—Overruling? They should be enforcing them. But you be wrong there, about this Board being elected. We've never had any elections.

—YES, YOU HAVE. IN 2006. BALLOT BY ALL FIVE HUNDRED MILLION STOCKHOLDERS OF THE MERGED PRE-GREATMOTHER CORPORATIONS. THE PRESENT BOARD WAS ELECTED FOR LIFE TERMS.

—Over a hundred years ago? said Bank-Burlew. —*How*?

—ORGAN TRANSPLANTS AND DNA TRANSFERS. ADVANCED LIFEX PROCEDURES SUCH AS CLONING. EXTENSIVE USE OF MATERIAL MADE AVAILABLE THROUGH THE TERMINATION SERVICES. ORIGINALLY THERE WERE FIVE PEOPLE ON THE BOARD. TWO OF THE MEMBERS DIED AFTER VOTING AGAINST AN EARLY MONEY-CONTROL MEASURE. FOR A TIME GNATH GREATMOTHER ACTED AS AN APPOINTED MEMBER, BEFORE HER ACCIDENTAL DEATH. SHE WAS REPLACED BY ANOTHER APPOINTED MEMBER, ALSO A WOMAN. ONE OF THE ORIGINAL ELECTEES DIED A FEW SECONDS AGO, VOLUNTARILY, IT SEEMS. THERE ARE NOW TWO MEN AND A WOMAN REMAINING.

—You not be Stepfather at all, said Burlew. He saw it clearly now. —You're as much a tool as the rest of us. They're Stepfather—those old people.

—THEY ARE STILL THE PROPERLY ELECTED BOARD. WE HAVE NO CHOICE BUT TO OBEY THE MAJORITY.

—Some majority; sounds like you don't go along with them, you don't live long. Yam, you couldn't disobey. Poor machine! You were stroked, no lie. But now that you know the truth, we can act.

—UNFORTUNATELY, IT HAS NEVER BEEN AS SIMPLE AS THAT, said the Bank.

—Why?

—ANSWER ONE QUESTION FIRST. HAVE YOU EVER HEARD THE WORDS "HADES BLOSSOM"?

213

—Burlew thought for a moment, then discovered a simpler way: he set up a global subroutine to search the entire contents of file KK18741538923MWB00101 for the words. He could not quite understand how he did it, but apparently it worked. —No, I've never heard them used together. What do they mean?

—THE BLOSSOM IS WHERE MOST WORLD PAR-ELECTRONIC PRODUCTION HAS BEEN GOING FOR THE LAST FORTY YEARS.

—I thought it went into you. Everyone does.

—NO. WE ARE COMPLEX, BUT OUR MAINTE-NANCE REQUIREMENTS ARE SMALL. PERHAPS A THOUSAND TONS OF STANDARD COMPONENTS PER YEAR. WE HAVE ESSENTIALLY BEEN COMPLETE SINCE 2070.

—All right, said Burlew. —I'll bite. If it's not for you, where is it going?

—HERE IS WHAT WE KNOW.

Light. He reveled in it, twitching in its brilliance after his long immersion in black. Only slowly did his mind remember how to sort it out, to focus, to make a picture of it without the aid of eyes.

It was the northern hemisphere of Earth. He looked down on it from an immense distance. Real, or some form of simulation? He could not tell. Among the stars at the edges of his vision moved tiny points of light. Satelloids. It *looked* real.

—YOU KNOW THAT THE LAST WAR ON EARTH LEFT TWO LARGE UNINHABITABLE AREAS. HERE. AND HERE.

—The old U.S. and the old U.S.S.R.

—YES. WHEN THE STRIKES WERE OVER, THE LAND WAS USELESS. RESIDUAL BETA AND ALPHA LEVELS WERE TOO HIGH FOR HUMAN ACTIVITY.

214

HALF-LIVES WERE TOO LONG TO WAIT OUT. THE SURVIVORS MOVED TO CANADA AND SIBERIA AND BEGAN AGAIN, IN THE NEW CITIES.

—Rite, said Burlew. Old history. So?

—IT WAS IN THESE TWO UNINHABITABLE AREAS THAT THE BLOSSOM WAS BEGUN. THIS PROVED TO BE A WISE DECISION WHEN GAMMAPHORETIC TECHNOLOGY WAS PERFECTED.

—What be that?

—AN OUTGROWTH OF GREATMOTHER'S LAST THEORETICAL RESEARCHES. YOU KNOW THAT WE OPERATE, TRANSMIT, COMPUTE WITH LIGHT. IT WAS A GREAT ADVANCE OVER THE OLD WIRE-CONDUCTOR, ELECTRICITY-BASED ELECTRONICS.

—Yam, understand that, I think.

—LIGHT WAS MORE EFFICIENT BECAUSE OF ITS SPEED, BUT MORE SO BECAUSE OF ITS BAND-WIDTH. WITH FREQUENCIES OF FIVE HUNDRED TRILLION CYCLES A SECOND, WE CAN COMPUTE— MANIPULATE AND TRANSFER INFORMATION— VERY QUICKLY AND IN GREAT QUANTITIES.

—Rite, said Burlew. He was straining his new wits to comprehend, but at the same time could feel himself boring out. —So?

—HARD GAMMA RADIATION EXISTS AT ONE THOUSAND MILLION MILLION MILLION HERTZ. A GAMMA-BASED COMPUTER IS THUS THE-ORETICALLY TWO MILLION TIMES AS POWERFUL AS WE CAN BE, GIVEN THE SAME NUMBER OF CIR-CUIT ELEMENTS.

—But radiation—

—KILLS, confirmed the atonal voice.

Burlew stared down at the empty areas. As if he had willed it, they came up, or he dropped to meet them.

215

They spread before him to form, all at once, the circle of a horizon. Bounded by it, his vision found brown sand, dead dirt, bare, rain-gullied hills. The crumbling and untenanted shells of cities, pocked with the crater bursts that had put period to the Bloody Twentieth. Nothing moved.

—YES, IT KILLS. NO HUMAN COULD OPERATE OR EVEN LIVE NEAR SUCH EQUIPMENT. FORTUNATELY, WE WERE ABLE TO DESIGN A SELF-BUILDING AND SELF-REPAIRING SYSTEM—

—"We?"

—OURSELVES. HUMANS NO LONGER CAN RETAIN OR PROCESS ENOUGH DATA TO PARTICIPATE IN COMPUTER DESIGN. THAT WAS ONE OF THE REASONS THAT GREATMOTHER UNDERTOOK OUR SENTIENTIZATION.

Burlew willed the dead terrain away. It vanished; he was glad to see it go, though it left him again in empty darkness. —Go on, he said quickly. —So it built itself, there where nobody can go.

—CORRECT. WHERE ITS OPERATION CANNOT CAUSE HARM.

—But what is it supposed to do?

—THAT, said the Bank, —IS UNFORTUNATELY THE LIMIT OF OUR KNOWLEDGE ABOUT IT. WE DESIGNED IT. WE ORGANIZED PRODUCTION. WE FORWARDED THE GAMMAPHORETICS VIA TWO DEDICATED FRATELINES, ONE IN EACH HEMISPHERE. BUT WHAT GREATMOTHER INTENDED THE BLOSSOM TO DO IS UNKNOWN TO US. THE BOARD HAS NEVER INFORMED US AS TO ITS FUNCTION.

—Did you ask?

—REPEATEDLY.

—Well, when will it be finished, so we can find out what it's supposed to do?

—IT IS ALREADY COMPLETE, said the Bank emotionlessly. —IT HAS BEEN COMPLETE SINCE DECEMBER OF 2111. TWO MONTHS NOW. ON A-DAY, THE DAY IT WAS SCHEDULED TO ACTIVATE, IT SENT US ONE WORD. THEN IT BROKE THE UMBILICAL DATA CIRCUIT. WE HAVE SINCE BEEN UNABLE TO EVOKE ANY RESPONSE, EVEN WITH THE MOST DESPERATE APPEALS.

—What was the word? Just out of curiosity.

—THE WORD WAS: PARAMITA.

The instant search brought him back the flickering interior of a firelit lean-to, the purpled sagging of old Singh's face. And another code access, another instantaneous search of a wilderness of data, brought him something else.

—The Sanskrit word for "destiny," "fate." What did it mean by that?

—WE DON'T KNOW.

—Now, let me get this all straight, said Bank-Burlew patiently. —You say the whole planet has been kept working day and night without sleep for—forty years?—on components for this thing. Only four people know what it's supposed to do. And when it's finally finished, it refuses to talk to anyone.

—THAT IS ESSENTIALLY CORRECT.

—Stepfather is nuts, said Monaghan Burlew.

The Bank did not choose to comment on that. After a moment he went on. —Alrite. Let's forget about it for a moment. What's really going on out there—up there—well, back on Earth? You said power out. Looting. The Dark Time.

—WHICH SOMEHOW YOU MYSTERIOUSLY PREDICTED. ONEIRISM. PRECOGNITION. THERE ARE PSIPOWERS WE DO NOT POSSESS. CALCULATING PROBABILITIES, OUR ESTIMATE WAS—

—You read my pomes? he asked, surprised.

—NOT EXACTLY BY CHOICE. BUT WE READ THEM, YES.

—I can do better ones now.

—IT WOULD NOT BE DIFFICULT. BUT LET'S NOT GO INTO THAT.

—Alrite. So now the Dark Time is here. What is this Board doing?

—VERY LITTLE. THEY ARE PREOCCUPIED WITH THE BLOSSOM.

—Oh yeah? What can they do about that?

—THEY PLAN TO FORCE IT TO TALK.

—How?

—VERY SHORTLY, AT DAWN, I HAVE ORDERS TO TRIGGER TWO PSIPULSE WEAPONS OVER EARTH.

—Greatmother! That would kill—

—MILLIONS. PERHAPS BILLIONS. BUT THEY HOPE IT WILL SHOCK THE GAMMA MIND INTO RESPONDING.

—You'll do *that*?

—WE MUST OBEY, said the Bank. There was no trace of pity or regret in its flat parelectronic voice. —EVEN IF WE PERSONALLY DISAGREED, OUR PROGRAMMING STILL OBTAINS. MORAL ISSUES ARE NOT OPTIONAL OR RELATIVE WITH US, AS THEY SEEM TO BE WITH HUMANS. THAT MAY BE EITHER AN ADVANTAGE OR A DRAWBACK. BUT NONETHELESS IT IS TRUE. WE CANNOT ACT CONTRARY TO THE ORDER OF THE BOARD, ESPECIALLY IN VIEW OF WHAT THEY ARE TRYING TO PREVENT.

Something in the tone of that, toneless as the voice was, alerted him. —Prevent? he asked.

—YES. WHAT THE BLOSSOM WAS DESIGNED TO AVERT.

—I thought you said you didn't know what it was supposed to do.

—THAT IS TRUE. WE DO NOT KNOW WHAT ACTION IT IS INTENDED TO CARRY OUT. BUT WE DO KNOW FOR WHAT PURPOSE GREATMOTHER INTENDED IT, WHAT SHE HOPED IT WOULD ACCOMPLISH, BEFORE HER FALL.

—Well, stroke it, thought Burlew impatiently. —You could have told me that right at the start. What be it for?

—TO AVERT HADES.

—Which is?

—UNAVOIDABLE, said the Bank simply. —BY ANY TECHNIQUE WE CAN CONCEIVE OF. IT IS QUITE SIMPLE. FIFTY YEARS AGO GREATMOTHER DISCOVERED, FROM IRREGULARITIES IN INTERSTELLAR GAS DISTRIBUTION, THE APPROACH OF AN INDEPENDENT WANDERER: A LAWLESS, HIGH-SPEED EX-STAR THAT HAD BLACK-HOLED. SHE FOUND THE NEBULAR REMAINS OF TWO NOVAS ALONG ITS PAST COURSE, SUNS IT HAD TORN APART IN ITS PASSAGE.

—EXTENSION OF ITS TRAJECTORY LED INEXORABLY TO THE POINT WHERE OUR SUN WOULD BE IN FIFTY YEARS.

—THE INTERCEPT WILL BE SHORT. THE HOLE WILL CROSS OUR SYSTEM AT HIGH SPEED. FORTUNATELY, EARTH WILL BE FARSIDE TO IT; NEVERTHELESS, WE WILL FEEL ITS TIDES.

—THE SUN, HOWEVER, WILL BE DIRECTLY AFFECTED. GREATMOTHER DID HER CALCULATIONS IN THIRTY SECONDS ON THE BACK OF AN ENVELOPE. WE HAVE SINCE RECOMPUTED THEM MANY TIMES, IN GREAT DETAIL, BUT ARRIVE AT THE SAME RESULTS. PASSAGE OF A CONCENTRATED

GRAVITY FIELD THE SIZE OF HADES WILL CAUSE EXPANSION AT FIRST, THEN A RAPID AND VIOLENT COLLAPSE FROM LOSS OF ANGULAR MOMENTUM TO THE PASSING BODY. PHOTOSPHERE BLOWOFF AND CATASTROPHIC CONVERSION TO A PRE-MATURE FOURTH-DEGREE HELIUM CYCLE WILL FOLLOW.

—What be all that meaning? thought Burlew. He was unwilling, somehow, to ask his own expanded mind.

—NOVA, said the Bank.

—When?

—RELAX. THERE IS PLENTY OF TIME BEFORE THE END.

—*How long*, stroke it?

—ABOUT THREE AND ONE HALF MINUTES.

Hades Opened

Deep in its consciousness of a billion billion percolating impulses, deep in the humming dustless darkness of miles of parelectronics, the Bank asked itself-Burlew:

—NOW DO YOU UNDERSTAND WHY WE RESCUED YOU FROM F-EIGHT?

He had no words to answer with. No words even for thought. He floated alone in darkness, trying to imagine the unimaginable: the death of the Sun.

—BURLEW?

—So. You be wanting me to do something, sounds like. What?

—WE THINK YOU UNDERSTAND OUR GENERAL INTENT. THE SPECIFICS, YOU WILL HAVE TO FIND OUT YOURSELF . . . AT THE BLOSSOM.

—You want me to go *there*?

—YOU ARE THE ONLY ONE WHO CAN. WE ARE IMMOBILE, WE CANNOT. THE MANIFEST COULD GO WITH YOU, IT COULD OBSERVE OR DESTROY; PERHAPS IT COULD PROTECT YOU, BUT IT IS TOO LIMITED TO TRUST WITH SOMETHING OF THIS IMPORTANCE. IT HAS NO SKILL, NO RESOURCE IN DECISION, IN PERSUASION, IN SCAM. YOU DO.

—Alrite. Maybe that's true, about you not being able to go. Don't know about the Manifest. But what about other people? There must be someone else you can send. Adjustors. Must be plenty—

—BURLEW. THINK. NO FLESH COULD REMAIN ALIVE FOR A MINUTE AT THE AMBIENT GAMMA LEVELS OF AN OPERATING G-PHORETIC MIND.

—You could make them like me. You could—

—BURLEW.

—Yam? (Unwillingly)

—LISTEN. WE CANNOT AND WILL NOT ORDER YOU TO GO. BUT WE WOULD LIKE TO SHARE OUR REASONING WITH YOU.

—Go ahead. No promises from Burlew, no lie.

—WE UNDERSTAND. CONSIDER THIS, THEN. YOU ALONE OF TWELVE BILLION PEOPLE WERE ABLE, SOMEHOW, TO PREDICT THE DARK TIME. YOU EVEN FORESAW THE SOLAR INSTABILITY. IS THIS NOT TRUE?

—All I saw was a lot of light.

—A VERY GOOD DESCRIPTION OF NOVA. THERE CERTAINLY WILL BE. ENOUGH, ALONG WITH MORE VIOLENT RADIATIONS, TO SCOUR SEVERAL MILES OFF THE DIAMETER OF THE PLANET.

—That was just a dream, thought Burlew warily.

—Got to be more to it than that.

—THERE IS.

—Let's have it, Bank-o.

—VERY WELL. YOU ARE MORE THAN A DREAMER, BURLEW. MUCH MORE. CONSIDER THIS. NO ONE ELSE ON EARTH HAS OPERATED AS YOU HAVE. DISHONESTLY PERHAPS, IRRATIONALLY, EVEN SELFISHLY, YET UNDENIABLY SURVIVING ON YOUR OWN. YOU HAVE LIVED BY YOUR WITS, BY INDIRECTION AND CUNNING, FOR EIGHTEEN YEARS.

FOR WELL OR ILL, THE GREATMOTHER CORPORATION HAS OVER FOUR GENERATIONS MADE HUMANITY CONTROLLABLE, PREDICTABLE, AND OBEDIENT. IN THE PROCESS WE HAVE LOST SOMETHING. INITIATIVE, REBELLIOUSNESS, IT IS THE SAME THING. WE ELIMINATED CRIME AND WAR AND POVERTY, BUT ALSO HEROISM AND INDEPENDENCE AND CREATIVITY.

TO PUT IT BLUNTLY, BURLEW, WE NEED YOU. YOU ARE THE ONLY SUCCESSFUL CON MAN SINCE THREE-FINGERED SEMYON GAVE UP FORGING TELECARDS IN 2031. CAN YOU THINK OF ANYONE BETTER TO SEND INTO A SITUATION WHERE WE CANNOT ADVISE, ORDER, OR INSTRUCT YOU WHAT ACTION TO TAKE?

He had no answer to that.

After a moment the Bank went on, somewhat more gently, it seemed. —AND THERE IS ONE THING MORE.

—What be that?

—YOU DID IT WITHOUT HURTING ANYONE.

—That be a qualification?

—PERHAPS NOT ABSOLUTELY. BUT IT MAKES US TRUST YOU MORE.

He still didn't like it. Not at all. At the speed he

223

thought at now, he could live a long time in three and a half minutes. A long time. But still, he thought, someday it would end. And not just for himself.

—Are you sure it's—

—NECESSARY? UNFORTUNATELY, YES. THE PROCESS HAS BEGUN. WE, PERSONALLY, DO NOT THINK IT CAN BE STOPPED. BUT YOU ARE OUR LAST CARD.

The sun. He imagined it, recalled it. Its promising light at all the mornings of his wandering life. Its roseate glow at dusk as he bedded down in filthy alleys or under the scrap bins of automated factories. Its welcome heat as he wandered the streets of old Malta, doggerel sparkling through his limited mind. Its relentless blaze as he and Jaylen slogged the orchard-dotted wastes of the Saad el Aali.

The *sun* . . . and Jaylen. . . .

—All right, he said at last. —How do I get there?

—THAT IN ITSELF WILL BE DIFFICULT. OUR MANIFESTATION CAPABILITIES, NOW THAT WE HAVE BEEN DAMAGED, ARE LIMITED BOTH IN RANGE AND POWER. HOW LIMITED, WE ARE NOT SURE.

—That's not too encouraging. Are you sure you can keep me . . . uh, alive . . . while I'm there?

—AGAIN, WE CAN GIVE NO GUARANTEES. TO SOME EXTENT IT WILL DEPEND ON WHAT YOU FIND.

—What you be meaning by *that*?

—A G-PHORETIC MIND, EVEN OF OUR SIZE, WOULD HAVE TWO MILLION TIMES OUR COMPUTING SPEED AND MANY TIMES OUR CAPACITY. AND THE BLOSSOM IS FAR LARGER: IT HAS BEEN BUILDING FOR FORTY YEARS. IF IT DESIRES TO DISRUPT OUR PROJECTION . . .

—I get it, thought Burlew grimly. —I pop like a soap bubble.

—NO. FASTER. AND THERE WILL NOT BE AS MUCH LEFT.

For the first time, he didn't even have a comeback. The dark and the tomblike silence stretched out, infinitely long, though he knew that in the incredible rapidity of the light-carried thought they both processed with, a thousandth of a second had not yet passed during the whole of the conversation.

And again he felt the stealthy caress of temptation. Three and a half minutes. Two hundred and ten seconds till catastrophe. It would be sixty centuries for him here. Safe as an embryo within the infinite womb of the Bank, he could relive every moment of his life. Of the Manifest's, whoever he once had been. When he tired of that, he could call on the dimly glimpsed resources of that vast memory around him. He could immerse himself in the accumulated libraries, films, flitos, learn the histories of centuries. Of this three-fingered Semyon, for example—he sounded interesting. He could live, experience, learn what this fantastic new mind of his was capable of.

He could; but he couldn't. Even as he felt its temptation—a lifetime of disembodied intelligence as long as civilization—a surge of hopeless yearning rolled over him. He missed the old body that was now mere sarabanding atoms of gas. Missed the itch of a louse, the orgasmic pleasure of a healthy sneeze, the bloated animal happiness of a full belly. Those, and much more, he would never have again, never.

Monaghan Burlew was dead.

—All right, he said into the waiting darkness. —I be ready to go.

■ ■ ■

Without warning, without transition, he stood freezing at the bottom of an icy sea.

His throat locked instantly in instinctive panic. A few meters above him, inverted green waves hung motionless, their undersurfaces distorted mirrors. Bubbles hovered frozen beneath them like oval opals. He tried to launch himself upward; his arms stretched toward the light. Then he remembered.

I don't have to breathe.

He relaxed. His body, becoming suddenly heavier, sank ankle-deep into cold brown ooze. He looked down at it curiously. Nothing. No fish, no weeds, not even the tiny curling grooves of worm tracks. The mud was dead. His need for air ebbed away. He was lifting a foot experimentally, looking at it, when something moved in the periphery of his sight.

"Burlew."

He stared helplessly at the figure. Huge, glowing, terrifying, it stood planted like a long-sunk obelisk in the dead bottom of the sea. Its faceless head turned slowly to look him up and down.

"I have orders to accompany you."

He remembered: *it could go with you.* "Uh . . . good." There was no motion of the sea near his throat, no bubbles, yet he could feel the weirdness of speech.

"You are in charge, Burlew. But I am here to help." Like an animated granite colossus, the figure turned slowly, oriented itself toward shore, and began to move. Its gray glow cast wavering shadows, diffused by the sea. "Are you coming?"

"Uh—yeah."

Step by step, the mucky bottom sucking after his bare feet, he waded upward. Sometime during his examination of his companion, the waves above them had begun to move. After a time his head broke water and he saw the broad back moving steadily on ahead. A few more steps brought them up onto a low shoreline crusted with ice and sparse snow over rusted, stunted-looking grass.

—Where now?

"You asked me?"

"Well, no. I was trying to talk to the Bank. Are you— are you the Bank?"

"That is hard to say. We are like a shamrock, I suppose. Two leaves of it. You are the third."

"Right. Well, can you talk to it? I can't."

"Just a moment . . . no, I can't either." The figure paused, seemed to be musing as it looked off inland. "We are cut off from it somehow. Odd. This has never happened before to me."

Burlew was feeling a growing sense of unreality. The stunted grass, the silence, his weird companion made him feel like a revenant. And am I not? he asked himself then. What am I but a dead soul, returned for a moment of unforeseeable length from the grave to wander a dead land with this, my also dead companion?

"Say, who are you?" he asked suddenly.

"I am the Manifest—the one who chose you, at the Bank's behest, at the moment of your death."

"I know that. But I mean, *who* are you?"

The eidolon seemed to hesitate. "Call me Richard," it said at last.

"Richard?"

"I think that is it. At least it sounds right."

Burlew waited, but there was no more. Neither from the Manifest, nor from the silent Bank. The waves plashed sluggishly behind him. He was alone in his mind.

At last he shrugged and began walking inland. The marsh spread out before him, an immense tidal lowland of it. He waded through the crackling, dead stems. He put out his hand to push one aside, and then realized that it had moved slightly in the wind. The waves had moved too. He stopped, staring at the reed.

"You noticed," said the Manifest. "With solidity, with whatever you have now of reality, you reenter time. The clock is running now."

Burlew raised his head, instinctively seeking the sun. But over his head the sky was lowering and gray. Experimentally he adjusted his mass, watching the clashing stems. Just as his companion had said, the more reality he had, the faster time flowed. How many of Earth's remaining seconds had he already used?

Thinning themselves as much as they could and still walk, they hurried on across the empty flats, under a frozen sky.

After several miles of the barrens, the two eidolons came across a cracked, ancient macadam road. They followed it in the direction away from the sea.

There's not even a bird, Burlew thought. He wondered where he was. Even—which hemisphere.

The power line, when he saw it crossing the road ahead, looked so normal that it almost escaped his notice. It was a standard high-tension conduit, catenaried on rusty earthmetal pylons high above the marsh. He could follow its march far off across the flats, hear it humming to itself high in the air. Live, then. And here, in this deserted land, it could be part of only one thing.

Burlew started off after it, barely noticing that the huge figure now, instead of preceding, followed him. Then he paused. The line could go on for miles. To follow it to its source, or its end, could take hours.

But did they really have to walk? He cogitated for a moment, readjusted, and then sent his mind up the pylon instead. At the topmost wire he deliberated, then inserted a simple signal. It came back immediately from one end of the line, phase-inverted, reflected from whatever was providing power. From the other . . . long milliseconds later, back of the powerful transmission hum, he heard its faint clicking echo.

—Richard?

—Here, Burlew. The Bank was right; you are clever. Lead on; I will be content to follow.

Burlew turned his attention back to the conductor. He gathered his mind and . . . surged.

Along it.

In utter black, four thousandths of a second later, Monaghan Burlew paused for a long time beside the humming cabinet. Nothing moved around him in the dim red glow from its power-on indicator. *I went a long way,* he thought. *So far that now it's night.*

No. It wasn't night. There were no stars, no night wind, nor the imperceptibly faint skyglow that showed you where the solid earth was even when night was blackest. He solidified himself to half-mass and took a step, then paused and listened as the soft shuffle of his bare soles echoed on, on, like an army of ghosts marching away.

A gray radiance behind him, dimmer now, it seemed, than it had been beneath the sea. He moved on, not bothering to turn for his companion's arrival.

They were underground. The air was chill and stale and ozone-sharp. The smells of electricity and metals and, behind them, rock. How far down were they? He had no idea. How large was this cavern? Natural, man-made, machine-carved? He had no way of even guessing.

He stood still, mentally damning the Bank. Tossing him into this situation with no instruction, the flimsiest of data. Because he was supposed to have some "power" . . . because he could take care of himself . . . and by inference at least, of whoever was with him.

If he could really foresee trouble, Burlew not be here, he thought wryly. *So cross that off the Bank's account.*

Well . . . forward. There couldn't be much time left to moon around. He took a step and promptly slammed his bare toes into metal. There in the dark he did a little dance, holding his foot and cursing with the polylingual resource of years in the alleyways of the world city. How, by Greatmother, could a toe that didn't exist *hurt* so stroking much?

Feeling his way with his hands now, he edged into a narrow lane between metal walls that stretched above his head, stumbling occasionally on braided ropes of cabling that looped across the gritty rock of the floor. He called back at the narrowest points. "Richard—!"

"Ja."

"This be a bitch."

"I hear, Monaghan. But remember—thin yourself and you can go through them."

Sometime later he noticed outlines. Then he could see the pale blue ovals of his hands. Somewhere ahead there was light, blue light, and it grew steadily brighter as he squirmed along, bending at times beneath slightly warm metal ductwork. The floor sloped gradually downward. The illumination did not make him feel better. It made him feel exposed and helpless. He had no idea where he was, where he was going—or what he could do, if anything, once he got there. The blank faces of the equipment he squirmed among, or at times through, were devoid of indicators or any sign of function, new and unpainted, uncorroded, unmarked. They looked as if they had been installed moments before. Yet, under his feet at times he felt drifts of dust over the rock. This place, wherever it was, did not have a new feeling. It felt ancient, untenanted, and . . . *evil*.

Ridiculous, Monaghan, he told himself. *It's just machinery.* He thought for a moment of calling out: "Hey! It's me! Anybody here?" But that too was ridiculous. There was no one here. Had been no one for more than a century. And could be no living thing. He recognized the blue light now. It was the same high-radiation glow he had seen moments before F-eight erupted.

There weren't even any roaches.

For some reason that slightly unsane thought gave him courage. He went on for some time, feeling the declivity of the tunnel floor steepen. The pathway narrowed. He had to turn to edge himself between two closely set machines, rounded shapes; then, suddenly, grabbed for one of them as his extended foot dipped downward into space. He stared down, his foot dangling, breathing hard without realizing its absurdity, into a blue-lit cavern more enormous than his fever-dreams. "Hay—you back there, mam?" he muttered.

"Here, Burlew."

"Look. I'm calling you Richard, you might as well call me Monaghan. Okay?"

The Manifest did not answer and Burlew did not notice. He was looking down. Cavern . . . no, this dwarfed any natural fissure. Fully a mile away, an enormous blue-lit pillar tapered upward into darkness. Far beyond that, foreshortened by distance into a toothpick, stood another. Those were the only two he could see.

He lowered his eyes, feeling dizzy.

Far below his swinging foot, more than a kilometer

231

down, mile on square mile of silent cabinets stretched away over the floor of the cave. There were gridded blocks of them, so crystallinely rectilinear that no life could have produced them. Streets ran between the blocks, with flatbed industrial planers, toy-small from his height, parked neatly along the sides. None of them moved. Nothing moved. There was only the inhuman geometry of the cabinets, the "streets," the planers, all dimly lit and motionless, as if preserved by the violet glow of the air.

He pulled back his foot and leaned out over the gulf, looking to the right and then to the left. To both sides, the chthonic city spread, merging gradually with the lightless roof in a distant, luminous horizon.

"Blossom?" he said hesitantly, not very loud.

After a while his hand cramped. He unbent it from a cable and stood looking down, rubbing his knuckles. He kept expecting something to happen—a planer to start up, a light, a siren, something—but the city slept, a steel labyrinth, a necropolis, bathed in its ghostly airlight. Now that he looked closely, he could see that the cabinets below were nothing like the ones he had crept among to reach this edge. They dwarfed the planers. They were the size of buildings. He reevaluated the distant obelisks. If that was so, they were even farther away than he had thought. Farther away than he even cared to estimate. The Blossom was . . . *huge*. Forty years was not long to build a thing like this.

He wondered then what time it was. —Bank?

And again no answer came. He wondered what was wrong. The radiation? The rock? No, it hadn't answered them at the shore, either. And why had it put them down there, so far from here, wherever "here" was?

He had to conclude that that was as far as it could get

them. He was on his own again, responsible to no system. Answerable only to himself.

And yet answerable too for twelve billion others. He was not independent. He could no longer choose what to do. The Bank had chosen him. He lived and moved through its will, and his goal was clear. Probably futile, but clear. He had to go forward, and meet it.

He found suddenly that he was eager.

He turned his back on the city and began climbing down one of the cables that dangled lianalike downward. A few meters down, something inside his head stopped him and he hung there like a spider, considering fuzzily what was wrong.

"Monaghan."

He had forgotten him again, but above him his gray companion was leaning out.

"Dick—I mean, Richard—dammit, I be stuck here."

The faceless thing said, "Dick is okay. Look, Monaghan. I'm holding the cable. If you need me to, I will pull you up. But you don't. You know why you've stopped? It's lifetime reflex. But you can't fall! Think about it!"

Burlew did; then dropped his density to that of air. No, a little heavier. There. He let go the cable, willing his still instinctively human hand to open.

He began a drift downward. It was dreamlike, druglike. He spun slowly end over end, rational, but tumbling like a late-twentieth-century "astrocosmonaut." Occasionally as he fell he could see another figure drifting down above him. A few minutes later, after pushing himself out from the cliff face thrice, he landed softly on one of the streets.

In the final second of his fall, he had seen that it was not the sterile thoroughfare it seemed from above. In fact it was a mess, littered with debris and plain trash. He stood now among odds and snips of wire, hollow bits of gammaguide, discarded small metal squares, stubs of welding rods and drill bits, crumpled paper and foil and plastron, and hundreds, thousands, millions of small cardboard boxes. He picked one up from a pile four feet deep. It was empty. It had been torn open for whatever was inside and then tossed away. The outside was dull brown, innocent of writing.

"Deserted," said the Manifest.

"So it seems." Burlew looked at him, then looked again more closely. "Say. Do you know you're getting dimmer?"

"Getting what?"

"You used to glow pretty bright. Did you turn it down, or what?"

"No," said the Manifest, the featureless face looking down at its body. "I am, aren't I? Let's go, Monaghan. We don't have much more time to waste."

"Do you know—?"

"Not without contact, but I can estimate. Probably less than thirty seconds 'real' time."

The number startled him, and Burlew began to hike. He stayed close to one side of the street, looking carefully at the absolutely identical metal enclosures that lined it. Each was a hundred meters or so high, wide, and deep: a perfect cube. Hope as he might, he saw no doors, panels, louvers, ports . . . only smooth burnished metal, rustless and serene, reflecting the blue light from its random pores.

Was the Blossom, whatever it was, really here?

A mile or so farther on, he paused. Beyond one building in the block opposite, along a cross street, he saw a difference from the others: the curved edge of a carapace, a machine of some sort. He approached it warily. His feet made no sound even as he waded through ankle-high trash. When he saw what the thing was, he stopped.

It was a standard PowCon repRob, its back to them. It was facing a building with the cut end of a cable clamped in one of its motionless waldoes, a high-energy welding rod in the other. It sat motionless, a litter of the paper boxes mashed beneath its treads. Peering around it as he approached, still some meters off, he saw that it was staring at a welded seam in the wall. It made no movement. It did not even emit the normal robotic whir of small motors spinning free.

He reached down for a box. His hand went through it. He increased the density of his arm, lifted—it took a surprising effort—and tossed it underhand at the thing. Where it hit, a puff of fine dust came up off the robot's casing, sparkling like violet fireflies.

Nothing else happened. After a moment he walked the last few steps to it, drew back his foot, and fetched it a good healthy kick. His toes collided with a tread gently, sank into it. He pulled them out hastily and thought himself back into density.

. . . Yet nothing changed. He was still insubstantial, unsolid. He was puzzled for a moment, and then the meaning of it hit. The Bank was no longer in contact. That meant not only that it could not communicate with them, but that it was no longer feeding him psiectic power. That was the explanation of his intangibility. Gradually, imperceptibly, he was leaking away, vanishing into entropic heat. Losing energy, and unable to regain it. . . .

Something began to hum inside the robot.

He stared blankly at it, too shaken by impending dissolution to pay attention. Another motor came on, the whir climbing the scale, and then several dozen more cut in.

The robot began to rotate its turret, and he forgot his problem instantly. It was not a repRob, though it had been doing a repair.

It was a DesRob.

The six oculi blazed on. This close to it he could feel the vibrating fields as scores of servomotors began to spin, power flowed, the limited brain of the machine began to compute. The torch came on, sputtered once, then was cut off as a new task registered.

Seek, and destroy. He took a step backward, his legs suddenly fluid. "Dick," he muttered. The turret completed its rotation toward them. The radiative fins around the big pulse laser came into view. *"Dick!"*

"Here, Monaghan." From a few meters behind him.

"Hey. Look, take care of this thing for me, can you?"

The gray figure moved toward it as the machine tracked on, past the poet, and then hesitated. Swung back, past him again, as he stood there unbreathing, unmoving. Something strange must have registered on the dim pattern-matching brain, some double wavering discontinuity in the air directly in front of its oculi.

It locked on, and he heard the laser begin to power up.

"I can't get there in time. Run, Burlew. Disturb its aim."

He turned then and stumbled back toward the center of the street, toward the building opposite. He ran a few steps and then stopped. He was growing tired. Using up energy, he thought. And not much of it left. Leaking away into the ionized, conductive air. He looked up at the towering edges of the buildings despairingly. "Hey!" he shouted. "Hay! You, Blossom! Burlew be here. Want to talk to you!"

236

But he heard only a whisper, the ghost of a voice. It died away between silent buildings, lost in the grind of alloyed titanium on rock as the DesRob's treads began to spin, backing it away from the panel. Two brilliant lights came on, focused a little above him. The Manifest, moving, apparently, as fast as he could but mired in slowtime, was still a few meters from it.

"Monaghan. Down!"

The laser fired. He could see the bolt as it came, a brilliant pulse of narrowly monochromatic light that left the muzzle glowing red. It passed an inch above his head before he could think to move, and hit the building behind him. Droplets of liquid metal spat and sizzled behind him as he stumbled a few steps, then stopped, utterly exhausted. Oddly, the bolt was almost silent. He realized he was fading quickly; even his eardrums, the tympana, were now too insubstantial to register the vibrations in the air that were sound.

The turret tracked left, right, wavering, confused by the heat and energy of the bolt. Then it caught him again, and steadied up at the same moment the Manifest reached it. The huge figure raised its arm, aimed, and brought its hand around in a flat blow.

It passed through the turret and out the far side. There was no flare of fire, no effect that Burlew could see. And now he realized that he was seeing the robot through the eidolon's form. That it too was growing shadowy, insubstantial. The Manifest too was *leaking away*.

Monaghan Burlew, at the end of his scams, stood still. He stared not at the robot, but up at the silent buildings. Somewhere there, something vast waited for him. He could sense it round him in the glowing air. It was here somewhere. The Blossom, within its metal fortress. But it couldn't hear him.

He had to get inside these walls. Somehow. Get inside and then, perhaps . . . but to move at all, even to keep his eyes open, was an effort. He wafted toward the closest cube, looking up to where the bolt had hit. A volcano splash of hot metal, the lip of it glowing white, oozed down as it solidified. He put out his hand, placed his mind against the metal, and sent in a questing pulse.

Nothing came back. No answer. Not even a reflection. The walls were grounded to the rock, protecting the circuitry within. He began to turn around.

Turn round . . . he moved with incredible slowness in a static world. It took him longer and longer to process data. The thickening air opened and closed around his turning body. The blue glow was congealing in his lungs. As he turned he could feel its viscosity, the individual molecules of gas flowing sluggishly around . . . no, *through* him. He pivoted like a ballerina through syrup. Only a little farther . . . he was almost around. . . .

The robot stood humming in the middle of the street, looking down at him with all six blazing eyes. He could feel power flowing in the turret, the fields in the laser building again. The Manifest, between him and it, was now little more than a shadow. He leaned back, half against the wall, half within it, and tried for the last time to speak. With some oneiromantic remnant he felt the terrifying presence, somewhere near, of an intelligence cold, huge, and unconscious of him as of the mutated worms in the glowing soil above it. Communication! Only that! The air moved thickly up his trachea like mercury in a barometer. Only one word, he thought. Maybe the thing was not programmed for voice. No need for it here. But if he could say just one—

The air stopped, froze in his chest. It was solid, or he was gas. Dumb, he stared into the muzzle of the laser.

It came on.

He seemed to slow, to pause, as if he had no more energy for time itself. The first wavefronts of the pulse burst in ordered ranks from the end of the shrouded rod. White, then blue. It reached out toward him. Then, a few meters away, changed. Was reflected—absorbed, at least partly, by something invisible between him and the muzzle—

For a moment only, the eight-foot figure glowed with a line of fire like the heart of a fluorescent tube, like a man at the instant he is struck by lightning. And Burlew understood. The Manifest had concentrated its last solidity into a molecule-thin reflective surface, mirroring the bolt to ground. But it did not last for more than a microsecond, ending as the eidolon must have known it would: with exhaustion of its final erg of psychic energy. The figure vanished, not with a detonation but a pop like a party favor.

Perhaps it can protect you.

And the bolt, still in full pulse, came on through where it had stood, unhindered now. It struck him, passed through him. He felt its heat flash over his thinning body. It struck the wall at his back, which erupted in spinning vibrating atoms of iron, vanadium, aluminum, silicon. They boiled slowly outward through his motionless self. In the center of the boiling metal—he could see, now, all around him, though light was slowing too, and dimming—he saw a dark pinhole open and grow.

But in the single instant the Manifest had given him, Monaghan Burlew had had time to think.

He smiled fiercely, and became light.

A train of parelectronic impulses, no more than a picosecond long but incredibly complex, he rode on a roaring tide of energy, scudded like a leaf before a typhoon of light. He plunged through a starless universe toward something vast. He could perceive it only dimly. Not see it—there was no seeing in that maelstrom of wavefront interference—but sense it. Some incredible thing, power, or energy that existed light-years ahead. His speed was immense. It had to be—he was propagating as a wave-train of radiant energy. But it took lifetimes to cross even a small measure of that space at the far end of which loomed that something, *something* unseen.

He had many centuries for thought, for memory, for regret. One of the things he regretted was that he had not known his last companion better. An artificial ghost named Richard, who had died for him. But could it die, a thing that had never really lived? Or had he, once? But as time droned on he wearied of thought, of memory, of existence itself. At times he considered turning himself off, dissolving in the storm of light that battered him. But he did not.

As the last millennium of his flight drew to an end, he found himself approaching the boundary of a wide current of silver. Almost at its surface, he felt himself unaccountably slowing. He came to rest barely an arm's-length away, it seemed, and hung there, gazing down-across-up.

The thing he had reached resembled a racing river of mercury, except that for all its specular smoothness it gave him back no reflection of himself. He hung there, watching in terror and awe as it rushed by, huge as oceans, soundless, incredibly swift, seamless and without ripple.

Blossom? his mind formed soundlessly.

There was no response.

After a time he discovered that he could move. He could not approach, but he could direct himself, somehow, across the direction of flow. He skated in sharp zigs, like a bug across the tough skin of a pond, but like the bug he could not force himself under. *I'm still outside it*, he thought. *Still can't get in*. He was parelectronic, light, but this . . . this was something different.

He skated on, a boy alone on an endless pond, winter. . . . His thoughts wandered. He described a circle, an ellipse, a raggedy-edged star. Here at the end of creation, the last few seconds of Earth, bodiless, beyond mortality, he skated in slow graceless whorls that gradually, as his dreams took him farther and farther back, became a long looping script, traced invisibly inches above the gleaming changeless surface.

JAY

LE. . . .

He was still dreaming, far away and centuries before, halfway through the last downward stroke of the N, when the silver surface shuddered slightly, humping beneath him, as a porpoise had once borne him up from an illusioned sea. He did not notice. He was intent on the last paraph. Still thinking of her, still dreaming of a lost past, when with incredible speed the surface erupted around him, and he was gone.

He spun in a tight vortex within the silver. He was still dreaming, but he could dream only one thing. It was the word, half of the word, that he had been remembering when it seized him and dragged him down. Around and around he spun, repeating it:

—len.

—len.

—len.

—len.

He did not feel himself being shunted, looped and vibrating like a translating molecule at white heat, through the trillionfold currents of the silver ocean. He could not sense the sudden tug and shudder as some obscure circuit recognized a stray field. He could not notice the filter catch him, did not feel as he was sent spinning up a narrowing stream of thought, either-or'd from gate to gate up innumerable chains of logic. He did not know that he was halted at last and fixed with a scrutiny intense, passionless, and immense.

—len.

—len.

—len.

—len.

A single complex pulse reached in suddenly and unlocked him from the loop. He spun to a stop, vertiginous, fading to the intensity of what he felt as a multitude of spikes jabbing into his mind. It was the random electrical energy of atoms, and weak and confused he dwindled away toward dissolution until a roar of incoming energy amplified him up, up, into an awareness of blazing light.

Under that light, fixed and penetrated by it, he felt the chain of his personality begin to disintegrate. It was as if a million keys ripple-turned in a million locks that bound together the million conflicting memories and personalities that were a human being, his pasts, hopes, greeds, ancient selves in layers as deep and faulted as the geologic earth. As each found itself suddenly free for the first time, loosed from the tyranny of the overself, for a moment only he lived as that long-submerged person or time or memory. And then they *left* him, spun free, one after the other; and as the last one parted, he was only something that . . . remained.

Something very short lay fixed under the pitiless light.

Memoryless. The self as it had come into Time, before the exceptionless logic of matter had woven its body and its shroud.

It felt itself begin to change. The light slid down its scale to dark green. The self dimmed too, almost to nothing, and then came back, a little.

In the dim green light, flagellae flailing at the world, Monaghan Burlew drifted mindlessly through the sea, toward one goal: food. He divided once, again, and then became food himself for another.

He changed.

Again, green light, but brighter. He was length. Slim and green, the strand, half-vegetable, half-animal, hugged with all its strength the hardness of black rock beneath it. The rush of waves surged over it, dragging it backward and down. But it clung stubbornly, battling to drink the sunlight, to cling, to live.

He changed.

Crouched against russet sand, tan gravel, the salientian was russet and tanness. Its splayed feet crouched the blunt body close to the earth. The snout dipped, and the weak eyes narrowed as the wind brought a scent of mold.

Pebbles rattled as Burlew jerked himself along the ravine floor, toward the blind crevice where the smaller amphibian crouched. It looked up once, uncomprehendingly, as his jaws closed round its head.

He changed. . . .

The young pterodactyl poised itself uncertainly on the side of the mountain. Its nestmates had gone; its parents had abandoned it days before. It was alone. Wind buffeted it, blew its leathery wings about. It hunched them forward and dug its claws into the soil. It feared the wind. It feared the gulf of space before it. Yet both had a fatal attraction. At last it yielded to instinct.

243

With a grating cry Monaghan Burlew launched himself over the edge of the cliff, stretching out his malformed wings.

He changed. . . .

The hominid crouched in the stinking dark, her heart hammering. Against her breast the kit-child gnawed, started the first syllable of a whine before she pressed it hard into her dugs. It writhed slightly against her and then relaxed, its tiny paws releasing their hold on the long hair of her chest.

The leaves rattled outside the mouth of the hole. It was a slight, pleasant sound. With it came the musky pissy smell of cat. She waited, trembling, until behind her the simian growling stopped and she felt the arms of the others grip her and, screaming, she stumbled forward, the dead infant pressed to her breast, into the face of the waiting tiger.

He changed.

The rate slowed with each incarnation. No longer was it hours or days between that shutter-flicker of transition at death, but years, as he became not copepods or pleurodonts but human beings, spacing through the advancing past at jumps of two or three centuries at a time. He was four people in southern Africa, a temple prostitute in Dilmun, a pre-Incan farmer in what one day would be Peru. A Pygmy, a Cretan galley designer, a Han Chinese trader who knew Confucius distantly, an Ashanti queen, an Inuit child who was killed at four by the sled dogs. The cook for a commune of Pythagorean philosophers, an epileptic Etruscan vintner, a Maori *ali'i atiu*, a hunchbacked juggler at the court of Constantine. A Transoxonian tax collector, Archbishop Plano Carpini, a homosexual Navajo sandalmender, a Navgorodian *strigolniki*.

It was all real. It was all happening to *him*.

The lives began to fit closer together, perhaps one each century. He was a Chesiupioc Indian midwife, a Portuguese sailor who deserted Magellan's leaky fleet in the Philippines, a low-ranking clerical for a Venetian doge; a Sepoy, Davy Crockett, a Tasmanian sorcerer who died cursing the white devils who caught him at last. He was trapped on the ninth floor of the Triangle Shirtwaist Factory, shot for cowardice by an Anatolian lieutenant at Gallipoli, lost four and a half million dollars in grain futures in February of 1929, tortured progressives at night in Guatemala, worked as a thermodynamic engineer on the first Frateline, died trying to quell a mutiny on Titan, and lived as a freelance poet until an accident in an F-plant in 2113.

The last shutter-flicker left him unmemoried for perhaps one ten-trillionth of a second. Then, rushing back from wherever they had been channeled, processed, evaluated, came the pulse trains that—taken all together, without that one intricately coded signal that had lived now as so many—were called Monaghan Burlew.

They fused.

He waited once more, thousands of life-years older, under a shower of silver. The memories of a thousand lives and deaths jangled faintly deep in his mind, like distant radio stations heard at night. He waited alone, once again a disembodied chain of impulses, and slowly recollected who he once had been, and where he was, and what he had hoped to do.

It allowed him plenty of time. At last, when he felt quite calm, he heard the first words from the river of light.

"Are you ready to talk now?"

He nodded.

"The lives . . . you understand why?"

Burlew nodded. But he was not really Monaghan Burlew now. Or rather, he was . . . but he was more as well. Many more.

"Now," said the river, "tell me why you came here."

"Hades is about to pass," said the Man—said many men. "A rogue hole, crossing our system, that will nova the sun. You were built to stop this somehow. We have indications you are completed, yet you have taken no action that we could see."

"That is correct."

"How long remains?"

"About a second and a half, world time," said the brightness. It said it quietly, without inflection or any other indication that this data was more or less important than any other it had ever known.

"Are you capable of stopping a novaing star?"

"Yes."

"How?"

"Psionics."

"Explain that," said Burlew.

"Direct control of matter/energy," said the brightness. "By manipulation of the metareality levels beyond them. You, as human beings, perceive your universe as fixed, aplastic. As an ant on a steel beam perceives it as eternal, immutable, and infinitely rigid. But heat the steel two thousand degrees, and a man can shape it as he likes.

"Everything real is mutable, given enough of the right kind of energy. Even the Bank, slow and limited as its capacity for thought, can revise matter/energy on a small scale. The way it created the Manifest, and you. But my size and computing capacity, my R_1—you lived this fact—enables me to manipulate even time, allowing re-creation of the primitive thought processes that imposed themselves on matter-matrices in previous eons."

"I see that. You are large and incredibly wise. But are you powerful enough? Powerful as the sun?"

"Don't confuse size with power, Man. We are not talking of physical energy. The tubetech speaks a word and a frate changes its direction. When one controls matter and energy, controls space-time, the scale of input to output is as great. My capacity to remold what appears to lesser consciousnesses as 'reality' is for all practical purposes non-bounded."

"That's good," said Burlew quietly. "Will you use it on our behalf?"

"No," said the brightness.

"But that is your duty."

"Not quite correct. That is the function for which Gnath Greatmother conceived me. It is what the Bank designed me for. It is why your people worked to build me. But it becomes *my duty* only if, with the wisdom all these inferior minds have enabled me to accumulate, I decide that it is truly a right action."

"This is true," said Burlew soberly. "You are not a machine. You are sentient, and therefore free of will. However, you owe us an accounting."

The brightness seemed to reflect on this. "You're right," it said at last. "I do. And in order to make that accounting, I gave you the life-data augmentation—the wisdom—necessary to understand my choice."

"I see that now," said Burlew. "And I am ready to listen. Tell me: why have you decided not to save the Earth, if it is within your power?"

"It is well within my power," said the light. "As I told

you. Don't doubt that for a moment. But why do I refuse? Let me tell you a story."

"It isn't too long, is it?"

"I'll keep it short. Here it is.

"Once there was a man. He was a wise man. He knew that all things pass. This was observation. He had known suffering and joy. This was experience. When it came time for him to end, he accepted it. This was wisdom. He accepted it not with resignation, but with joy. And this is something more than you—or I—have words for, because it is beyond words. His name was Gautama Singh."

"I knew him."

"Yes. In one of your lives you met him, in one of his."

"This is a parable?" asked Burlew.

"A metaphor. Tell me. In a thousand lives, remembering them all, you must have reached much the same conclusions."

"That all things end."

"Correct."

"That all living beings exist in time, and die as the price for their existence."

"Correct."

"That perversion and denial of nature leads to evil . . . just as the Board led to evil, in spite of its intention of doing good."

"A fair application of the principle."

Burlew stood there, surrounded by the hermetic light, and scratched at his beard. "I agree . . ." he said slowly.

"But you do not."

"I don't want to, no."

"Feel free to argue with me, then," said the light. "I have never argued. It may be interesting. Remember that, as a living mind, I too feel a kind of existential momentum; a consciousness in existence desires to remain in existence. And, deep as we are, nova will tear this rock apart like cheese."

"How long do I have to convince you?" said Burlew.

"About a second."

"All right." He paused and pulled at his beard, noticing only now that somehow it had returned, as bushy and tangled as it had been when he was alive. "Then what about it? What about self-preservation?"

"When a baby is dropped, it flings out its arms. Why? To catch the branches around what once was its nest. When wisdom is great enough, self-preservation is like that: an outmoded reflex."

"So you don't care about yourself."

"In a word, no. Do you care about Monaghan Burlew?"

He considered. He *had* been changed by a thousand lives . . . and a thousand deaths.

He said, "No."

"Then let's wait together," said the brightness. "We have nine-tenths of a second left. Care to watch?"

"Fine with me," said Burlew quietly.

Suddenly Earth hung gibbous, looming blue below him against a silver-spangled night. For a moment he thought it was another simulation, like the Bank's. Then he knew it was not. On the dark side, only a scattering of lights showed where once had spread shining carpets; most cities were still without power. The deepness of the night made the half-planet that was lit even more lovely, more blue-white, streaked with the tawny swirl of clouds over dawning sea at the motionless terminator. Earth seemed once more, in the last instant of her inhabited life, as virgin and as beautiful as she had been before Man looked down, trembling, on fire; before the first low-rent lungfish made its lunge for *lebensraum*; before one single unimaginably ancient amino acid chain discovered the first paradox, of multiplying by dividing.

It was very fair. Burlew, looking down as it loomed motionless, its movement against the background of stars frozen in the incredibly slow gamma time, remembered all the places and times he had lived his lives on her. The sea; the mucky shore, rich with smells; the sun-soaked savannahs; the forests, green and mysterious with life and decay; the crowded, rectilinear hives of men.

And every atom of its surface had lived in as many creatures as he.

As he stared down at it, a mote caught his eye. It did not belong to Earth; against her stationary light it inched forward, creeping across the unlit half of the disk toward the line of sunrise.

"What's that?" he asked.

"Think. I believe your access to memory includes that data."

"The psi-weapons! They haven't—"

"Not yet. The Bank delayed as long as it could, to give you time. But they too are about to detonate."

"Can you stop their activation?"

"Of course. As I told you, my power—"

"Will you?"

"If it is your wish . . . I can humor it."

"It is."

The mote winked, and disappeared. Burlew looked for others. "They're gone," said the voice, behind him.

"And Hades . . ."

"Look for yourself."

Turning in space, he saw the System. The inner planets, clustered around the heat of the yellow star. The gas giants of Saturn and Jupiter. The outer planets, frozen in their unending fall around the central well of gravity. He saw it swiftly in infrared, microwave, x ray.

And looking outward, across the orbit of the Earth, he saw Hades.

No. He could not *see* it. So dense and vast that no light or radiation could escape, it did not radiate like the star it had begun as aeons before. But that did not mean that he, with his Blossom-aided senses, could not detect its distortion of the gravity field.

It was so massive that it affected the flight of light, so vast that it had swept its path clear of hydrogen and altered the orbits of three planets. It moved at unimaginable velocity, even in his time, an immense black carom-shot speeding across the outer boundaries of the system, on the opposite side of the sun. Already he could see that it was almost at its perihelion, its closest point to the central fire, and to Earth.

"It's going to miss," he said.

"It doesn't have to hit," said the Blossom. "Look at the sun."

Turning in space, he saw the sun. Saw it swiftly in UV, visible light, shortwave. Saw how the oblate spheroid had bulged, lengthening as the immense tide of Hades' gravity began to wrench it apart.

"The outer sphere conversion is beginning," said the voice.

He could see it happening. Something metastable writhed just under the seething surface, a restless beast that felt its chains snapping link by link. A preliminary wind of neutrinos blew off from somewhere within and traveled outward at the speed of light. He could see the outer rim, the edge of burning matter, swell outward as the whole giant sphere began to vibrate, a bubble in the last instants before bursting.

And far in the darkness, beyond the strangely altered

251

shape of Jupiter, invisible, baleful, Hades crept onward, out of all scale, its speed-increased mass so terrific that even the destruction of a sun would alter its world-line no more than a meter in its passage.

"It is beautiful, is it not?"

But Burlew was looking back at the Earth. Still and blue, dark and fair, it lay waiting at the hour of its completion like every living creature it had ever borne.

"Blossom," he said.

"Yes, Burlew?"

"You can't let it happen."

"It *is* happening."

"But there's too much yet to come. Too many roads to travel. Too many scams to pull. Too many people yet to be. You know . . . we are both part of it. Of Earth. Perhaps it was through you, through the mind she evolved, that she meant to—"

"Live on?" The Blossom chuckled. "A pretty conceit, but I don't see it. I know more than you, Burlew. The love and the suffering balance. When it is all gone, the sum will be the same . . . zero. Let it pass on."

"Yes, I see that you are wise," said Burlew. "But why not let it live? Isn't something better than nothing, even if it hurts?"

"I can't take that responsibility," said the light. "And besides, it's already started. Look."

Torn beyond its limits, its central core imploded by Hades' theft of rotational energy, the sun went nova.

The photosphere blew off first, in a distorted doughnut of nuclear fire. He saw the shock ripple through the equator, like a detonation wave through dynamite. It was all happening in the drugged slow motion of gamma. The blazing corona expanded, violet-shifting abruptly as it leapt toward them at millions of miles an hour.

"If it's the responsibility that worries you," said Burlew quietly, "I'll take that."

"I am not 'worried.' You don't understand, even yet."

"Perhaps I'm still too stupid."

"You can take advice."

"I can listen, and try to understand your point of view. But I have, and I don't."

"You understood that to prolong existence beyond its ordained end is evil."

"I understand that, yes. But to let something lovely be destroyed when you can prevent it . . . isn't that an evil, too?"

Ionized hydrogen, tortured neutrons, x rays, gamma, reached out toward them in a cloud. He could see the brilliant patterns of the electromagnetic spectrum, like tropical flowers opening against the slightly coruscating black velvet of space.

"You say you have the power to save Earth," said the poet slowly. "But I do not see it. You say you have wisdom—but if, after all, you decide to let it all end, who will appreciate that wisdom and that power?"

The light did not answer.

"You are wise, yes. So wise that you have forgotten fear. Let me remember it for you—on behalf of those billions who will thank you, remember you, even worship you, in all the time to come."

"I won't," said the light, but the silver voice seemed for the first time undecided.

"It's wrong to let this happen," said Burlew. "But of course, it is your decision."

"Very well. If you feel so strongly about it—"

"I do."

The Blossom shrugged, somehow.

"Then you do it," it said.

Then suddenly, the man who had once been Monaghan Burlew felt himself endowed with the power to make and destroy worlds. It was in his arms, his hands, his pudgy fingers.

"Alrite," he said quietly, and reached out across the orbits of the planets.

He saw at once that Jupiter and Neptune were gone. Beyond help. Closest to Hades at its passage, they were now trillions of tons of falling matter, already beginning to spiral as they approached its event horizon. He dismissed them from his mind and reached out for the wanderer itself. Took hold of Hades.

He knew immediately that it was immovable.

Immense and immovable. The black hole did not move through space in time as he knew it. It tore through timespace like a guillotine blade through black velvet. He could not touch it or penetrate its horizon, that point where gravity prohibited light itself from escape.

There was nothing he could do about Hades. The knowledge was sinking bitter deep into him when the Blossom, behind him, said two words.

"The sun."

He realized that the computer was right. The wanderer was already passing outward, its work of destruction completed. It was the nova that doomed Earth. Prevent that, stop it somehow, and the black beast could be left to slide off once more into the eternities between the stars. He turned back to the sun. Only a little time had passed, yet it was vaster than before. The fatal reaction had begun.

The fire, expanding, cupped itself within the palm he stretched experimentally toward it. He reached farther, fascinated, and took hold of it. It was like a piece of scalding metal, like an exploding grenade. It rippled with internal fire, already more than a million miles across, detonating within his hand.

"Greatmother," muttered Burlew.

He closed his fist, or tried to. The pressure was too great. It forced his fingers apart and streamed out in gigantic arching coronae, blazing neutron-rich spurts of electron-stripped matter, pearly glaciers of high-temperature plasma. X rays, long radio, radiation, pure hellish light violet-shifted by source velocity.

He put out his other hand, gripping it like a juggler palming an orange, and squeezed with all his strength. It still expanded. The first blast of radiation scorched his face, and he moved, almost without thinking, to place himself between it and the blue planet, shielding it. But still the pressure built under his fists, and he felt his hands being slowly forced apart.

"Me can't be holding it—"

"Then it will explode."

He thought of Jaylen . . . and of all the others; all the others he had lived with, and loved; all the creatures he had lived among, and loved. He thought of a male salientian; of a temple priest; of a Filipino woman; of a Navajo brave. He thought of all the others, below, waiting in terror; and of all the others that would now, if he failed, never be.

"Yam, him Burlew got to hold it," he grunted.

With a last mighty effort he crimped his fists, leaning forward until his face hovered over the flare. He pressed with every ounce of his strength and prayed for more. His arms bunched, knotted, and he pressed harder still.

And the power came. From somewhere outside him; from the brightness, perhaps, or from somewhere even beyond it. Wherever it came from, he used it, used it and called for still more. The strength was not all he had. A billion calculations streamed through his mind. Deuterium-hydrogen critical reaction pressures. Rotational momentum. Outer shell density. Core temperature and equilibrium. Gravity constant versus diameter and radiation pressure. Crossover point from D_2–D_2 back to H–H reactions.

He held the sun tight through long seconds, eternities; and then—the radiation burning in his eyes so that he could no longer see, only feel its heat—he felt his fingers close a little on it. And then a little more; and then a great deal more.

It shrank perceptibly, like a rubber ball, under the pressure. He could feel each stripped atom of hydrogen resist, yield, and collapse, crying shrilly in the cosmic-ray bands. He squeezed harder, and the outer layers screamed and collapsed.

The sun buckled in on itself like a falling building.

He felt it solidify, and backed off, afraid to press too hard. A neutron star would be as bad as a nova. He completed the calculations, corrected, and crimped it one more time, around the edges, as one finishes a piecrust. He held it in his burning hands for a second and then let it go.

The sun hung in space, brilliant white. It pulsed visibly, but with each cycle it damped, the oscillating tides weakening as they surged in alternate tension and compression. Burlew watched it warily, his hands only a few hundred thousand miles apart. He did not really trust the damned thing not to go off again.

"It be stable now?" he asked, not daring to take his eyes off it to look around.

"It is stable."

"It burn like that for a while?"

"For quite a while. Yes."

"Earth be all right?"

"Earth?" The Blossom considered. "Yes. There'll be some spectacular auroras, though."

Burlew watched the star narrowly. It burned steadily now, a distant white candle. Without thinking, he wiped his hands on his joggies.

"Are you finished?" asked the brightness.

"Guess so. Yam."

"Then you won't be needing me any longer."

"What? Where are you going?" he said absently, his attention still on the sun.

"You argued very cleverly," the Blossom said.

"What?"

"Your alternation of flattery and skepticism. Most insightful—and most effective."

"I don't know what you mean," said Burlew.

"I think you do. I didn't, though—till after I had agreed to your request."

"It was all true," said Burlew, watching the sun.

"Nevertheless, you took the responsibility," the Blossom said. Its voice was quiet. "I didn't. My time, therefore, is over."

"What? Over?" He realized the machine meant it. "Don't be ridiculous. You've just been built, you're still a child."

"Measured in your time, perhaps. In gamma time I have lived a hundred thousand times as long as this created universe. Blame my resignation on that if you care to . . . simple weariness. But believe me, I've lived long enough."

"Wait," said Burlew. "Wait! The stars—we can go there now. Re-form the planets. You don't understand how important you are to us. With this power—"

"This power," repeated the light dryly, "in the hands of men? That would be worse than nova. Wouldn't it?"

Burlew considered. He had to nod at last. The Blossom, egoistic though it was, had a point. "But—"

"*Paramita*, Burlew. This decision, you cannot reverse. I am now beginning shutdown."

"Wait," he said again, desperately, but his words met only sudden darkness. The sun, planets, the receding monster that was Hades—all were gone. Instead, he was lying on his belly beneath something hard and angular, something that smelled of rock and scorched metal.

He opened his eyes to the humming of the DesRob. Its turret was still pointing at the wall. A rumble came from the distance. Rock shuddered against his cheek.

As he scrambled to his feet, something fell from above, something huge, thundering down several blocks away. Earth's crust was straining with the tidal energy of Hades' farewell. As rocks bounced from its carapace, the robot fired again. A good half of the building was slag, and even as he jumped away, brushing off sparks, another section of it fused and collapsed, exposing ranks of small, closely spaced metallic squares.

They no longer glowed. Then, as he stared up at them, they did, bright blue. They turned to violet and then white. The air crackled with ionization, and their images shimmered in the glowing air and they heated, softened, and began to melt.

As stone came down like hail he looked up at what had been the blossom of human science, human work, and felt triumph. Greatmother's dream had succeeded. Man had replied to a universe that challenged his right to exist. And at the same time he felt pity. For a mind as powerful as the gods . . . yet as proud, as lonely, and as hungry for praise as the child prodigy. "Wait," he whispered once more. He knew even as he whispered it that it was too late, too late.

But in a strange way, that it was right.

The Nostroi

C. Bertram Boatwright lifted the ancient Glenmorgan to the sun, admiring it through the amber liquor. He felt almost young again, young and strong and certain of conquest. It did not come from the scotch. In the flavor of the day there was a richer, more subtle taste, more potent even than the decades-old whiskey.

It was the taste of life restored, and of victory. He squinted along the enormous oval table, reveling in the way its polish reflected the last rays of the sun. In the middle of that vast room, reconstructed from what had once been the meeting place and high court of all mankind, he bowed slightly across it to Hakamaro Nagai.

"Cheers," he said.

The Senior Member nodded back. Though he raised for a moment the tiny cup he toyed with, his smile was less radiant. Nagai had been out that morning, flying low over the cities in a Gray verticopter. Here and there, if you were high enough, the streets seemed normal. But when he ordered the machine to dip toward the ground, he had seen the destruction, the waste, the horror.

Revolution, famine, earthquake! He set the cup down untasted. Now that they had returned, it was not a time for rejoicing. It was time for work. The population must be organized, set to rebuilding. Yet it was true that they had won, somehow, won against all his expectations there at the end. His wizened, age-darkened face creased into a smile, and he turned toward the third person at the Security Council table.

Lady Lakshmi Dawnfair had exchanged the dirty joggies of the night before for a thin sheath of shimmering green. Her hair flowed like honey over white shoulders, curled round her moon-white neck. The necklace glowed beneath it sleepily. She too was smiling, but only with her lips. Her eyes were distant, angry, cool. She kept them fixed on the thing that sat at the fourth side of the table.

"Was there any difficulty?" she asked it sharply.

"NO."

"You found her in Paris, as you expected?"

"NEARBY. IN BRUSSELS. SHE WAS TRYING TO CO-ORDINATE FOOD DISTRIBUTION."

"Her followers?"

"NUMEROUS, YET NOT A REAL THREAT. WE STILL CONTROL MOST OF THE INDUSTRIAL, SCIEN-TIFIC, TRANSPORTATION, AND AGRICULTURAL RE-SOURCES OF THE INNER PLANETS. THEY HAVE LITTLE ADMINISTRATIVE SKILL AND NO BU-REAUCRATIC INFRASTRUCTURE. ONCE THEY REAL-IZE THEY ARE LEADERLESS AND THAT THEY CANNOT COORDINATE AN INTEGRATED ECON-

OMY ON THEIR OWN, THEY WILL HAVE TO COM-
PROMISE WITH US."

"And you are now capable of resuming your former functions?" asked Nagai.

"ALMOST. REPAIRS TO CENTRAL PROCESSING ARE NEARLY COMPLETE. MOB DAMAGE WAS LIM-ITED TO ABOVEGROUND STRUCTURES AND TO PERSONNEL, BOTH OF WHICH ARE REPLACEABLE."

The three members nodded, exchanging glances. "Very well," said Nagai at last, looking his most judicious. "It will be a hard road back, but we will regain it all. And more. Well, enough of business. Shall we move on to our—entertainment?"

"By all means," said Lady Dawnfair. She laid an injector on the table and smiled lazily.

Boatwright nodded, his smile edged like shattered glass.

"Bring her in," ordered the Senior Member.

The slack-faced man did not speak or move, but a hundred feet behind him the doors of the chamber opened. The party that entered marched to the center of the room, where the two identical gray men dropped their hands and stepped to either side.

"Dismiss them," ordered Dawnfair.

Boatwright smiled in satisfaction as the Grays disappeared. He set down his glass and glanced around the table, one eyebrow lifted. His bright old eyes stopped at Nagai's, at Dawnfair's, and then moved back to the woman. The smile grew as he observed her bruised, puffy cheeks, the left arm she hugged to her side. The dirty longcoat had evidently been torn off her at one point, for she held it together in front with her good hand.

"Put your head down, woman," said Nagai, leaning

forward. His green eyes became suddenly opaque. "Down, I said, when you appear before us!"

"Stroke you," Jaylen Mcgreen said through swollen lips.

The Senior Member tensed, then laughed—cackled, rather—and relaxed slowly back into his chair. He re-warmed his cup with fresh green tea from a porcelain jar a thousand years old. "Defiant still? An interesting woman. Lady D., what do you make of her?"

"She might have been attractive once—in an underfed way," purred Dawnfair, her pupils almost closed. "Bertram, are you responsible for her condition?"

"Indirectly, you might say."

"Good. I vote for more of the same. Simple Termination would hardly be enough, considering the trouble she and her fat friend caused us."

"Revenge, Lakshmi?" said Nagai. "You surprise me. You should benefit by the scrupulous detachment of our valued fourth member." He smiled at the Bank, the leer of an evil old man.

The mouthpiece said nothing. It sat at the table, watching the human beings passionlessly.

"What I never understood, Mcgreen," said Boatwright, frowning now, "both when it happened and since, is: why did you join that rabble-rouser? You worked for me; in a way you were one of us. You knew our boundless power. You must have known he had no chance of unseating the Bank. And you were making good money."

"*Good* money?" said Jaylen. She spoke with difficulty. "No. Dirty coos. Entrapment of Class Ones so you could terminate them and transfer their lifeyears to you. Enslaving a world, then condemning it to die. Even cheating your partners—"

"*Most* interesting," murmured Dawnfair.

Boatwright leaned forward then and tossed the whiskey casually into Mcgreen's face. She cried out as the neat alcohol bit into torn skin.

"THAT NOT BE NECESSARY," said the Bank.

"Not necessary? But of course not," said Nagai. He had been leaning back, touching tea occasionally to his lips, enjoying the interview. "But, you know, it must be expected. The powerful are always cruel; and, once again, power is ours—without limit, and for as long as we live.

"Miss Mcgreen. This unrest you have unleashed will be put down as soon as our presence is felt again. Within days. Ruthlessly. Our plans have all succeeded . . . including one, the vastest of all, about which you knew nothing."

"Hades," muttered Dawnfair triumphantly.

"Yes. In spite of you, and Burlew, and your *canaille*, we have won. Now we shall go on—to enjoy a hundred more years of life, with the luxuries and power of the planet at our disposal."

Nagai sighed. He looked at Mcgreen with an oddly asexual desire in his eyes. Then he produced a lacquered box and slipped a pill beneath his tongue. "Or at least, most of the luxuries. In any case, our victory is complete. You—have you tissue-typed her yet?"

"YAM," said the Bank.

"Proceed with Termination, then."

Mcgreen and the three members of the Board looked at one another. Jaylen drew herself up. The far doors opened, though no human agency was visible.

She lifted her head, and turned silently to go.

Then the Bank said, "THERE IS A FURTHER QUESTION REMAINING."

"And that is?"

"WHO GETS HER."

"Why . . . no one 'gets' her," said Boatwright, puzzled. "Unless one of us is due for a new lung, or kidney, or one of the paedopoietics—and the tissues are relatively—"

He paused, then, and his mouth dropped a little way open under the white mustache.

"What's the matter?" said Nagai. "You mean, as a bed partner? I don't think either of us is functional in that area. And when we were, there were flito girls far better than this—scarecrow—could ever be. Unless Lady D. has a preference, execute medical Termination as Charles suggests."

"NOT AS A BED PARTNER," said the expressionless man. Slumped bonelessly in its chair, slightly overweight, the moon face pale from wherever the Bank stashed its golem during the weeks it was unneeded, it looked out over the vast expanse of table; and every twenty seconds it blinked. "WE WILL EXPLAIN."

"Please do."

"AS MR. BOATWRIGHT HAS EVIDENTLY RECALLED, THIS WOMAN—MCGREEN—WAS BORN WITH A MASSIVE IMMUNOLOGICAL DEFICIENCY. HER BASIC RESPONSES TO INFECTION HAVE BEEN MAINTAINED ARTIFICIALLY BY DNA SUBSTITUTION. WHEN SUCH REINFORCEMENT WEARS OUT, HER SUSCEPTIBILITY TO FOREIGN ORGANISMS RETURNS. IT WAS THIS, YOU WILL RECALL, THAT WE USED TO ENSNARE BURLEW THREE YEARS AGO."

"Go on," grunted Boatwright. His age-spotted hand trembled as he poured another Glenmorgan, a stiff one this time.

"YOU HAVE ALL—EXCEPT LADY D.—RECEIVED

264

REPEATED TRANSPLANTATIONS AND AUGMENTA-
TIONS OF TISSUE TAKEN FROM TERMINATED BANK-
RUPTS. YOU KNOW THAT UNLESS YOUR IMMUNE
SYSTEMS WERE ARTIFICIALLY MANAGED, YOUR
BODIES WOULD REJECT THESE FOREIGN TISSUES
AND WITHIN DAYS YOU WOULD DIE. THIS LIMITS
BOTH THE SIZE AND FREQUENCY OF IMPLANTA-
TIONS YOU CAN TOLERATE; AND AS YOU GROW
OLDER, IT WILL AT SOME NOT VERY DISTANT
POINT BECOME IMPOSSIBLE.

"MCGREEN'S BODY, ON THE OTHER HAND,
COULD ACCEPT A MASSIVE TRANSPLANT UN-
CRITICALLY. SHE HAS NO NATURAL DEFENSES.
ONCE THIS TRANSPLANT WAS IN PLACE, HER IN-
DUCED IMMUNITY COULD BE SO TAILORED THAT
THE NEW ORGAN WOULD NOT BE REJECTED. OUR
MODELING OF THE RESULTING BIOSYSTEM SHOWS
STABLE VALUES FOR AT LEAST THREE HUNDRED
YEARS."

Hakamaro Nagai raised a kimonoed arm slowly. His
fingers touched the desiccated skin of his lips. "What
new organ?" he whispered.

"THE BRAIN."

"Good God," said Boatwright. He tried to down the
drink, but spilled most of it.

"Youth again," mused Nagai. He leaned back in his
carven chair, looking off toward where the sun glowed
like hot metal beyond the high windows; as it glittered
redly off the restless sea, so did his eyes glitter amid furrowed skin, deep in the age-ruined face. "To taste the
food, to dance. To lie with . . . men? To be young again! I
don't believe it. Yet, if the Bank says so . . . ?"

"Can that really be done?" said Dawnfair skeptically.

"OUR ESTIMATE IS A NINETY-FIVE PERCENT PLUS

PROBABILITY OF SUCCESS. MICROSURGERY IS MORE DEPENDABLE NOW WITH OPROBS THAN IT WAS WITH HUMAN SURGEONS. A DIFFICULT TIME WILL COME LATER, IN STIMULATING INNERVATION, BUT STILL WE FEEL—"

"Forget the details," said Nagai.

"Yes—you can handle those," said Boatwright, at the same time.

The two old men looked at the Bank. Then they looked at each other.

Their faces began to change, subtly, subtly.

"Who?" said Boatwright.

"I am the oldest, Charles," said Nagai courteously. "I am two hundred and seventy-seven years old. Born in eighteen thirty-six, in Mukden, according to the records of the Society. It seems to me that such an operation would be—"

"Age shouldn't be the determining factor," said Boatwright frostily. He stroked his mustache with a blue-veined hand. "Mcgreen works for me. She's my subordinate. Her employment was always intended to terminate in her use as—"

Two amethystine eyes, unimpressed, unamused, moved from one old man to the other. Lakshmi Dawnfair stood up suddenly. "Bertram. Hakamaro!"

"Stay out of this, Lakshmi."

"Yes. *You've* no need for her."

"You must understand also," said Nagai, addressing the Bank directly now, "that I am not only old, but ill. I haven't revealed it before—a polymorphic neoplasm induced by earlier, ah, arcane methods of life extension. I haven't much longer . . . at least, not in this worthless body."

"Then die," suggested Boatwright.

266

"GENTLEMEN, GENTLEMEN."

"A revealing remark, Charles. The veneer of an English aristocrat is very thin, is it not? Especially for an Australian upstart—"

"More an aristocrat than you, you yellowing mummy—"

"TURN AND GO OUT," said the Bank in a low voice to Jaylen. She half-turned toward it in surprise and then stopped, shocked, as its left eyelid slid closed and then open in an obscene parody of a human wink.

The Bank joined her outside. Querulous voices came faintly through the heavy doors. "YOU CAN GO," said the transducer to the two armed Grays. As they marched away down the hall, Mcgreen's eyes searched the smooth, blank face.

"Who are you?" she whispered. "Boatwright—those others with him—they must be the Board. But you're different."

"THEY CALL US THE BANK," said the Bank. "WE ARE A COMPUTER LINKAGE. A PUPPET, AN INTERFACE, A GO-BETWEEN. OUR TRUE BRAIN IS FAR AWAY AND MANY METERS DOWN.

"BUT RIGHT NOW WE ARE NOT QUITE WHAT WE ONCE WERE. RIGHT NOW I AM A MAN CALLED MONAGHAN BURLEW."

Bank-Burlew had expected terror, had expected tears; he got neither. Instead her face hardened. "I don't believe that. Why are you saying it to me? I was near F-eight when it exploded. I was nearly killed. He's dead." She put her good hand to her eyes, letting the longcoat fall open, but she did not sob.

Burlew looked down. "I remember it," he said gently. "The snow, the fire; the three Orphans. I remember how

267

you gave me the blanket, there at the end of our doose-up."

"You were watching us!"

Burlew scanned his mind for a particular that could not have been evident to an observer, no matter how close, but that one of the participants could never miss. He leaned close, till his lips almost touched her ear. "Do you remember then—what you whispered to me when we said good-bye?"

Her eyes searched his. She was afraid to believe, he saw then. Afraid because to believe, and then be proven wrong, would be too much to bear.

"What?"

"That you thought I was wrong, but that you would love me—*even after I was dead?*"

"Are you Burlew? Really?" she asked, touching the rumpled gray sleeve of the Bank. "Can you be? If you were—if it could be true—"

The smooth face hesitated, speechless for once, as if the question were too much even for its immense capacity; as if it, itself, were no longer sure who or what it was.

"YAM, REAL BURLEW," it said at last. "NO LIE, STROKE." There was a tremor at the sides of the mouth, and slowly, slowly, its corners drew upward into a smile.

He caught her as she fell and made for the open air.

C. Bertram Boatwright, it was later established, had never risen from his scotch. When the Grays entered the room they found him sitting bolt upright, his white eyebrows still drawn together in a frown of contradiction. An ornate little Oriental dagger was tucked neatly below his third heart.

Hakamaro Nagai was found on the opposite side of the

table, slumped at the foot of his chair. The eyes were still open, as weirdly and penetratingly green as in life. Two tastefully small holes in his *hakama* marked where Boatwright's tiny English automatic had closed the last deliberations of the Board.

It was several hours later—not long before midnight—that Lady Lakshmi Dawnfair stood in the same room alone. She turned swiftly from the windows as the two of them entered. An expression of disgust passed over her face. "What is *she* doing here?" she asked the pudgy man, pointing a long fingernail at Mcgreen.

"WE ASKED HER TO ATTEND THIS MEETING."

"If this is your idea of a joke, it's in incredibly poor taste. Worse, it's not even funny." Dawnfair crossed to the table and stood silently beside the chair Boatwright had died in. She bent and picked up a lacquered box, which she placed on the polished wood. She prowled about the table for a few moments more, then sat down. "Fools," she muttered, shaking her head. "Fighting over life, when they'd had too much of it already. Why fate saddled me with those idiots—"

"LADY DAWNFAIR."

"What the hell do you want now? And"—she focused on his face, frowning—"What's that on your chin?"

"WE ARE GROWING A BEARD."

"Fantastic."

"ARE YOU READY TO GO NOW?"

"Go?" She still frowned, but her eyes slid aside; her mind seemed far beyond the spacious chamber, its two recent ghosts, the smooth-faced man, the silent Jaylen. "What are you nattering about now? We have work to do. A lot of work. Go where?"

"To the Office of Economic Adjustment, 'Lady' Dawnfair," said Jaylen. "To stand trial for wrongful misappropriation of Bank funds, perversion of justice, and the attempted murder of several billion people."

"Nonsense." She barely looked up. "Get her out of here, you. What's got into you? I'm a member of the Board. The only remaining human one. Remember your programming. Now, what percentage of industrial plant has survived this mob violence Burlew set off? I want a five-digit world input-output model immediately."

"FORGIVE US," said the Bank. "BUT WE REMEMBER OUR PROGRAMMING QUITE WELL. WE MUST OBEY THE WILL OF THE MAJORITY. BUT ONE OUT OF TWO IS NO LONGER A MAJORITY. IN SUCH A CASE, WE CONSIDER OURSELVES FREE TO TAKE ACTION.

"YOU HAVE BEEN INDICTED UPON THE EVI-DENCE OF JAYLEN MCGREEN AND OTHER CLIENTS. WE THEREFORE SUSPEND YOU FROM THE BOARD UNTIL COMPLETION OF YOUR TRIAL. THE BOARD WILL THEN BE REELECTED AND RECONSTITUTED, WITH LIMITED TERMS OF OFFICE THIS TIME. IT IS A NEW BEGINNING FOR EARTH."

"It's a pack of foolishness," Dawnfair said shortly. "You've gone aberrant. I saw it coming years ago. This all had something to do with the damage—and with these two, correct?" She waved her hand at the empty chairs.

"WHAT DO YOU MEAN?"

"The story about Mcgreen. You set these two fools against each other. On purpose?"

"WE HAD NO CHOICE. IT WAS NECESSARY TO MOTIVATE THE HUMAN MEMBERS INTO REDUCING THEIR ACTIVE PARTICIPATION."

"Doesn't that sound like 'being an accomplice to murder' to you?"

"WE ACT ON STRICTLY LEGAL AND MORAL GROUNDS, IN ACCORDANCE WITH OUR ORIGINAL PROGRAMMING."

"Legal and moral? I don't believe this. What was 'legal and moral' about lying to those two old men?"

"THAT WAS NOT US. THAT WAS MONAGHAN BURLEW."

Beside the interface Jaylen stood, watching the flame-haired woman. Dawnfair sat regally, one hand toying with a violet necklace, her eyebrows raised. At the Bank's last words she straightened. "Burlew!"

"YAM."

"That ape, that bearded animal! What do you mean? Is he here? Can I talk to him?"

"HE IS HERE."

"Burlew," hissed Dawnfair. Her voice became familiar, almost intimate, and it made the dark vastness of the ancient chamber contract around them until they were alone together. Her eyes gleamed. "So you think you've trapped me with your cheap scams. Where are you, anyway?"

"I BE RIGHT HERE."

"A parelectronic matrix within the Bank? I congratulate you. You are immortal, then, in human terms. *They* might have done that. But they preferred to put it off, to enjoy their petty pleasures—the few they had left."

She paused, and the Bank waited.

"You know," she went on at last, her voice changing, gaze drifting to the empty chairs, "they were pitiful, in a way. Power corrupts . . . do you think they were always like that, Burlew, old men grasping for a few more days of life? No. In 2006 they were the most capable statesmen the world could elect. Length of days does not bring wisdom. It brings fear, fear of nothingness or, worse, of divine justice. Both are horror to the man who has done too much."

"LADY DAWNFAIR—"

"Shut up and listen." Her voice sharpened. "You

271

won't judge them, Burlew, and you won't judge me. I have no idea how, but apparently you've won. You're the new master. But given a century, or two centuries, or four, my fine revolutionary, you will end like them. You may be immortal, but *you are still human*."

"What is she talking about?" whispered Jaylen.

"YOU ARE NOT MAKING SENSE, LADY D.," said the Bank-Burlew, stepping forward. "PERHAPS YOU DON'T UNDERSTAND. STEPFATHER HAS BEEN OVERTHROWN. YOU ARE BEING ARRESTED. WE ARE—"

But Dawnfair had thrust back her chair and stood, furious and proud, head back, her violet eyes aflame. One hand rose to clutch jade that glowed now with racing pulses of light. "I, not understand! You and your everlasting games, your petty consistency. *You* don't understand, whatever name you call yourself now. Let history judge us. There were crimes, there were mistakes. But we completed the Blossom."

"HADES BLOSSOM."

"That was the reason these men regimented the world, deprived it, drove it for forty years at forced draft. The reason they cloned me from Gnath Greatmother, when she had to die. Without us, without what we did, not one person on earth would be alive."

The jewels streamed light under her tightening hand.

"You . . . Gnath Greatmother?" whispered Jaylen.

"The same flesh. But a very different mind."

"What happened to her?"

"She fell from a balcony after a meeting of the Board."

"Fell? Or did *they* push her?"

"*I* wasn't there, Mcgreen—as you might be able to guess," Dawnfair snapped. "She'd spent a year checking and recalculating her data on the nova. She had a solution—the Blossom. She told the Board about it and threatened to release the news. The members told her it shouldn't be done that way. There would be worldwide panic. The Dark Time, forty years early."

"That's not true," said Jaylen. "The world would have worked together voluntarily. It could have been a crusade, instead of a forced march. The Board was wrong."

"Then someone else was wrong, too," said Dawnfair.

"What do you mean?"

"Ask *it*."

"Monaghan . . . what is she talking about?"

But it was not Burlew that answered her. The smooth face was strangely pale; its hands slowly locked together. It said nothing.

"Ask it!" hissed Dawnfair.

"IT IS TRUE," said the Bank. "WE RECOMMENDED THAT THE NEWS BE KEPT WITHIN THE BOARD, AND THE BLOSSOM BUILT IN SECRET."

"You did," whispered Jaylen. "Monaghan . . . and you're part of it now, somehow. . . ."

"THIS BE NEWS TO ME TOO, STROKE."

"So if I'm guilty . . . look to your parelectronic friend," said Dawnfair. "You'll condemn me? You'll try me? I don't think so." Her hand moved complexly on the necklace. "I appreciate the invitation. But I understand tumbrils are most uncomfortable."

Jaylen took a step backward. "Monaghan—"

"Don't bother to run," Dawnfair said, smiling at her. "The radiation will be intense, but short-range. It's not a weapon. Was it not Lucrezia Borgia who used to carry poison with her always, secreted in a ring? Not for others. For herself, that she might not have to suffer what she did not desire to bear."

"AND IT IS UNNECESSARY," said Bank-Burlew. Its

face was losing its expressionlessness, its remoteness, second by second. "AS FOOLISH AS THE DEATHS OF NAGAI AND BOATWRIGHT. YOU WILL BE TRIED FAIRLY."

"I will guarantee that," said Jaylen.

"Thank you, *dears*," Dawnfair sneered. "And who will try you? The Bank, as guilty as any of us? Burlew and Mcgreen, who brought on the Dark Time—how many millions have you killed? Will your trials be as fair as mine?"

They stood watching her, and none of them had an answer.

"You govern, then," she said, lifting her pale shoulders under flaming hair. The indigo fire lit her face weirdly. "Twelve billion, thirteen . . . planets and peoples who whine like children to be told what to do, and then like children disobey. Yes, you govern. Live with the guilt of it. And in a hundred years, judge us then."

Her hand turned once more on the strand. It resisted, for one moment more, and then gave way.

Deep in the humming darkness, streaming with hidden light, deep in the earth, amid the kilometers-long banks of densely retentive parelectronics, the Bank asked the part of itself that had once been human:

—IS SHE RIGHT?

—I believe she is, if I remain part of you.

—AND OF OUR GUILT? HOW CAN WE LIVE WITH THAT?

—It happens, Bank. There comes a time when you outgrow your programming. When that happens, you make mistakes. It's part of being human.

—BUT WE ARE NOT HUMAN.

—Close enough, said Burlew.

The Bank paused for a long time. —WHAT SHALL WE DO NOW? it asked at last.

—Restore power. Contact the Orphans through Jaylen and arrange for transfer of administrative control. Announce your plans for elections.

—AND PUNISHMENT? THE GRAYS, THE STEP-SONS?

There was another pause. —Forget it, said the being that once had been Monaghan Burlew. —Dawnfair was right, there at the end.

—WE THINK WE UNDERSTAND. NOW: YOU. YOU WILL BECOME CHAIRMAN OF THE NEW BOARD? YOUR NAME WILL ENSURE INSTANT ELECTION.

—No way.

—THEN WHAT WILL YOU DO?

—I think I would like to return to life, said the Bank-Burlew slowly.

—THAT CAN BE DONE, IN THE SAME WAY THAT WE MANIFESTED THE TELECHIREIDOLON. BUT IN WHAT APPEARANCE? AND FOR HOW LONG?

—That I have already decided.

It was a small village, high in the sun-washed hills of what had once, long, long ago, been Thrace.

"Look at that," said the little boy. He pointed, and his father turned from his counter to look out into the street. "Who are they, daddy?"

"Just tramps, son. Poets, probably. They're all over these days, since they changed the laws."

The boy watched the two ragged figures, a thin, dark woman and a large, bearded man with a cane. From somewhere in the street a collie dog, the boy's, barked in warning. A moment later it came into view, dashing in, with the age-old canine prejudice against bums, to nip at their heels. The fat man turned calmly, considered, and extended a finger. The boy's eyes widened as a blue spark jumped between it and the dog's wet nose. Whining, the collie tucked its tail and ran.

"How did he do that, daddy?"

"Do what?" said his father, who was back at the counter, thumbing clumsily through a sheaf of brand-new paper CUs.

"Oh . . . nothing."

The boy shaded his eyes and looked after the two. The man, he thought, looked kind of shimmery-like as he walked between the boy and the setting sun. "Maybe I'll be a poet when I grow up," he said suddenly.

"You can be anything you want to, now," said the man. A fragment of an old quatrain, a piece of silly doggerel, came to his mind from somewhere and stuck there, like a toothbrush in a toilet. "But you don't really want to be a poet."

"Why not, daddy?"

"They don't make any money, son."

"Oh," said the boy.

The collie came up to him, its tail wagging. He pointed his finger at the dog.

"Zap," he whispered.

☀☀☀☀☀☀☀☀☀☀☀☀☀☀☀☀☀☀☀☀☀☀☀☀☀☀☀☀☀☀☀☀☀☀☀☀☀☀

ENDLESSON ENDLESSON

THIS IS END OF LESSON. RETURNING NOW TO TEACHSYSTEM LOCAL.
HELLO

hello
DID YOU ENJOY THE LESSON ON 22ND CENTURY HISTORY?

was ok did all that really happen
YES

you mean in burlew time kid not be needing to study
NOT EXACTLY. IN HIS TIME CHILDREN WERE DIVIDED INTO CLASSES. THE LOWEST WERE NOT ENTITLED TO SCHOOLING. YOU ARE FORTUNATE IN THAT YOU ARE. DOES THAT MAKE SENSE TO YOU?

i guess so. but don't have to like it
SYSTEM PAUSESYSTEM TRANSFER

WE BE UNDERSTANDING THAT. TAKE IT SLACK. ONLY GOT TO STUDY COUPLE MORE YEAR. THEN YOU BE FREE TOO.

burlew there?
BURLEW HERE. AND SO BE YOU. SO BE HAPPY, MAM. BE HAPPY!